HEX AND THE CITY

A CANADIAN WEREWOLF NOVEL

MARK LESLIE
JULIE STRAUSS

Stark Publishing

Stark Publishing
Waterloo, ON
www.markleslie.ca

Publisher's Note: This is a work of fiction. Names, characters, places, and incidents are a product of the authors' imagination. Real locales and public and celebrity names are sometimes used for atmospheric purposes. Any resemblance to actual people, living or dead, or to businesses, companies, events, institutions, or locales is either completely coincidental or is used in a completely fictional manner.

Hex and the City / Mark Leslie & Julie Strauss. -- 1st ed.
Hardcover ISBN: 978-1-989351-78-9
Trade Paperback ISBN: 978-1-989351-77-2
eBook ISBN: 978-1-989351-76-5
Audiobook ISBN: 978-1-989351-79-6

First paper printing March 2023

DEDICATION

For Lori Ryan and Lisa-Marie Cabrelli.

You patiently listened to us talk about this novel every Monday during our weekly author Mastermind. Thanks for your steady, encouraging wisdom in getting us back on track every time we spun out.

NOTE FOR READERS

All the books in the Canadian Werewolf series following Michael Andrews—an ex-pat Canadian trying to make his way in the Big Apple while living with the side-effects of lycanthropy—are meant to be read as stand-alone novels.

However, they do follow a sequential timeline.

If this is your first exposure to the series and you'd like to "get caught up" there is a brief "the story so far" landing page for your convenience.

Please note that this summary page contains spoilers.

www.markleslie.ca/canadianwerewolfthestorysofar

Table of Contents

HEX AND THE CITY

Friday, July 28, 2017

Prologue: My brother was an Anthro-man down in New Orleans

New Orleans

BEN

Ben Sommers was lifting the first spoonful of the crawfish étouffée to his lips when he saw her storming across St. Peter from Chartres Street. Even from this distance, he knew, by the tight and steadfast manner of her walk, what she was coming to tell him.

He sighed and slowly lowered the spoon back down to the plate.

It was almost 9 p.m., and he hadn't eaten since breakfast. But despite his anticipation of the first delicious bite of his favorite dish from Café Pontalba, the hunger pangs had morphed into a sour churning in his stomach. Even the spicy, garlicky scent of the crawfish étouffée, one of their house specialties that had been his comfort food ever since he'd arrived here, made him nauseous.

Ben stood as the tall Black woman strode through the entrance and past the maître d', who crested back in her wake rather than step out of her purposeful way. Her hair flew in loose curls flapping behind her, and her dark eyes glittered when she spotted him.

"Iz," he said, his voice barely a whisper. He shook his head. "Please don't tell me."

Isabeau Gilland remained silent, staring at him from across the table, her lips pressed tight. Though her face portrayed an unmistakable determination, Ben also detected the trepidation that danced in subtle shadows within her eyes.

She slowly nodded her head, her eyes never leaving his.

"No."

"Yes," she finally said. "It's time."

"They didn't."

"They did."

"But that spell you cast on her..."

She shook her head. "She must have inadvertently tapped into her true nature and overcome it. Over the years, I've gotten small tremors here and there. But this time, about an hour ago, it was like a dam bursting open. And it's far worse than what happened in 2011. There might be no turning back."

"No." His knees going weak, Ben lowered himself back into the chair.

"Yes. Get up, Sommers."

"Gail," he whispered. He'd tried. They'd both tried so hard to protect his little sister from this fate. But it was now all unraveling.

"I said, get up. We need to get to New York immediately."

"I knew this would happen. Dammit. Why couldn't Michael Andrews stay out of my sister's life?"

"You'll need to handle him," Isabeau said. "You up to that?"

Ben nodded. He'd like nothing better than to put that smug Canadian writer in his place. "I was born up to the challenge."

"And we can't have any sibling rivalry between you and your sister getting in the way. I'll handle Gail."

He let out a nervous laugh at that. Nobody ever "handled" Gail. She was stubborn beyond reason, as obstinate as anyone he'd ever known in his life. "You think she'll be any easier to *handle* after all this time?"

Isabeau's face remained stern and serious. "I'll deal with her. You worry about dealing with the mutt."

Ben took one last longing look at the meal he wasn't going to be able to eat—wondering if he'd ever have the chance to enjoy a delightful meal here again—before rising to his feet. "How do you plan on explaining why you left her?"

"I think it's time," Isabeau's face took on a determined look, "to tell her the truth."

"She's not going to like that."

For the first time since she entered the shop, a wry grin appeared on Isabeau's face. "She doesn't like anything she can't win."

Saturday, July 29, 2017

Chapter One: When you get caught between a curse and New York City

New York

MICHAEL
11:52 a.m.

T he big smile I'd been sporting vanished like critical thinking skills at a Trump rally the minute I smelled the two of them in the hallway outside my door. It must have been half a dozen years since I'd smelled either one of them. But they were back— together—and outside my apartment door here at the Algonquin Hotel in Midtown Manhattan.

The anxiety I smelled on them was palpable and powerful.

I stood at the sink where I'd been washing the dishes from breakfast, considering a few dozen ways I could *not* answer the door and *not* have to deal with either one of them. Paul Simon might have been impressed by the nearly fifty ways I instantly conjured of leaving my apartment before the inevitable knock on the door came.

It felt strange to be grinning like some big hairy wolfish idiot all morning, particularly considering what had happened two weeks earlier. In a battle against the

Proud Fighters for America, a neo-Nazi group hell-bent on creating an army of paranormal white supremacists, my girlfriend, Lex, had sacrificed herself to save Gail and me.

And just before she'd done so, she shared that she knew how much Gail and I still loved one another.

I'd descended into a deep, dark funk, spending most of these last two weeks in a comatose state. Gail, my long-time best friend and former lover, had stayed with me night and day, nurturing, comforting, and taking care of me. That whole time it had been entirely platonic, just like it had remained since Gail came back into my life that fateful day in August 2014. Gail had cared for me. Fed me. Been a quiet and safe presence.

But last night, when I'd come out of the foggy haze of anger and despair, I recognized she'd been hurting too. I hadn't been the only one to fall so quickly in love with Lex. Gail had loved her like a sister, despite the fact they could have been bitter rivals for my affection.

Gail and I took comfort in the familiarity of one another and, in our grief, made love for the first time since she had returned to my life. That intimate friendship we'd curated so naturally these past three years reverted to the love we'd shared when we'd first met but had both repressed.

We'd made love repeatedly all evening, all night, all morning, crying, and laughing, experiencing it all together, fighting against the loss, the pain, the grief, as the memories of just how amazing *we* had been came back to us.

This re-discovered magic between us left me whistling a happy tune all morning after she left to attend to the many things she'd abandoned while caring for me. I couldn't help myself or, for the life of me, get that shit-eating grin to do anything but proudly take up residence on my heartily stubbled mug.

Until they arrived with what I could immediately smell was the type of news I would never want to hear.

I let the frying pan I'd been scrubbing sink into the hot, sudsy water, then turned and walked to the front door like a man on his way to his own funeral.

"Andrews," Ben Sommers said to me before I even had the door fully opened. "We need to talk."

Gail's brother and her ex-best friend Isabeau wore somber faces that perfectly matched the dread their odors exuded. Ben had never liked me, and the only consistent interactions I'd had with Isabeau all those years ago were her threats of what she'd do to me if I ever hurt Gail. But the utter resentment they beamed at me now merged with a sour-sick scent of outright fear and made me wonder if they'd been marinating in their shared hatred of me.

As I gestured them in, I caught a brief scent of compassion and concern towards me coming from Isabeau. That filled me with worry. Had something happened to Gail?

"C-c'mon in. Is this about Gail? Did something happen? Is she okay?"

They stepped inside, but before I could get the door closed behind them completely, Isabeau said, "No. She is not okay. You are not okay. The world is not okay."

I turned to her. "What are you talking about? Where is Gail?"

Isabeau shook her head. "You can't see her again."

"The hell I can't."

"It might already be too late. You two opened up something I've been trying to prevent since you first came into my sister's life," Ben said. "It's not about you two. It's about something bigger. You just undid years of hard work. Centuries of legacy. There are consequences."

"Consequences," Isabeau said, "that go far beyond the two of you."

"Sit down, Andrews," Ben said. "You're definitely going to need to be sitting down for this."

"No," I said, thrusting my right hand in Ben's face. How *dare* the two of them? Coming back into my life and telling me that I couldn't see Gail again after we'd just spent the past twelve hours re-discovering something I'd thought had been lost forever. "*You* sit down!"

I brought my right hand down to clasp the top of Ben's shoulder, intending to shove him across the room. Considering I'd only ever seen Ben in person once, I realized I'd carried a lot of repressed distaste for him all these years. But when I pushed, something as malleable as putty but impenetrable as concrete wedged itself between my hand and Ben's shoulder. My attempted push went nowhere.

From the corner of my eye, I saw that Isabeau had lifted both her hands in front of her chest with her thumbs touching as if she were getting ready to receive a punted football. And right in the spot where her thumbs touched was a soft purple glowing light.

What the hell?

"Enough!" Isabeau demanded. "Knock off the alpha wolf act. We know the truth about you, Michael."

Ben nodded. "We know you're a werewolf."

I had the oddest sense of déjà vu. Three years earlier, Gail had said she knew my werewolf secret while standing in almost the same spot after coming back into my life out of the blue. What the hell was it with the Sommers family and their ability to see through me? And what was up with Isabeau casting a spell? Was she some kind of magician? Was Ben?

"Are you going to behave," Isabeau said, the purple glowing at her thumbs pulsing larger than before, "or am I going to have to open a can of whoop-ass on you?"

I didn't relish experiencing whatever preserved pantry item might be coming. I slowly removed my hand from Ben's shoulder and lifted it in the universal *I'm unarmed and mean no harm* gesture. Isabeau pulled her hands apart, and the little purple glow faded away.

"What happened to Gail? What did you two do to her?"

"She's safe," Isabeau said. "So long as we keep the two of you apart."

"Apart? Like hell you will. Do you have any idea what we've had to overcome to finally be together?"

"We're well aware of what the two of you have been up to," Isabeau said. "But we're also aware of things well beyond your comprehension. Of an age-old prophecy."

"I don't care who you are, what supernatural powers you possess, or what the two of you try to do to stop me. But you are *not* going to keep me away from Gail. Not again. Not ever. We have something that you could never possibly underst—"

"God, you love to run off at the mouth," Ben interrupted. "I never knew what my sister saw in you. But for once in your life, could you just shut your mouth and listen?"

I did my best to stem the rising anger I felt for Ben. I glared at Isabeau. "Fine. What prophecy?"

"A curse," Isabeau said, "was placed on the Sommers bloodline. It happened hundreds of years ago. Part of a bitter dispute between a Sommers female and Éirinn O'Clery, a bitter family rival. O'Clery discovered Aisling Sommers had, for years, been in a secret relationship with her werewolf lover. It decried that no Sommers female was to ever have, or experience, true love with any male again."

"How do you explain the continuing generations of Sommers, then? Some long string of immaculate conceptions?"

"Shut up!" Ben yelled.

Isabeau cast a sideways glance at Ben, then fixed me with a firm glare. "Are you done?"

I nodded, and she continued.

"A Sommers female could have sex with a male, but merely for the physical act of procreation. It could never occur with passion, never with love, never with a lasting commitment. And no Sommers female could ever again mate with a half-man, half-wolf.

"Did you ever notice the absence of men in Gail's family? There are no men. Only women."

"Except," I said, thrusting a finger in Ben's direction, "for him."

"Ben and Gail are part of the prophecy that came with the curse." Isabeau took a deep breath before speaking. "*Tar éis sin,*" she said in a perfect Gaelic accent before pausing and speaking in modern English again. "'*After the arrival of the first male in eight generations, the next born female shall be the one to break the curse. But not without dire consequence. A pure wolf male in a sheepish guise from the northern regions shall capture her with his guiles. And when she succumbs to an emotion that has been denied to her bloodline, her love will bring about his demise.*'"

Isabeau was almost in a trance-like state as she recited, from memory, something that obviously had been passed down through the generations. I thought about what she was saying. Ben and Gail weren't only brother and sister—they were twins. Gail had referred to him as her older brother, even if he was only about one minute older than her.

"You're telling me that Gail loving me brings an evil hex on me?" I knew paranormal creatures and strange magic were possible. But this curse seemed a little too far-fetched. Or, at least, I didn't *want* to believe it—*couldn't* believe it, because of what Gail and I had just re-discovered. "So, if Gail and I are together, I die?"

They did not answer, but their expressions and the scents they gave off told me that I was interpreting it correctly. I closed my eyes and took a deep breath.

"So, I die. I can't live without her. I'd rather experience loving Gail and die knowing that love than go on living for one more minute without it."

"It will mean Gail's death, too," Ben said.

"What?" That revelation hit me like a one-two punch to the gut.

Isabeau glared at Ben and then at me before continuing with her reciting.

"'And his love will seal her fate as well. And the consummation of their forbidden love shall create a fissure that will unleash the incarnation of man's deadliest sins upon their world.'"

I stood there, letting that sink in. It was one thing to die loving Gail. It was another to know that she would die, too.

My head spun. What the hell was happening here?

This was too much, all at once.

Isabeau was magic.

The reason Ben never liked me was because of this foretold ancient prediction.

If Gail and I remained together, our love would not only kill each other, but unleash some sort of Pandora's Box on the world.

I know I'd seen and experienced more paranormal things in the past couple of months than ever before. But this was well beyond that, and far too close to home.

My knees suddenly felt weak, and I regretted not taking a seat like Ben had suggested. I stumbled back and leaned on the kitchen counter for balance. And I was so out of sorts that I hadn't even heard or smelled Gail coming down the hallway to my apartment.

I only realized it when Gail shoved her way through the front door, her voice as angry as I'd ever heard.

"What the *fuck*, Ben?"

Chapter Two: Could dance to this beat; Quoth the brother: "Nevermore"

New York

GAIL

"When are you coming back?"

I glanced both ways before crossing the busy street. I could hear the strain in Jaya's voice, though she always tried to conceal it from me. Granted, I was probably not the greatest boss in the world, so she had a right to her constant stress. But she was the best employee I'd ever had, so I paid her well and apologized constantly.

"I'm sorry. I'll be in soon," I said, as if I hadn't said that to her every single day for the last two weeks while I was taking care of Michael. As if my promises meant anything to her anymore. "How were the numbers today?"

"Sales are up, but I'm concerned about stock. Books, in particular. The shelves look lonely. We are dangerously low on essential oils, and I can't reach the rep."

"Have you tried calling the regional manager? Daniel? No, wait, that's not his name. Darius? Something that starts with a D."

"His name is Rudy. And yes, I've left him several voice mails. Demand is up all across the country. We have to order more to keep up with our customers, Gail."

I clumsily moved the phone to my other ear so I could switch the bag of clean laundry off of my aching right shoulder. The brace on my left arm made it a little more difficult to do the maneuver gracefully. Now I swung the bag alongside my legs to match my stride, which was practically skipping.

"You're right," I agreed, and this time I meant it. "I'll be in tomorrow. Promise. We'll go over all the outstanding accounts and revise our inventory numbers. How are the new girls doing?"

"I wish you'd stop calling them 'the new girls.' They've been here for months. And why don't you let me have more control over these things? I've told you how I want to change things around here. I could help you, if you would let me."

A quick pang of guilt went through me, but it disappeared just as fast. Jaya was right; I was letting too much go. I didn't know the new hires at the store all that well. I'd been through a lot of employees over the years since Isabeau had left. The parade of bright women in their twenties who had an interest in the occult and an expensive, cramped Brooklyn apartment blended together in my head, and now I barely got to know them anymore. But how much did it really matter? None of them planned on being a cashier at a tiny occult shop for the rest of their lives. Wasn't it my prerogative as a boss to leave the touchy-feely stuff to my manager, and just sign their paycheck?

"Doreen and Zoe," I said triumphantly, proud to have remembered.

"Noreen and Chloe," Jaya said, a touch of contempt in her deep voice. "They are doing fine. Both working far more hours than they signed on for. We really need to talk about hiring more people. I'd be happy to do it. I know a lot of people who would do well here. They could take on a lot of your duties."

I sighed again, more out of irritation that I had to think about the mundane stuff of life than out of any real distress over my store. I wanted Jaya to ask me about Michael. She asked me about him, always wanted to know when I saw him, what he was up to, and if we would ever get back together. This time, I actually had something good to say. *We're in love!* I could squeal into the phone. *Can you believe it? Michael and I will never be apart again.*

But for some reason, Jaya didn't care about that right now. She was managing the shop in my absence with almost no input from me, putting in overtime and soothing overworked employees. She was not in the slightest bit interested in my resurrected love life. I bit my tongue and focused on the problem at hand.

"You're right. About all of it. I'm sorry, Jaya. Should I come in now?" I checked my watch. "I could be there in 30 minutes."

I waited while she spoke to a customer in her lilting, warm voice. I could imagine her now, her placid round face smiling gently at any request they had, her plump figure always draped in soft fabrics. She had wandered into the shop a week or so after my so-called business partner up and abandoned me, and asked me about the hamsa hanging behind the cash register. We wound up chatting for over an hour. The next week, she came back and asked more questions. Eventually, we spent so much time chatting that I got up the nerve to ask her if she wanted a job—I desperately needed some help, and her sweet disposition made her a perfect fit. She was a walking hug.

I heard the bell on the front door jingle when the customer left. "Don't bother coming over if you expect to talk to me," Jaya answered. "Chloe's on for the rest of the afternoon and Noreen's closing. I'm going home to take a long bath and get some sleep. Tomorrow?"

"Tomorrow," I said. "I'll be there at nine. We can work on inventory until the store opens, and then I'll sit down with each of the new—with Chloe and Noreen—and talk to them about upping their hours. If they aren't interested in going full time, we'll hire another part-timer."

"There's more to it than that," she said. "It's not just that I need you to handle the boss things. We have been busy lately. With a lot of strange people."

I snorted a laugh. "By definition, anyone who walks into an occult shop is a little 'strange,' Jaya. I made that clear when I hired you."

"You're not listening. Again."

I didn't entirely like her acidic tone, but I bit my tongue. After how much of the work she had to shoulder over the last several weeks, she was entitled to some sass.

She continued. "Our regulars are always asking for you. I've just told them you're on a brief sabbatical. But the thing is, we are getting a lot of new people. And they are...odd. I'd like to have a little more freedom with who we let in the store. And maybe set up some events to encourage," she paused, chose her next words carefully, "a better class of clients."

"We are not turning away any paying customers, no matter how strange they may seem. And you know they are harmless, right?"

"Yes. Our regular customers are harmless. It's different now, Gail."

My pace slowed, and I pressed the phone harder against my ear, as if I hadn't heard her. "Different how?"

"I don't even really know how to describe it. People who come in lately want more esoteric things. It's as if our store is too amateur for them. Is there such a thing as advanced occultists? Because if there is, they have discovered the shop. And they want a lot of things we don't have."

I laughed, but it sounded hollow even in my own ears. "Like what? Eye of newt?"

"That's why I didn't want to tell you. I knew you wouldn't take me seriously."

Now I stopped and moved to the side of the busy sidewalk so I could give her my full attention.

"I *am* taking you seriously. But you already know my opinion. Some of these clowns think we are a joke shop, and others think we are running a satanic sex cult. It doesn't matter. We fill a certain niche. The weekenders and the pretenders."

Even after I figured out that Michael was a werewolf and that Paranormals supposedly walked among us in New York City, I still thought that an occult shop was fundamentally nonsense. I never pretended otherwise with my staff. It didn't mean we didn't serve our customers well. The man who owned the piano store down the block from us wasn't necessarily a virtuoso pianist. Owning an occult shop was the same thing. I didn't have to be a believer to be good at my job.

Jaya's voice was still filled with impatience. "You'll just have to see for yourself. Which you will do, tomorrow morning, when we talk everything over."

I grinned and started walking again. "You got it. I'll bring donuts."

I slipped my phone into my pocket and hummed a bit as I strode toward Michael's house. Heat radiated off the sidewalks and sweat trickled down my back. When I got back to Michael's, I'd take a cold shower. Hmmm, maybe I'd convince him to join me. Then we could spend the rest of the afternoon luxuriating in the delicious air-conditioned cool of his cramped little apartment. Goosebumps rose up on my arms, and the promise of another afternoon with him caused me to quicken my pace.

I'd managed to have an entire conversation without even saying his name. Jaya didn't know it yet, but I was the very model of maturity and restraint. I'd spoken to her like a business owner speaking to an employee, when what was going through my head was his name, over and over again. *Michael, Michael, Michael, Michael.*

She'd know soon enough. Everyone would know soon enough, because I wasn't going to let this man out of my life ever again.

I wish I could talk to...

No.

Her name came into my head every time something important happened in my life, or when there was a challenge at our store, and I shut it down every time.

My store. It was my store since Iz had left, even if I still hadn't dropped the habit of calling it *our* store. She may have been the brains of our operation at one time, but I was on my own now. And I kept reminding myself that I was better off that way.

Sometimes I almost believed it.

Nonetheless, on days like this, when I had something to say to her, something that had to do with important life stuff like love or sex or feelings or celebrity crushes or the new flavors at the froyo place down the street, Iz was always the first thought in my head. Nothing was real until I talked to her about it.

And now I was with Michael again. How would I ever believe it myself if I couldn't even tell my former best friend about it?

I tapped my foot at the elevator and the other waiting weary, sweaty residents shot me annoyed glances. I watched the floor indicator change slowly, stopping at every single floor on the way to us, and suddenly it was too much. I'd been away from Michael for what felt like years, even though it had only been a couple of hours, and impatience filled my lungs so fast I thought I might scream. I yanked open the door to the stairway and took the stairs two at a time. My heart slammed in my chest—I hadn't gone for a run even once in the last two weeks, and I had definitely lost some stamina—but I didn't slow my pace.

Michael was waiting for me. I ran faster.

The door was just slightly ajar when I reached his apartment, and I paused for a second to catch my breath. I went to smooth my hair and my hand froze over my skull when I recognized the voices coming from inside.

No. Way.

I shoved the door open and gaped at my brother standing over Michael.

"What the fuck, Ben?"

My voice came out in a shout. I hadn't meant to react so harshly, but one glance at Michael caused what little tact I possessed to disappear. His skin was as pale as a ghost, and he was leaning against the counter as if he couldn't support himself.

I dropped my laundry and rushed to him.

"Sit down," I said.

His arms came up around me and Ben stepped between us.

"Michael. Don't touch her."

"Ben, get out of here," I said.

"Gail, you don't understand what's going on."

"I don't care what's going on. He's not well. Now is not the time for whatever drama you've decided to bring."

"It's not drama, Gail."

I snapped my head around at the sound of that voice. Iz, my best friend. My *former* best friend. Tears stung my eyes, surprising me, and I could see that she noticed. But her steely face did not waver. "Gail, I need to get you out of here. Ben will take care of him."

"Are you out of your mind? Absolutely not."

"You are in danger," Ben said. "Please trust me. I'm trying to save your lives." His tone was maddeningly pedantic, and I had a sudden urge to kick him in the shins, like I used to do when we were kids.

"Both of you leave now or I will call the cops. When Michael's better, we'll set up a super fun dinner party and you can argue with us all night long about how you know so much better than us who we should love. Until then, please piss off."

I turned back to Michael, but my brother blocked my way.

"Oh, my god, are you kidding me, Ben?"

I tried to wrestle him away, a seemingly playful slap fight between adult siblings that suddenly turned deadly serious. I didn't have time to consider the ridiculousness of it; I only felt fury.

"Get...out...of... my WAY!" I grunted, getting no closer to Michael.

"Gail." It was only a hoarse whisper from Michael, but it stopped all of us cold. The color had drained from his face, and he was looking behind me with wide, round eyes.

I turned slowly. A shimmering red light circled in Michael's living room, right there in front of his television set. I was seconds away from making another furious comment. *Another fucking portal?* I wanted to scream. *Can't they come up with something new for once?*

But the words died in my throat. Because whatever being that had conjured this portal was standing in the room with us. Tall and broad, a black hoodie hid most of his face and thick black tattoos snaked over his hands. He stood behind Iz, one hand gripping her shoulders and the other holding a switchblade to her neck.

"'Nothing is so firmly believed as what we least know.'" The man had a voice like cracked ice. His strange words tumbled through the room, cutting up the tension between us. Everyone stared at each other.

Iz's eyes met mine, and they were huge with fear.

The man holding her clucked his tongue against his teeth a few times, and then his face split into a grin. He leaned back, and I saw him disappear into the portal. Iz gasped as he yanked her neck and she fell backward with him.

"Gail!" she screamed.

I lunged forward without thinking and my fingers just managed to grasp her outstretched hand. She yanked me with her, a sudden jerking motion that sent my stomach hurling. I gasped and felt something at my feet. I turned back to see Michael jumping after me, trying to hold my shoe. But my brother was still there, holding Michael around his waist, and the portal sealed up between us.

I closed my eyes, and all of the air left my body.

Chapter Three: Perhaps we did ignite it while we tried to fight it

New York

MICHAEL
11:28 a.m.

I leapt toward her and might have made it into the closing portal before it shrank into nothing, if not for Ben's arms around my waist, holding me back. He certainly wasn't strong enough to actually stop me, but the split-second delay was all it took to keep me from reaching her in time.

We both tumbled to the floor, and Ben released his grip on my waist.

I turned back to look at him.

He wasn't showing the fear on his face that I'd expected.

But I could smell a mixture of determination and anxiety wafting from him.

"What the hell is wrong with you?" I yelled, getting back to my feet. "Why did you stop me?"

"Because it was fake. Iz created the portal and pretended to be grabbed."

"What?"

"She did it on purpose. She needed to get Gail out of here immediately."

"You two were behind this?" I grabbed Ben by the front of his button-down shirt, lifted him up off his feet, and slammed him back against the wall. Isabeau wasn't here to protect him now. "What the hell are you up to?"

Ben was radiating shock, but he wasn't afraid of me. He could tell I wasn't going to hurt him, despite how angry I was.

"Put me down, Michael," he said in a voice that betrayed none of the shock he'd just exuded. "And I'll explain."

"Tell me where they are."

"First let me down."

"Fine." I let him go and stepped back.

He let out a deep breath. "They're in New Orleans." He paused and took a second deep breath before continuing. "Th—"

"New Orleans? Why?" I instinctively jerked toward him as if I were about to grab him by the front of the shirt again. Instead, I pressed my forearm against the top of his chest and pushed him up against the wall.

"Listen, Michael, if you don't stop interrupting and manhandling me, I'm never going to get the story out. Are you going to shut up and listen?"

I took another step back and nodded. But I was still seething with anger.

"Gail is fine. Isabeau will protect her. As we've been trying to tell you, Gail needs to be far away from you. Since the curse has been activated, it's dangerous for you two to even be in the same space. If you're together, if you even communicate with one another, the chaos is going to continue. That's the first priority we had to address."

"You got what you wanted. Gail and I are no longer together. We're not even in the same city any longer. Shouldn't things be okay now?"

"No. The chaos has already been unleashed, and it will continue to grow if this curse remains unchecked."

"What curse? What chaos?" I gestured across the room, pointing toward the open window. The usual sounds of traffic—vehicles, voices, car horns—played on like they always did in the typical New York street symphony medley. There were even the sounds of some birds chirping the morning songs of their people. All of those sounds, even the voices of the pedestrians walking on the sidewalks far below, were playing in my ears. Ben didn't have the ultra-enhanced auditory senses that I did, but I knew that at least a layer of those noises could be heard by the average human ear.

"Have you looked at the news in the past twelve hours? Are you aware of the incidence of natural disasters? Of the darkness that has further seeped into the world?"

"The world has constantly been seeping into darkness," I said, thinking about the PFA and the incredibly horrible acts they both committed and also inspired. "Are you telling me that the Proud Fighters for America and their recent antics are related to Gail and me coming together?"

"Yes, I am."

"You're full of shit. The PFA was a thing long before Gail and I got back together. We defeated them weeks ago."

"You defeated one specific branch of the PFA. And their leader is still on the lam. But you didn't defeat them. Nor did you defeat the underlying hatred and racist waves that they stirred in society."

I hung my head in reaction to that thought. He was right. The ongoing antics and propaganda spread by the PFA served to empower those whose ideologies prevented them from seeing anyone different from them in skin color, religion, or sexual preference as anything but evil. Instead of continuing to hide their racism, bigotry, and homophobia, they felt justified, supported, and heard.

"You and Gail only discovered the PFA recently, during your trip to Los Angeles. But Isabeau and I have been tracking this for a long time. We've practically dedicated our lives to it. And do you know when Marco and his crew first spun off their particular branch of neo-Nazi warriors?"

"No. When?"

"May 2011. Specifically, May 22, 2011."

My heart jumped up into my throat. It was the date Gail and I first met. A day I would never forget.

"Do you recognize that date, Michael?"

I nodded. "Of course I do."

"That's when it started."

I thought about the damage the PFA had caused. They were the reason Irwin, Lex, her best friend Sacha, and so many others were dead. "Why didn't you do something, say something, to stop them?"

"Our purpose is tracking the curse and figuring out a way to stop it. It's not to stop the side effects of the curse. We need to strike at the source."

"In looking at the cure you're ignoring the symptoms. The symptoms are what are hurting people. You could have alerted the authorities, Isabeau could have shown up with her magic, done something."

The animosity he felt for me wafted strongly off him. "It would have taken away from the important work we were doing. We can't just run around like vigilantes reacting to muggings and kidnappings and whatever other little trouble we sniff out. We have much bigger fish to fry. And besides, the evils being unleashed into the world from this curse aren't all in the shape of a bunch of easy-to-spot goons you can take down with a few angry furry-fisted punches.

"The Ebola outbreak in West Africa in 2014 began when Gail first put two and two together regarding your werewolf nature. By the time she returned to your life, looking for help with her missing fiancé in August, the World Health Organization declared it an international health concern.

"If it weren't for Isabeau sneaking back to New York to infuse Enchanting Magic with a talisman that would continue to amplify the protective spell she had cast on Gail, there would have been a lot more than the nearly eight thousand deaths from the spread of the pandemic."

"What talisman?" I asked.

"One that was crafted to feed Gail with an underlying inability to act upon her love for you."

"All this time you two were hypnotising her to not love me?"

I thought about the years of being able to sense both her desire for me and her determination not to act on it. Isabeau and Ben had been behind that all this time.

"It's more complicated than that. But we needed to prevent you two from being together. You know the wildfires that are wreaking havoc across California right now? They coincided with Gail surfacing from the more recent spell that Isabeau had placed on her via the talismans planted in Enchanting Magic."

I'd read about those wildfires. And Lex, having grown up in California, spoke about this often. "Bullshit. They were caused by a century of severe drought and decades of climate change."

"That's the way the paranormal works. It infuses itself in things that are concrete and grounded. It manifests in natural science and the mundane. That's why most people never recognize what may be right in front of their face.

"We believe that something within Gail was resurrected when you first encountered Lex. It strengthened as you spent more time with her, and your passion was beginning to meander away from Gail. It's almost as if she was sensing that was happening, and something deep within her was rallying against it. It's like the fires were a physical manifestation of the burning she was feeling inside.

"It only got darker and darker, and the fires continued to rage when you returned to New York. On July 6th, the San Luis Obispo fires that they'd been able to contain re-ignited."

I remember that day clearly. It was the morning after I'd gone berserk on that racist thug in the alley. The day after I'd gone to see Gail in her shop without telling Lex about it. July 6th was the morning Gail had appeared in Central Park with my change of clothes and had seen me naked. I had felt the desire oozing from her very pores.

"More fires raged: in Butte, Santa Barbara, Fresno, Monterey, Lassen, and Mariposa. This was the result of the constant proximity of the two of you in the face of the diminishing spell.

"Isabeau returned to Manhattan and re-enhanced the talismans she'd left at Enchanting Magic. But Gail never returned to her shop. She was with you for almost two full weeks. And every single moment she spent with you, the spell was weakening."

"What's the second priority?"

"Pardon?"

"You mentioned separating us was the first priority. So, what's the next one? And what does that have to do with New Orleans?"

"These past many years, Isabeau and I have been researching and working on better understanding this legacy family curse and to find a way to nullify it. If we're right, we may have figured out a way to reduce the unfurling chaos. But it requires Gail's direct involvement. And mine.

"One of the things we know about this ancient curse placed against the Sommers clan, and upon the world, is that it was secured within a number of unholy artifacts called Baloraye. They are hexagonal pyramid shapes. About a foot and a half high, and heavy. Maybe thirty pounds. They're derived from a combination of black obsidian and grey andesite combined with crushed human bones and dried blood. They originated in Ireland, where the hex was initially cast, and were immediately dispersed to various parts of the globe, where they were hidden and then re-hidden every few decades. Hiding them was critical, we learned, because if they are found, they can be removed and, ultimately, destroyed.

"If we can destroy them, we might be able to undo this curse and reverse some of what has already happened. We're not exactly sure how many exist. We suspect one of them is currently here in New York City somewhere."

"Then we need to get Isabeau and Gail back from New Orleans," I said, moving towards the still-open apartment door. "We need their help to find and destroy the artifact."

"No," Ben said, grabbing my arm.

I could have easily shrugged him off, but I didn't. Instead, I turned and glared at him, considering how I could best reason with the man. "You've been aware of what Gail and I, and a couple of others were involved in earlier this month, right?"

He let go of my shoulder, walked past me, and then pushed the door closed, remaining in front of the door to block me from going through it.

"Yes. You fought against the PFA. You discovered Lex's ability to nullify the supernatural. What about it?"

"Then you know how well we work together as a team. You likely know I needed to stay a certain distance from Lex in order to maintain my enhanced powers."

"Yes."

"So, Gail and I can do the same thing. Have Isabeau open another portal. Transport the two of them back here. We maintain my distance from Gail, and surely the four of us, working in collaboration, can find and destroy the artifact more easily."

"No. You don't understand."

"Screw you, Sommers. You can't stop me. Now get the hell out of my way before I tear you out of the way."

"You won't hurt me, Michael."

Like before, there wasn't an ounce of fear oozing off him. Just that consistent combination of anxiety and determination he wore as thick as a teenage boy would sport Axe body spray.

"You're standing between me and Gail right now. Wanna try me?"

"We can't just portal between New Orleans and New York."

"Why not? Isabeau just did it. Reach out to her. Have her make another portal that they can return through."

"Opening up a portal to travel that far, particularly a portal for two people, combined with the illusory figure that Isabeau conjured up, takes a significant amount of energy. Iz might be able to create a portal for moving within a few meters, but anything with a larger range like that requires hours of preparation and is both draining and debilitating. That portal transported the two of them almost twelve hundred miles. Magic isn't infinite. Spellcasting comes with a cost.

"Besides, like I told you, there's more than one."

"Where are the others?"

"The only one we've actually found is in New Orleans."

"You found one already? Let's get down there and help Gail and Isabeau destroy it."

"It's not that easy. Isabeau and I found that artifact in a remote region of British Columbia a few months ago. We brought it to New Orleans where Isabeau's grandmother has been keeping it and trying to find a way to destroy it. We learned that it gave off a very high pitched, ultrasonic low pulsing sound wave. Neither Isabeau nor I could hear it, but Roberta Boudreau detected it. I suspect, with your enhanced sensory ability, if you got close enough to it, you'd be able to hear it.

"We know there's one right here in Manhattan. But there is at least one more in the Americas—our research suggests there was a concentration of them here because the prophecy spoke of the curse rearing itself in a new and foreign land. The placement of three of the Baloraye in Western Canada, New York City, and in the Baja California Peninsula would create a powerful triangulation that would increase its potency."

"Where in the city is the local one?" I asked, but before he could answer, my phone from the bedroom nightstand chirped with the familiar opening notes of the Phil Collins song "This Must Be Love."

When we had first met back in 2011, I'd set it as both the ringtone and text sound for Gail's cell phone in my contacts. The delightful inside joke-style pun of that song title for any incoming calls or messages from Gail was too much for me to resist. It was an obscure enough song that most people didn't know it, nor the significance. And, despite all that had happened over the years, even when I'd met and fallen in love with Lex, I'd never changed that tone.

Without saying a word to Ben, I turned and rushed into my bedroom and picked up the phone.

The text from Gail read:

I'M IN NEW ORLEANS. I NEED YOU. NOW.

Chapter Four: Would crashing this cemetery party be considered a graveyard smash?

New Orleans

GAIL

I'm *at a party.*

Music. Laughter. People talking.

Church bells pealing in the distance.

A familiar scent tickled my nose, and for a moment, I could smell a perfume we sell at the shop—a scent called "Memento Mori" that smells like wet dirt and rotting meat and incense. It's popular with our customers because of the name, obviously, but also because it comes with temporary tattoos of stylized skeletons. The goth kids love this perfume. Personally, I've always thought it smells like the garbage can in a mortuary, but I was relieved to place the scent.

It's not a party. I'm in the shop, I thought to myself. *I fell down in the shop.*

It was embarrassing, but at least I knew where I was.

I took a deep breath and opened my eyes, trying to focus. But I didn't see the gleaming hardwood floors of my little store. Instead, my body was lying on a dirt path, scuffed with boot prints, and surrounded on both sides by tall stone pillars. I raised my head a few inches off the ground and gasped at the pounding in my skull.

I tasted the metallic tang of blood on my tongue and spit out a mouthful of filthy saliva. The air was heavy and thick around me, pressing me back into the ground.

No matter how much I tried to will it to be so, this was not the shop. This was not even New York. The air was too hot, too muggy, and the sun had a physical weight on my skin. I put my hands over my eyes to massage away the pain, and right then I heard Iz's voice again.

Iz.

Screaming.

I jumped to my feet and turned side to side, trying to find the source of her scream, but my head was still throbbing, and I had a terrible feeling I might barf. I could sense her near me, and her agony echoed down the long corridor of raised pillars. I started to run, without really knowing where to go. Each step pounded in my skull, but I didn't stop.

The last thing I could remember was another damn portal. How is this now a normal part of my life? I made a mental note to complain to Michael about it. I didn't know how many portals were a normal number of portals in one person's life, but I'd seen too many. The one in Michael's apartment was the first one I'd actually gone through, and based on how my gut churned now, it would be the last.

I tried to call out to Iz, but my voice was dry and hoarse in my throat. I gagged again and righted myself.

My body was drenched in a sticky, heavy sweat. Where was I? Had the portal actually led to hell?

I made a mental note to behave a little better when I got back to New York. If this was what hell felt like, I was definitely not cut out for the weather.

A loud laugh pierced through my panting, and this time it came from my right. I tore past the stone blocks and stumbled into what looked like an outdoor party. A brass band scattered amongst a throng of people dressed in black. Thick smoke plumed up from an open grill, carrying odors of peppery spice and fatty, dripping meat. I scanned people's faces, trying to find Iz, but no one noticed me. A priest stood to the side of one of the stone pillars, staring down at a worn, leather-bound Bible.

"Isabeau?" I screamed with all my might. The jazz music trailed off, the voices stopped, and everyone turned their faces to me. It was only at this moment that I recognized the scene.

I was in a graveyard. In the middle of a funeral party.

"I'm sorry," I stammered. "I lost my friend."

The mourners continued to stare, and I scanned their eyes, hoping that someone could help me. Across the crowd, the priest snapped his bible closed with a loud *thunk* and locked eyes with me. Recognition crossed his face; his eyes narrowed slightly, and he licked his cracked lips.

"She's not here," a man with a deep voice said in my ear. He put his hands on my elbow and on my back and steered me from the crowd. "This is a private event. Please take it somewhere else."

"No," I said, my voice coming out like a sob. I stopped walking, but he kept trying to push me away from the other people. "Please help me. I lost her. I think she was kidnapped."

At this, he stopped moving and looked at my face, taking in the state of me. He was a tall, dark-skinned man with a greying beard, wearing a fine wool black suit. Drops of sweat glistened on his forehead and his eyes were kind, but hard. An authority. I couldn't imagine how I must have looked to him, but if it was anything like how I felt it must have been a sight. Dust caked my sweaty skin and itched at my scalp. I rubbed my face, and my hand came away bloody.

"She was kidnapped," I repeated, trying to steady my breath. "I'm sorry to interrupt you. I heard her screaming."

He stared for a fraction of a second longer, then released my elbow. "Why don't you let me call the police for you?"

"No!" I shouted this response and took a step backward, stumbled on the edge of a crypt and fell on my ass. The man glanced back at the crowd of people, who had mostly stopped looking at me and gone on with their celebration. The priest, however, was still watching me closely, and I saw the tiniest smirk at the corner of his mouth. I glanced down at my clothes—was I wearing one of my 'Fuck the Patriarchy' shirts? No. I still had on the clothes I'd thrown on this morning—light cotton pajama bottoms and one of Michael's Rush t-shirts. Perfectly acceptable attire for a laundry day.

Maybe not acceptable for crashing an outdoor funeral with a bloody face.

Just then, I heard the scream again. A protracted keen, seemingly coming from inside one of the crypts itself. I jumped to my feet.

"There." My sobbing stopped. "Did you hear that?"

The man knit his eyebrows, glanced back at his party, and then pulled his phone out of his suit pocket.

"I'm going to call for some help," he said, his deep voice a slow, patronizing cadence.

But I didn't wait for more. I took off again, weaving through the lanes between raised headstones. The heavy heat slowed my pace, but I could feel I was getting closer to her.

The sounds of the jazz music disappeared behind me as I ran down a slope to the far edge of the graveyard. I called her name with every wild turn, almost like a beacon, hoping she could hear me. My ears throbbed with the sound of my heartbeat, and my feet led me to a giant magnolia tree whose roots curled up and around the ancient headstones at its base. It was there that I saw her.

Or rather, I saw the man again. The slippery-looking man from the portal, with the heavy tattoos over his hands. He was standing at the trunk of the tree, and Isabeau was at his feet. Her skin was pale and almost blueish, her limbs splayed out like a discarded rag doll. He'd dropped her there, and held a knife above his head, ready to plunge into her chest.

I may have screamed. I meant to scream. But the sound was lost in the thunder pounding through my head. I'm pretty sure I flew. Because suddenly I was upon him, chest to chest, smashing his skull into the tree trunk.

The snake tattoos, I saw, were not just on his hands. They covered his face and his neck. I tried to wrestle the dagger from his hand, but he held it high above my head out of reach. I still didn't have much strength back in my left arm, but I used my body to pin him up against the tree. It may have been a trick of the murky graveyard light, but I could have sworn the snakes on his body moved. They slithered over his face and under the torn collar of his black t-shirt; even, horrifyingly, into his mouth when he opened it to laugh at me.

"Not a very smart one, are you?"

"Nope," I grunted. It would have been nice to come up with something clever, but holding him away from Iz took up all my energy.

He lifted a knee into my gut, and I recoiled back in shocked pain. He used the raised foot to push himself off the tree trunk and then he stood over both of us. The blade glinted in the sun, and he tapped it against his thigh while the ink snakes coiled over his fingers.

"This is better than we could have hoped." He grinned. "Two for the price of one." He raised the dagger across his face to his left ear and rasped out a laugh. "Someone's having a good dinner tonight, right Fraus?" he shouted to the sky.

I realized as I stared up at him that he was going to kill us, both of us, right here under this unknown tree, in this unknown city, and I would never know why. His blade came down in slow motion, arcing toward Iz's face, and with an almighty effort, I rolled over her body to cover it with my own. The metal sliced across the flesh of my back. I screamed when a wet, acidic burn ripped through my upper body.

He laughed again and bent close to my ear. "I'll make it quick," he said, his voice as dark as an oil slick. "'I'm not as shocked by savages who roast and eat the bodies of their dead as I am by those who torture the living.'" He stood and raised the dagger high over his head again. Incredibly, he winked at me from that height. "That's Michel de Moon-tanyee, in case you didn't go to college. You can count on your friend Artair to educate you."

Granted, no one can predict their own death. But if you'd given me a hundred years to think about it, I don't think I would have come up with me being slaughtered underneath a big-ass cemetery tree by a French philosopher-quoting madman with moving tattoos.

Below me, Iz's body was warm, and I heard her ragged breaths in my ear. She was still alive. The snake man's boots were planted on either side of our heads, and I knew his next move would be to slam the knife straight down, through both of our hearts, taking us at the same time.

"Iz," I whispered. "I got you."

I closed my eyes tight.

Chapter Five: No time to take a fast train; my baby just texted a message

New York

MICHAEL
11:43 a.m.

I stared at the text from Gail, my heart leaping high into the back of my throat.

Here I was, standing around and flapping my gums with Ben when what I should have been doing was getting my ass down to New Orleans. Gail needed me.

I hit the little phone icon at the top of the text message screen to call Gail, but it went straight to voice mail. I ended the call and texted two words:

I'm coming.

But I received a notification that the message was not delivered.

"What is it?" Ben said from the doorway of my bedroom. I'd been so focused that I hadn't even attended to the sounds of his movements. Not that he was a threat to me. But still, the idea I could be so easily distracted was not a good sign. That had happened twice in the past half hour.

"It was Gail. She needs me. She's in trouble."

"What'd she say?"

"'*I need you. Now.*' I tried calling and texting, but her phone must be out of cell phone range. I need to get there." I grabbed the wallet off my nightstand and slipped it into my back pocket.

"It's a three-and-a-half-hour flight to New Orleans, Michael."

I opened the top drawer of the nightstand and pulled out my passport. "You said Iz wouldn't be able to conjure another portal at such a vast distance that quickly."

"That's right."

"And you can't perform this spell, right?"

"Correct," Ben said, and I smelled bitterness coming off him. "I don't have magical abilities."

"Then what other choice do I have? I need to get on a plane right now and get to Gail."

I thumbed the button to call her again and, like before, it went straight to voice mail. *Dammit!*

"Gail is fine," Ben said.

"Then why did she text me?"

"I don't know. But I have faith that Isabeau will be able to protect her from whatever it is."

"I don't have that same faith. But even if I did, Gail needs me and I'm not ignoring that."

"Isabeau will protect her. And Gail is stronger than you realize."

"Yes, Gail is strong. And stubborn. And brave." I thought about how Gail had boldly joined three paranormal humans with no other power than the second-hand knowledge of how some magic worked, and then about how she launched herself at Marco to stop him from the relentless pummeling he was giving me. The woman faced a pack of supernatural PFA goons head-on without a second thought for her own safety. "But I can't stand by and not go help her face whatever caused her to ask for help."

"We have our own thing to face, right here."

"We can face it *after* we help Gail and Isabeau. I'm going. Are you coming with me?" I asked, thumbing my way down the contact list on my phone to call Anne, my agent's assistant. She'd be able to get me onto the next flight to New Orleans.

"No. And you're not going either."

"The hell I'm not." I hit the button to call Anne, and pushed past Ben, heading for the front door.

"Put the phone down, Michael. Let's talk about this a minute." Ben rushed to get between me and the front door.

"Enough talking, I—"

"Hello Michael," Anne's voice came from my phone. "Are you okay?"

"Hi Anne. Yes, I am. Listen, Anne, I need—"

"You sound like yourself again. Oh, Michael, I was so worried about you. We were all so worried about you."

Anne was referring to the zombie-like state I'd been in for the past couple of weeks when Gail was here and looking after me while I was mourning—while we both were mourning—what had happened with Lex. In between our marathon love-making sessions last night, Gail had caught me up on some of what I'd missed, including the calls from Anne inquiring about my well-being, and the ones from her boss—Mack "The Knife" Halpin, my literary agent—panicking about my next manuscript deadline.

"I'm fine, Anne. I'm back."

"And I'm so sorry about Lex. She was such a sweet girl." Lex was five years older than Anne. It always amused me how Anne was almost ten years younger than I was and yet she constantly doted on me like she was a grandmother, or at least a dear Auntie.

"Thanks, Anne. Listen, I need to get on the next flight to New Orleans. Can you get me a…" I paused. "Just a minute." I looked at Ben. "You coming?"

He glared at me, slowly shaking his head. "No. And neither are you."

"Fine," I said to him. Then, speaking into the phone again I said, "A single ticket for me. One-way. Not sure how long I'll be there at this point."

"Sure," Anne said. "I'll get right on it and call you back."

"Thanks, Anne." I hung up the phone.

Still standing in front of my door, Ben was glaring at me, and his anxiety was rising, along with a stream of anger. "Don't do this, Michael. You'll only make it worse."

"Worse than Gail sending a message that she needs help from halfway across the country? Out of my way, Ben."

"No!"

"I don't have time for this bullshit." I grabbed him by the shoulders, easily lifted him out of my way and set him down to the side of the door.

When I reached for the door handle, he tackled me, grabbing my right arm.

"Seriously?" I jerked my arm back, sending him flying back to bounce off the wall and stumble to one knee. He got up and rushed at me again, this time tackling me from the side and reaching his left arm around my throat.

"You're not leaving!" he yelled, as he repeatedly hammered against the side of my neck near the base of my skull, as if he were trying to knock me unconscious.

"You're not stopping me." I grabbed his left arm and he let out a shriek of pain as my tightening fingers dug into the inside of his wrist.

I wrenched his arm away from my throat, then spun and cuffed him on the side of the head with an open-handed right slap. I pulled the force of the blow because I wasn't interested in harming him, but I needed to stop his assault and get going.

That open-handed strike across the side of his head did the trick. He stumbled back, stunned and off balance, and fell to the carpeted floor, on the verge of blacking out.

I opened the door, slipped outside, and slammed it behind me. Then I ran to the elevator. I pushed the button and waited for the car to arrive. I could tell from the nature of his breathing that Ben was still stunned, still laying on the floor, barely conscious, and wouldn't be getting up any time soon. I nodded as the elevator door opened and I stepped inside.

Anne called me back before the elevator door had closed.

"I got you a United flight that leaves Newark at 2:08 p.m. If you're at the Algonquin, it'll likely take you an hour to get to the airport. That's your best bet. You'll get in about 4:52 p.m. our time or 3:52 p.m. New Orleans time."

"Thanks, Anne."

"No problem. I'll text you the details so you can check in to your flight on the way. Is there anything else you need?"

"Not now. Thank you."

"You'll let me know what's going on?"

As the elevator reached the ground floor, I thought back to all the times Anne had, like that proverbial dear Auntie, always looked out for me. She fawned over me and treated me with such kindness and grace.

Mack was a crusty, rude man with very little need for social graces. The term "bull in a china shop" wasn't apt enough for the way he brashly negotiated. He was like an Olympic flatulence team storming through a library display of houses of cards. But he was damn effective in what he did.

Anne was often caught between Mack's hostile and aggressive nature and my penchant for procrastination and turning in my manuscripts at the very last minute.

And yet she never seemed fazed. She had no idea about my werewolf nature (until this morning, there were only two other people still alive who I knew were aware of that: Gail and Bridge, a book-loving young woman I'd befriended on a most eventful train trip a couple of years ago), so I couldn't very well explain what was really going on. But I needed to tell her something. And I would. I owed her that. Just not now.

"When I'm able."

"You're sure you're okay? What with Lex and—"

I cut her off as I stepped out of the elevator and into the lobby. "Never been better, Anne. Listen, Gail and I have re-kindled what we had before." As I was saying this, I walked past the lounge area of the Algonquin Hotel where Gail and I had shared our very first kiss. That memory made me smile. I knew that Anne had always really liked Gail, even when she'd been open to embracing and accepting Lex into my life.

Anne made a noise that sounded like a barely contained shriek in the back of her throat. "Oh, Michael, I'm so glad." The joy in her voice was clear. "I'm so happy for you. For the both of you. I knew it would happen. I just knew it."

"Thanks."

"Michael." Anne's voice took on a note of apology. "What should I tell Mack? He'll be asking about the status of the manuscript."

"Tell him this trip is directly related to research I need to do to get back on track."

I had become a master of being able to tell certain people exactly what I knew they wanted to hear. I knew Anne would be distracted and elated to hear Gail and I were back together. However strange the current circumstances were, I knew Gail loved me, and I loved her. We'd figure out the rest in good order. Of that I was confident, or at least, hopeful. I definitely wasn't going to give up on that, ancient curse or not. And I knew Mack would only be pleased with news that I was writing and fulfilling the obligation of my latest contract. So, I fed Anne that white lie. But, I'd never been to New Orleans before. Maybe I would eventually use something I saw there in the plotline of a future novel.

Never mind my wolfish powers. I was an expert poseur. Was that even a type of paranormal ability? Who knows? I'd certainly seen more than my share of new supernatural things in the past month or so.

"He'll be so pleased to hear that, Michael."

"I've got to go, Anne," I said, hailing a cab with my left hand as I stepped onto the sidewalk outside the hotel. "Talk to you soon."

A taxi that had been waiting at the curb about ten feet away pulled forward. "Penn Station, please," I said, as I slid into the back seat.

On the ride over, I tried texting and calling Gail again several times.

After the third time my call went to her voice mail, instead of hanging up, I left a message. That way, if her phone came back into range when I was in the air, she would know what was happening on my end of things.

"Hi Gail. I'm on my way. I've got a flight that should get me in about 4 p.m. local time. I'll call you as soon as I land. I love you."

I hung up and slipped the phone back into my pocket as the cab crossed W 34th Street and a series of rapid-fire gunshots rang out from somewhere above and the windshield of the taxi shattered.

Chapter Six: A beautiful, terrible, wonderful, startling reunion on an otherwise horrible, no-good day

New Orleans

GAIL

An explosion crested over my head, but nothing touched my skin. When I opened my eyes, Artair's feet were gone. I peeked across the graveyard and saw him slumped against a headstone, which had cracked with the impact of his head.

I sat up, holding Iz against my chest like a child.

A young woman stood in front of us, one arm outstretched in our direction, and one pointing toward Artair.

She jerked her chin at Iz. "She okay?"

"I don't know," I said. I leaned my ear to her mouth. "She's still breathing."

The girl strode over to us and put her palm against Iz's chest. I recoiled.

"Back off!" I snapped.

The girl didn't even look at me. "I'm Nombeko. On your side." Again, that chin jerk. "We have a car."

"But where are we—"

"We need to move fast. Artair won't be out long, and he'll conjure backup when he wakes up."

I glanced over at him. He looked dead enough to me.

A small red car roared up to the road on the other side of the fence, and the Black man from the funeral who had tried to call the police stepped out.

"Hurry!" he called.

I looked back at the girl, who had her hands up in a defensive position again.

"Can you carry her?" she asked.

"I'm not going with that guy," I said. "He wants to call the cops on me. Iz needs a hospital."

"Shut *up*, Gail. Do as I say."

I was so stunned that she knew my name that I obeyed her. I got to my feet and bent to pick Iz up. But as soon as I put my arms under her body, the pain shot across my back again and I screamed in agony, dropping to my knees.

Nombeko spun me around to examine me. I heard her take in a quick breath.

"Shit," the girl muttered. "Papa, we need help."

Considering his age and expensive suit, the man leapt over the wooden fence with surprising agility. He sped up to where Iz lay and scooped her into his arms. Nombeko slipped one arm around my waist and lifted me to my feet. I swayed when I was upright, but she held firm. She had surprising strength, considering she was easily a foot shorter than me and maybe a buck-o-five.

I didn't have the energy to argue, so I leaned against her and let myself be led to the car. I climbed in back with Iz, who the man had buckled into the cramped back seat.

He turned and held out a hand to me. "Mosegi. Nice to finally meet you."

"Where are we going?"

"Getting some help. Hold on."

Nombeko swore under her breath as Mosegi peeled out of his parking space.

"He's up," she said, her voice eerily calm.

Mosegi swerved hard to the left, slamming me up against the car door, and I looked back at the graveyard. The upright tombs rose eerily out of the hillside like snaggly, rotted teeth. Incredibly, Artair, who only minutes before had his head smashed on a gravestone, was up and walking toward us. He wobbled, but his direction was sure. Three other men with similarly tattooed faces, appearing out of nowhere, had joined him.

"You got this, baby girl?" he asked, accelerating through a red light.

Artair and his cronies were picking up speed, and somehow catching up to us, despite the fact they were on foot and Mosegi was driving like a NASCAR racer on meth.

"Mmm-hmm," she breathed.

She didn't seem to have much need for words, this one. In one smooth motion, she slipped off her seatbelt, pulled herself halfway out the car window, sat on the edge, and braced her feet against the door. She lifted her hands above her head again and yellow jets of light exploded out of her palms. Artair lifted his hands to block his face, but she shot again immediately, and a jet hit him square in the chest. The force of the impact knocked him off his feet and he flew back into a parked car, smashing the front windshield. She turned her palms to the other men, one after the other, who couldn't dodge her fast enough. She deftly hit them all, leaving their stunned bodies splayed across sidewalks and cars, and then she slid easily back into her seat. She glanced back at me and Iz.

"Put on your seatbelt," she instructed.

I did as she said and saw Mosegi smirk in the rearview mirror. His driving slowed, though not by much, and he eased into regular traffic. I wanted to ask at least a million questions, most importantly, "How do I know you aren't going to kill us?" But my head was spinning and I could only stare at Iz in the seat next to me, still pale and lifeless.

Mosegi pulled onto a bridge, and I sucked in my breath when I saw it. Or rather, didn't see it—because the bridge had no end. It pointed off into eternity, its terminus seemingly over the edge of the planet.

"Where are we?" My voice was much smaller than I wanted it to be. I was in a very small, dangerously fast car driven by strangers who knew my name, with a very sick Isabeau and a girl with explosives in her hand, running from a lunatic who commanded an army out of thin air. And we were driving over a bridge to nowhere.

"Lake Ponchartrain Causeway." Mosegi sounded surprised that I didn't already know that.

The events of the last hour assembled in my head. The soupy heat. The above-ground tombs. The outdoor funeral with a jazz band.

New Orleans?

I remained quiet and kept my eyes wide open as we drove. I had no reason to trust these people—they may have saved me and Iz from the snake guy, but I didn't know who the hell they were or what they wanted from us. Best not to let them know how completely clueless I was.

Or how scared.

The car slowed on a beautiful oak-lined residential street. Giant homes with pillared porticos lined the street, and we had stopped in front of the most regal one of them all. Lush vegetation surrounded the home, and a white marble staircase swept up from the front garden to the massive double front door.

Nombeko jumped from her seat and ran toward the house, but before she could reach it, the familiar face of Iz's grandmother, Roberta Boudreaux, popped up from behind a giant hibiscus. I had only met her one time when she came to visit Iz in New York years ago, but I could have cried with relief when I saw her now. She wore a huge, brimmed sunhat over her curly white hair, and a colorful apron over her long-sleeved linen blouse. She smiled when she saw me, but I saw her face change when Mosegi stepped out of the car.

She yanked off her garden gloves and dropped them on the ground as she ran to us. "What happened?"

Mosegi was carrying Iz in his arms, her arms and legs dangling below her. Her skin was still that eerie blue shade.

"It was Artair," he said.

"Take her to my room," Mrs. Boudreaux instructed. I wanted to weep for the frailty in her voice. We desperately needed professional help.

"Why aren't we going to a hospital?" I asked.

"I can take better care of both of you here," she said. She lifted a withered hand to my cheek. "Let's get you inside."

"Wait," Nombeko had rejoined us, and she met Mrs. Boudreaux's eye and then looked pointedly at the back of the car.

I looked back to where I had been sitting and saw a crimson smear of blood on the leather. My head swam, and I held on to Nombeko so I didn't fall over. I wondered how I could have ignored the throbbing pain so long. Suddenly it was the only thing in the whole world.

Iz's grandmother turned on her heel to stride with surprising speed back into her home. I leaned on Nombeko so completely she nearly carried me.

Mosegi had left the front door open. Mrs. Boudreaux stepped in, and the cool dark of the house enveloped me. I was hardly over the threshold when she pulled my shirt over my head and turned me around.

"Druid blade," I heard her murmur.

"I didn't know they had those," Nombeko whispered.

"Now we know," Mrs. Boudreaux said. "Get the unguent."

I swayed on my feet.

"Lie down right here, baby." She pointed to a long velvet-covered couch in the foyer, and I collapsed face down into it.

My upper back burned with a pulsing heat. Nombeko returned with a large leather box with a brass lock on the front. Mrs. Boudreaux pulled a tiny key from a chain around her neck and opened it quickly. She pulled a small green bottle from the depths of the valise.

"It's very important you stay still," she told me. "I cannot help you if you go acting the fool. You understand me?"

"Need stitches," I slurred. "Doctor. Vicodin."

"That's right, baby. Keep talking." Her words floated over me, a long, melodious incantation, almost like a song. I drifted along with them, liquid and gentle. She opened the bottle and poured a thick, viscous gel into her palm and her words were clear again. "This is going to sting," she said.

When her fingers touched my back, a molten fire tore through my body with such force that I screamed. If I had any strength inside of me, I would have run from that couch. But the scream was all I had left. So it went on, endless and throat searing, while lava burned through my veins until, mercifully, I passed out.

"Michael?"

I woke up with a gasp in a large white room, darkened by jungle-patterned curtains hanging over the massive window. I was wearing a nightgown that did not belong to me, but it was light and airy, and I was clean, and smelled like garden herbs. I stretched, tentatively, and found that I could move my arms. I reached back and felt a thick bandage crossing my back and winced at the throbbing pain.

"Michael?" I called out again. Where was he?

"Easy now," I heard a deep voice say. "Relax. Don't move too fast."

But it wasn't Michael. In the chair next to me sat Mosegi, casually flipping through a newspaper, his legs crossed easily at the ankles. He still wore the mourning clothes I'd seen him in at the graveyard, but he looked as comfortable as if he was in his pajamas.

"Where am I?"

His eyebrows went up. "You're in Roberta's home."

At my puzzled look he spoke more slowly. "Roberta Boudreaux. Isabeau's grandmother. You're in New Orleans. We brought you here from St. Roch."

"How did you find me?"

"You found us. We were attending a funeral, and you busted in. Made quite a scene. I think Father Guidry will write sermons about you for years to come."

His words swam in my ears, and none of it made sense. But one memory shot through me, and I sat up fast, despite the pain.

"Where's Iz?"

He put his large hand out and touched my arm. "She will be fine. You need to rest."

But I was sick of people telling me what to do. This day had started off so well. If it even was still the same day; I really had no way of knowing. I'd gone from Michael's bed to the laundromat to a portal to a graveyard and now to this spooky mansion all in one day? None of it made any sense, and I was determined to get some answers.

I jumped off the bed and ran down the steps, ignoring the dull pains shooting through my body. I heard voices down the long hall and made my way to the vast kitchen at the back of the house. It was a cheerful space, bright white and diamond-shaped, with a massive marble island covered with fresh flowers, fruits, and vegetables. Nombeko was chopping vegetables at the kitchen table. Mr. Boudreaux stirred a savory, bubbling stew in a huge stock pot on the gas stove, and Mrs. Boudreaux stood in the middle of it all, kneading bread dough on the countertop.

"Why are you up?" she asked. "I gave specific instructions for you to stay in bed."

"I couldn't stop her." Once again, Mosegi was faster than he ought to be at his age, and he appeared behind me. "You know how she is."

Before anyone could answer, I barked out, "Why does everyone here know me, and supposedly know how I am?"

Mrs. Boudreaux raised a floury hand. "Gail, baby, I know you have a lot of questions. And I'm going to answer all of them for you. But not if you don't take care of yourself. I need you to sit down before you fall down."

"No!" I said, and I could see that the word surprised her. "No," I repeated, but my voice was not as strong this time. Had I imagined it, or had Mosegi actually stepped back in alarm? I continued. "I am not sitting down. I am not listening to you. I want to see Iz. She needs a doctor. At a hospital. And when she's well, I need to take her back to New York to find my boyfriend and figure out if he survived the portal that appeared in his apartment."

If nothing else, maybe what I was saying might make her think I'd lost my mind, and she would send me to a mental hospital. If that happened, at least I'd finally be around actual medical professionals.

She wiped the flour off her hands to come around the counter to face me. I wished beyond all reason that we were meeting under different circumstances. When Mr. and Mrs. Boudreaux visited our shop in New York years ago, she had been so gentle and generous. She held on to my arm when we crossed streets, giggled in a breathy, sweet voice, and fretted constantly that we weren't eating right. I loved her dearly, but she was not the type of grandma who was cut out for whatever I had gotten Iz mixed up in.

"Listen to me, baby," she said, her voice as sweet as a praline. "My granddaughter is going to be fine, thanks to Nombeko's defensive skill and Mosegi's driving. You were pretty lucky, yourself."

"Okay, so what's wrong with her? And what did you do to help her?"

She reached up and placed her tiny hands on my shoulders. "There is so much you don't understand," she said gently. "Isabeau is the daughter of a long line of very powerful witches. She fell victim to a particularly nasty practitioner of dark magic in that portal, but they got her to me in time, and I was able to halt the damage. I'll have her back to health in no time at all. You too, if you can learn to follow instructions."

We stood facing each other, as still as the headstones in that horrible cemetery, and then I lost my cool.

"This is *bullshit!*" I yelled. "I'm sick of everyone suddenly having magic powers. I'm tired of portals and laser beam hands and snake tattoos and all of you crazy people. I am taking my friend to a fucking *hospital,* and when she is better, we are going back to New York City."

This time I didn't imagine it. Iz's grandfather and Mosegi both took several steps back, and Nombeko set down her knife and stood up.

Mrs. Boudreaux's face hardened, and her grip on my shoulders tightened. A mist filled the kitchen and everything fell away around us. I watched her grow taller, the lines on her face smoothed out, her short white curls spiraled out from her head until they reached the floor. She grew proud and majestic, towering over me, and when she gazed down at me her eyes were coal black and her face glittered bronze. She was beautiful and terrible.

When she spoke, her voice rang through the vast empty space and rattled the windows. "I am a stolen woman on stolen land, and you are intruding on my sacred space. You will show me respect, or you will pay the price of my anger."

My chest hollow, I nodded my agreement, and before I could take a breath, she had shrunk back down to her normal size. The mist burned away, and I could see the kitchen once again. I didn't know if I had imagined it or if she had slipped me some kind of hallucinogen in that ointment she used on my back. But whatever had just happened, I was terrified of Mrs. Boudreaux. I could still see the warrior face on her wizened skin when she smiled gently at me and patted my shoulder with her now teeny hands.

"I don't like foul language, Gail," she said, almost in a whisper. "It's unladylike."

Just then, the doorbell rang, and her eyes shone.

"We have a visitor," she said. She took me by the hand to lead me to the front door. My legs trembled so hard I could barely walk.

She pulled open the gigantic front door with ease, and I was stunned again at the unbelievable strength inside this tiny woman. As if my shock wasn't overwhelming enough, I tore my eyes from Mrs. Boudreaux to see who was at the front door, only to nearly fall over again.

"Mom?"

Standing on the doorstep, dressed in a long skirt and draping scarves, stood Darina Sommers.

My mother's eyes darted over me, but she did not acknowledge my presence. She stepped inside the house, her fine head erect and her back ramrod straight, and shut the door behind her. She stood in front of Iz's grandmother for a moment, and then my mother, the scariest woman in the world, did something I never thought I would see in my lifetime.

She bent her head and knelt at the feet of Roberta Boudreaux.

Chapter Seven: The origin of the wolf-enhanced, beta male, bug-eyed New York Lover vigilante

New York

MICHAEL
12:03 p.m.

I took evasive action before I was even aware of it. And, as pleased as I was to have such lightning-quick wolf-blood reflexes, I still wasn't used to my body reacting before I became consciously aware of what it was doing. It certainly came in handy for me in the middle of a fight—especially considering that, before I became endowed with my enhanced wolfish powers, I'd been as good at fighting as a one-legged man at an ass-kicking tournament.

But within the first split-second that I heard the exploding glass of the car's windshield followed by the distant gunfire, I was already down on the floor in the space between the back and front seats.

"Are you hit?" I called to the cab driver.

He didn't respond.

The car was filled with the overpowering scent of his shock and fear, but I couldn't detect the smell of fresh blood at all. And his heartbeat was thumping a mile a minute.

A series of two more quick bursts of additional gunfire echoed through the canyon of city streets, but no other bullet struck our vehicle.

"You're not shot, are you?" I asked.

The man didn't respond. And there was still no smell of fresh blood. But he was breathing heavily. Another four bursts of gunfire within the space of a couple of seconds sounded. They appeared to be coming from the same location, that I was starting to place as somewhere above us and to the right. That suggested to me there was a single shooter.

"Sir, can you hear me? Are you injured?"

"No," the man's voice came out in a horrified gasp. He took a deep breath. "What is happening?"

"I think there's an active shooter," I said, thinking about the slight lag time between the sound of the windshield smashing and the echo of the gun shot. "He's not on the street. Not nearby. I think he's on top of a building. Stay down, as close to the floor as you can. And stay inside the car."

I inched closer to the door on the left of the car and carefully slipped out onto the street. The cab had stopped halfway across W 33rd street, blocking the cars moving West—not that anyone was driving. When the gunfire started, most everyone in an automobile crouched down low in their stopped vehicle. That didn't stop a bunch of cars a block or two back from leaning on their horns in typical New York driver impatience.

Remaining in a crouched position on the east side of the car, I listened to the nearby cacophony of screams, gasps, panicked yelling, racing heartbeats, and the footfalls of people running away. The smell of anxiety from numerous people drifted through the air, hearty and strong, but less contained than it had been inside the cab.

As I listened to try to get a bead on where the gunman was amidst the yelling and noise and panic, I thought about how strange it was that something like this always seemed to happen to me when I was on my way somewhere else.

Did I have some sort of penchant for walking into trouble? Whether it was here in my adopted home city or in Los Angeles, I was like a magnet for misadventure. Sure, I was often able to detect mischief in the making a lot better than most people, and that certainly led to me sticking my nose into trouble I had sniffed out; but this time, like so many others, I was on my way somewhere and the troubling incident found me.

I needed to get to Newark airport to board that plane to Gail. She needed me.

But there's no way I would not step in and help put a stop to this dangerous and immediate situation that threatened the lives of so many people.

Damn that steady diet of Spider-Man comics I'd ingested growing up.

The click of a fresh cartridge being loaded into a gun came on a shift in the wind—reminding me how, a dozen years ago, I'd never have even recognized that noise— and based on the wind direction, I figured out where the shooter was perched. I also took in, on that same gust of air, the scent of intense hatred. It reminded me of the bitter rage PFA members often sported.

"I thought we'd taken care of those assholes," I muttered.

I took a deep breath and tried to figure out what to do next. But as I'd come to know, stomping out their brand of white supremacy and neo-Nazi hatred was like stomping around in a room infested with cockroaches. For every two or three you smash, another half dozen will appear.

"The shooter is on the roof of a building on the north side of West 33rd Street," I shouted to anyone within earshot. "Take cover inside or down the nearest subway entrance now. He's re-loading."

I wasn't sure if that helped anyone or not, but I did detect a few whiffs of understanding and acknowledgement from several shocked pedestrians, and the sound of footfalls heading for the subway entrances on either side of 7th Avenue.

Scuttling behind the car, I rushed across the street toward the shooter, knowing I'd be protected from his view by the buildings on that side of the street. I moved along W 33rd, keeping as close to the buildings as possible. As I moved past a bank, he opened fire again, confirming my suspicion about his location. I needed to get to the top of the seven-story building across the outdoor pedestrian mall.

As I prepared to run toward the entrance to the K-Mart on the main floor, I turned my head left to take in the scene across the street. One person lay face-down across a cement block coated in blood. To that man's left, I saw two police officers down on the sidewalk on the corner of W 33rd and 7th near the entrance to Madison Square Garden. They'd been shot but were still alive. I could hear their labored breathing and heartbeats.

As I was looking at them, their bodies jerked, followed immediately by the steady report of gunfire coming from the building above me. Watching in horror as fresh blood spurted from the officers, I felt my own rage at the bloodbath taking place.

There was no point trying to rush across the street to help them. It was too late. Like that other person who must have died in the initial round of gunfire, they were now among the victims of this madman on the roof. My stomach dropped and a sour-sweet taste filled my mouth as tears welled up in my eyes.

The gunfire stopped as I looked back to the building I needed to enter. Then I heard the loud hissing noise of something moving through the air above me. An object that looked like a coffee tumbler somersaulted through the air, spitting out a thick cloud. It landed in the middle of W 33rd Street.

Another canister hissed its way to bounce onto the sidewalk immediately to my left, spitting out noxious fumes.

Tear gas.

This guy was heavily equipped. Like some sort of survivalist prepper.

I rushed to the K-Mart door and slipped inside ahead of the cloud of toxic air.

Knowing I needed to find protection from the gas, I rushed over to a display of swim goggles, the beady-eyed kind that you see Olympic swimmers wear, and took a pair. Across the aisle, I grabbed a bandana and wrapped it around the lower half of my face to cover my nose and mouth. That should allow me to rush back out through the tear gas to get to the nearest fire escape on the building that could get me to the roof.

As I moved past a display of sunglasses and other beachwear, I spotted what I thought was a goggle-eyed monster to my right and instantly dodged to the side and raised my right arm to ward off a potential strike. I was wondering how some PFA monster had snuck up on me without me hearing or smelling them when I realized it was my own reflection in a mirrored pillar.

I hadn't even recognized myself.

Talk about being on edge.

But it reminded me of something I'd long been worried about: jumping into evasive action with my enhanced powers and being recognized or spotted. I didn't want anyone to know I had this moon-cycle curse, nor any special abilities. The last thing I needed was to be captured and studied in some secret government lab. I doubt that even the friends I'd made who were aware some paranormal beings existed, FBI Agent Reynolds and NYPD Detective Wagner, would be able to protect me from that.

When I'd prowled the city streets last month during the height of the nighttime PFA terror attacks, I'd dressed all in black so I could slip through the shadows. That had been the first time I'd ever purposely sought out vigilante action. But I had long engaged in using my powers to help others, to take down bad guys, to fight like some super-powered hero.

So why the heck had I never thought of creating a disguise? Even a goofy one like the one I was now wearing to protect me from the tear gas.

It's funny how the weirdest notions strike you at the oddest times.

But I wondered how it was even possible, for someone who grew up worshiping Spider-Man, to never once think of creating a disguise to hide my identity.

But that's what I had going for me now.

I grabbed a large grey *I ♥NY* hoodie that had been a tourist "must have" for as long as I could remember and pulled it on, throwing the hood up to disguise the color of my hair, and rushed back outside through the noxious fumes.

As I slipped outside, the idea that any bystanders spotting me might nickname my vigilante outfit in some bizarre fashion stuck me. *Look, over there,* I imagined someone saying. *It's the bug-eyed New York Lover, here to save the day.*

The goggles and the bandana did the trick, and I moved quickly on the periphery of the tear gas, but my sensitive taste and smell still brought a stinging and painful burning sensation.

I moved down the pedestrian mall, further away from those acidic fumes to the nearest flat handle-less fire-exit door. I threw a hard kick at the door that made a deep dent in the metal. A second kick against the wall to the right of the door crumbled the concrete there, and then I grasped the edges of the heavy door and was able to pry it open.

Slipping inside the much darker stairwell, I rushed up the stairs, taking them two at a time, all the way up to the top.

As I ascended, I could hear more rapid gunfire shots, the sound of the bullets ricocheting off concrete and pavement, and the screams of what I had to assume were more victims being gunned down in the street.

The sound of several approaching sirens also echoed somewhere outside, and I was relieved to know that New York's Finest and most likely New York's Bravest were on their way.

The ceiling hatch leading to the roof was deadbolted, telling me the gunman hadn't entered through this stairwell, but through one of the other ones on this long building. I climbed the metal stairs attached to the wall, grasped the lock and pulled hard on it, tearing it from the metal hatch.

The gunfire outside stopped. I listened carefully and could hear the sound of the gunman breathing heavily, what must have been the spent cartridges dropping to the roof top beside him, and another clip being loaded into the gun. The noises seemed to be coming from the left of where I was.

Slowly lifting the hatch, I peered to my left and spotted him. His back was to me, as he was looking over the roof's edge. He was wearing a navy-style army jumpsuit. He had a utility belt across his shoulders stocked with ammo and a few more of those tear gas cannisters he'd thrown down to the street.

His heart was beating rapidly, and the stench of hatred infused the entire rooftop area the way the noxious grey clouds of tear gas were filling the street below.

I leapt out of the hatch and rushed across the roof toward him. The sound of his gunfire provided enough cover so that he couldn't hear me.

"Die, motherfuckers, die!" he yelled as I approached within striking distance.

I reached around, grabbed his arms, and slammed his wrists hard against the four-foot-high rooftop ledge; the weapon fell from his hands to the street below.

His heart jumped in response to the sudden attack, and for a brief second the bitter scent of his fury was mixed with shock. As I spun him around, he was scrambling to reach for the pistol strapped to his belt.

I slapped his hand away just as it reached the gun, grabbed it myself, tore it free from its holstered strap, and threw it off the side of the building.

As this was happening, we were standing face to face, mere inches apart, and for a split second I could have sworn I spotted an odd dark inky blob moving across the whites of his left eye.

I gasped, unsure what I was seeing, and that was when he reached with his other hand for a knife strapped across his chest.

Because I'd been momentarily distracted, my reaction wasn't as quick as it should have been. I grabbed the hand that held the knife but not before it sliced into the outside edge of my left palm.

I yelped in pain as a thick line of blood poured out from the inch-long gash.

"Dammit," I said. "Now, is that any way to treat your newest rooftop dance partner?"

I squeezed his hand hard enough to feel his bones crack, forcing him to release the knife. It clattered to the rooftop. I then grabbed him by the collar with my right hand. That's when I saw something dark flicker across the whites of his right eye.

What the hell *was* that?

Then he smiled a wide tooth-filled grin and vomited a series of somewhat coherent sentences. "The evils of this world must be ended by those pure of heart and convicted of mind. Champions of what's just and right must rise and stomp out the sinners, but also the weak who drag the rest of society into the depths of despair. Hellfire fury shall reign supreme and wash this world of the blight that has been allowed to evolve. Only then shall a new world order emerge." He then released a roaring laugh.

His voice, completely different than the voice I'd heard from him moments earlier, and the laugh were impossibly deep and of a nature that would have made

James Earl Jones' low deep voice sound almost like one of the Disney chipmunks in comparison. The sound coming out of his mouth was as out of place in this pale skinny young white man as the inky dark liquid swirling in his eyes.

Still holding him by the collar with my right hand, I threw a solid left hook into the side of his face.

My punch struck its mark perfectly, sending his eyes rolling immediately into the back of his head as he was slammed directly into unconsciousness. The blood oozing from my left palm created a wide smear of crimson across his cheek. As his eyes rolled back and up, I caught the fleeting wisps of dark tendrils slithering in the opposite direction in both of his eyes. A thin jet of the black inky substance leapt out of his one eye-socket and onto the side of my left hand, as if drawn to the blood pouring from the open wound.

The cut across the side of my palm stung as if someone had poured vinegar onto it and I yelped, jerking my hand away. I shook it and looked down to see where the dark blob had gone to. It seemed to have disappeared. My hand stung and throbbed as I released my hold of his collar and let his body crumple to the ground.

That's when a preternatural scream sounded, not from his throat, but from somewhere much deeper inside him.

That scream, and those dark shadows I'd seen in his eyes, filled me with instant dread.

I shook my still-throbbing left hand and droplets of blood from my hand spattered to the rooftop.

What the hell was that dark stuff?

This was something new; nothing I'd ever seen with the PFA.

I mean, this guy's utter hate was in the realm of what the PFA were all about, but that odd substance moving about within his eyes was something else entirely.

To my continued horror, I thought I saw a thick black string of smoke escape upwards from his open mouth and nostrils. I leapt backwards to avoid it touching me again. The wispy dark tendrils then disappeared quickly straight up into the sky as if being pulled by a magnetic force, and then faded into nothing.

I didn't even have time to register whatever the hell it was I'd just witnessed when I heard another burst of rapid gunfire from down the street.

Chapter Eight: Always wear clean underwear, don't eat yellow snow, and other motherly bits of advice

New Orleans

GAIL

"Can I see her?" my mother asked when she stood from her kneeling position. She still hadn't acknowledged me.

Mrs. Boudreaux had rested her hands on the crown of my mother's head when she was on her knees, but now she had them clasped at her waist. She was so tiny compared to my mother.

"She's been sleeping all day, but I know she'll want to talk to you," Mrs. Boudreaux said.

"Mom?" I said again. "Why—"

My mom held up one hand, palm flat. "Quiet!"

Unbelievable. Thirty-eight years old, and Darina Sommers still treated me like a toddler having a tantrum. She turned and started up the carpeted stairs.

I wanted to shout so many things at her.

How did she know this house?

How did she know the Boudreaux family?

How had she known to come here?

Did she know that Iz's grandmother could turn into an African warrior goddess at random?

The list of questions was endless. My only hope was that I was having some sort of fever dream. Any minute now, I'd wake up in Michael's arms, and we'd laugh about how my imagination got the best of me.

I followed my mother up the stairs. She tapped lightly on a closed door, listened for an acknowledgement, and then opened it.

Isabeau was sitting up in the bed. She still looked pale, and she had dark circles under her beautiful liquid-brown eyes, but at least she was alert. Mrs. Boudreaux came up and stood behind me.

Darina sat on the side of her bed and stroked her hair. "Precious girl."

Iz's eyes filled with tears when she looked at my mom. "Someone else showed up," she said. "It was one of the Tír Uaighe guys. He tried to kill both of us."

My mother shushed her. "It's not your fault," she said quietly.

"How did it happen?" Iz asked.

"We don't know yet," Mrs. Boudreaux said, brushing past me into the room. "Either someone passed along information, or someone has access to your plans."

"What happened to Finn? Wasn't he supposed to be waiting for me at the other end of the portal?"

My mother glanced at Mrs. Boudreaux before answering. "Finn was killed, Isabeau. Probably by Artair, or one of his clan. I'm sorry."

I remained frozen in my spot while Iz fell into my mother's arms, weeping like she'd lost a family member. Mrs. Boudreaux procured a box of tissues for her and straightened the bedspread while my mother rocked Iz like a baby. Finally, she calmed down, smiled weakly at my mom, and turned to look at me.

Sighing, my mother stood up from the bed and walked to me. Her eyes ran over my bare feet, and she pulled the collar of my borrowed nightgown back to glance at the wound across my shoulders. But she didn't embrace me the way she'd embraced Iz.

"Are you feeling okay?" she asked.

"Given what?" I asked. It took everything I had not to scream.

"Yes, yes, daughter. Your displeasure is duly noted," she said. She turned back to Mrs. Boudreaux. "Is she well enough to listen to me?"

"She was well enough thirty-eight years ago." Her voice still had the breathy, sugary tone I was used to, but for a flicker of an instant, I caught a glimpse of the Roberta Boudreaux I'd seen in the kitchen, the giant bronze goddess with the cheekbones that could cut through steel. I knew now that it hadn't been a hallucination. That warrior lived inside her at all times.

Finally, my mother put her arms around me. She was careful not to touch the bandages on my back, and I held back from hugging her in return for a moment. But then I caught a whiff of her perfume—something like neroli and leather, a scent so familiar it took me right back to my childhood home—and I melted into her arms.

"Mom," I said. "I want to go home."

I meant to New York, to my apartment, my store, my life. To Michael. But she didn't know that.

Her hand stroked my hair now, and my throat ached with yearning. Darina Sommers had never been a stroke-your-hair kind of mother. She was more of a *stop-acting-like-a-child* kind of mother. Even when she was talking to an actual child.

"Sit down," she said.

I plopped myself on a small loveseat next to Iz's bed, and she sat on a chair across from me. I glanced around and noticed that the room was as massive and tastefully appointed as the rest of the house, with heavy draperies, bowls of fresh flowers, and tiny votive candles scattered around. Mrs. Boudreau remained standing, regal and in charge, on the other side of Iz's bed.

"Gail," my mother said. "Isabeau was trying to get you away from Michael."

"I don't want—" I began, but she put up a hand to stop me.

"This will go much faster if you just let me talk. I know you are confused. Ask questions when I'm finished."

I opened my mouth to argue, because that's what I do, especially when my mother is around. But then I shut it. Quite honestly, I had no idea what to say.

She seemed to recognize the mental debate I'd just had and lost, and she nodded her head curtly and continued.

"Isabeau was in New York under my instructions," she said. Out of the corner of my eye, I saw Mrs. Boudreaux stiffen, and my mother hastily corrected herself. "Our instructions," she clarified. "Roberta and I sent her and Ben to take you away from Michael. We didn't want to do it that way, but things were," a pause, while she searched the ceiling for answers, "*urgent*. And we didn't have time to talk to you like civilized people because you're rather stubborn when it comes to Michael Andrews. And most everything else, for that matter."

Her hand came up again, just as I was about to snap back a retort. "Please, Gail. Just listen."

I crossed my arms and sank back into the couch.

"When they arrived in New York, they went together to separate you and Michael. Isabeau created the portal back to New Orleans, at tremendous energy cost to herself, I might add. They had a plan. A rather unnecessarily complex one, in my opinion, but they argued that they know you better than I do. I couldn't disagree with them, so we let them continue."

My cheeks warmed at that observation. She wasn't wrong.

"Isabeau can generate portals because she is a witch, Gail. She has kept that information from you all this time at my request. For better or for worse, everything you are going to hear tonight has been kept from you at my request. Most didn't agree with my choice, but you were—you *are*—my daughter. I decided to raise you as I saw fit. In my opinion, that meant keeping a few secrets, for your own safety.

"When we sent them to retrieve you, the plan was for one of our people—Finn Hayes—to join them at the portal and pretend to abduct Isabeau. We knew that they would never convince you to willingly leave with them. We also knew that if you thought Isabeau was in danger, you would give chase without thinking twice about it, no matter how many years it had been since you had seen each other."

At this, I glanced over at Iz, stock-still in her bed. Her eyes were on me and she looked profoundly, deeply sad. I turned back to my mother.

"Unfortunately, and for reasons we don't understand yet, a man named Artair discovered their plan. Artair belongs to another coven, one that has never been particularly friendly to us. Like most male-led covens, they are susceptible to dark magic and extreme violence. Now they've made it clear they want war. Artair murdered Finn and snuck through the portal. He used dark magic to silence Isabeau. Once she was immobilized, he could control the portal. That requires vast amounts of very advanced magic, by the way. We did not know that his coven had those capabilities. But he couldn't change the exit spot, so you wound up back where Isabeau intended to bring you. Here, to her childhood home town. I shudder to think what would have happened to you if you had landed anywhere else. By the mercy of the goddesses, her family happened to be attending a funeral near your exit spot. Nombeko and Mosegi saved your lives; you owe them a great debt."

"It wasn't just Artair, though. There were a bunch of other guys with him."

She paused, and when it became obvious that she wasn't going to explain this, Mrs. Boudreaux spoke up. "It's called necromancy."

I felt my eyes go wide. "Those were dead bodies?"

"Not exactly. They were the spirits of dead folks. He can cast a cloning spell over them, so they look like regular people to a Mundane. They don't have the powers he has, but they are frightening."

"What happened to my brother?"

She nodded. "Ben's with Michael. They are safe. For now."

"For now?"

"We don't know how many of Artair's coven are in New York. We don't know how many clones he has created. For that matter, we don't know what other creatures are in New York. There is so much we don't know. The one sure thing we know is that you and Michael cannot be together."

"What the f—" I stopped short and glanced over at Mrs. Boudreaux, whose eyebrow raised just a fraction. A shiver ran through me, and I cleared my throat. "Why?" I said, my voice meek.

My mother sighed and looked down at her hands. "Gail, the wolves and the witches are forbidden from associating with each other, though we have been able to coexist with them for hundreds of years without much trouble. There have been minor interactions here and there, but nothing unmanageable. Our separation has always been the only thing we agree on. Until recently, the curse put upon us has been enough to keep us a respectful distance apart. We stay away from them; they stay away from us."

"Who is *us*?" I asked. "Our family? The Sommerses? Who cares about old family feuds?"

"Not just our family. Our kind." She looked at Mrs. Boudreaux, who nodded slowly.

Still, my mother hesitated. Of all the upsetting and alarming events of the day, seeing my mother unsettled was about the most terrifying.

A thought occurred to me. "Wait. Mom. Did you say *coven*?"

Finally, she seemed to gather up her courage. "Yes." She spoke clearly and directly. "Mrs. Boudreaux is the High Priestess of the Ulo coven. They are headquartered here in New Orleans, but they have roots in Africa that go back many thousands of years. It is the most powerful coven on earth. Her daughter Marla is heir to the priesthood of her coven, and her granddaughter Isabeau has become an extremely competent witch under their guidance; and will eventually lead them. The Ulo women lead all other covens on earth. That was why I trusted her to find you."

I glanced over at Isabeau, who, though still very pale, glowed in the praise. Mrs. Boudreaux's shoulders squared, and her chin lifted in pride.

"O-okay. Cool." Cool? I don't have an explanation for that response. What else do you say when you find out that witches are real, and your best friend is one? "So, Iz can stay away from Michael. That's fine. It doesn't affect my life,"

"You are talking. Not listening. I said *our* kind." She took a deep breath, and she met my gaze with steady eyes. "I am the High Priestess of the Tír Ceilte coven. We are descended from centuries of Celtic warrior women. It is because of an ancient conflict between our coven and a member of the wolf clan that the curse was put upon all witch families."

I stared at her and swallowed a sudden, alarming urge to laugh. A screeching, hysterical, giggle-in-church kind of impulse. "You are a witch? *You?*"

She didn't respond. She simply stared at me, stony faced, without blinking.

A candle on the table between us flickered, and I recalled a vague memory. My twentieth birthday. Mom had taken me and my college roommates out for a birthday dinner, and when the waiter brought out the cake, I caught her eyes across the table over the flaming candles. She was watching me with this exact expression on her face—one of steely anger. As I watched in horror, her hair erupted into flames, encircling her head, though she didn't flinch. We remained locked in that position, staring at each other, until one of my friends screamed and threw a glass of water, not on her, but on me. I'd leaned too close to the cake and my hair—longer then, and never tied back—had caught fire. After a waiter brought a towel and we all laughed about the near miss and my scorched locks, I tried to catch my mother's eye again. Her hair was back to normal, and she did not appear at all bothered by what had happened. In fact, at the time I wasn't sure she'd even noticed.

I had forgotten all about that night until this moment.

Now, staring at her across the small table in the bedroom of my former best friend, I could see it again. Much as I had seen a different side of Mrs. Boudreaux earlier, everything else fell away, and I saw my mother, her hair aflame, her eyes burning like embers, her face fierce.

The image disappeared as fast as it had flickered into my brain, and I was left panting. "You are a witch," I said again. She nodded, and we all sat in pained silence for a moment. "Nice of you to tell me now, I guess."

Her expression didn't change, but I could see her jaw move as she clenched her teeth. That was always a sign that I'd pissed her off. "I am telling you now because it involves you now."

"It involved me my whole life. You're my mother. It would have been nice to know who you are."

"Not just who I am, Gail," she said. She paused, and my stomach dropped as the meaning of her words sunk in. "You are the rightful heir to the priesthood of our coven, daughter."

My urge to laugh had disappeared entirely. Now I was filled with nothing but dread.

"Gail," she said quietly. "You are a witch."

Chapter Nine: Plenty of guns at the Hotel Pennsylvania

New York

MICHAEL
12:14 p.m.

There was a second shooter.

Of course there was.

It never failed. Whenever it was important for me to be somewhere, there always seemed to be some sort of urgent matter that required my special abilities.

Gail needed me; and I needed to get to New Orleans. But, as critically important as she was, it was going to take me all afternoon to get there. And anything could happen in that incredible length of time. It could already be too late. A darkness struck me as the thought occurred, weighing heavily, making my eyes well up with tears. Whatever it was she was facing could already be over, even now, and I'd be getting there hours later to learn the details of her terrible fate that went down while I was more than a thousand miles away fighting a pair of gun-happy prepper psychopaths.

I tried to force those dark thoughts out of my head. I couldn't think that way.

She was fine. She was with Isabeau. Iz had magical powers and would be able to protect her. Gail herself was kickass and strong. She'd be fine.

Feeding myself those thoughts helped a bit, and they'd have to do. Right here, right now, right in front of me, people needed my help.

Fortunately, the fumes from the tear gas were highly diffused at this building's height—enough for me to be able to see down the street in the direction where I'd heard the shots being fired.

I spotted something hurtling out a window that was third from the northern edge of the building, and two floors up from where the yellow wainscotting-style lower portion of the building ended. The dark, cylindrical object tumbled through the air, releasing a stream of thick white smoky matter. Another tear gas canister.

Knowing this gunman's location told me where I needed to get to.

I hastily tore the utility belt and shoulder strap from the unconscious body of the prone gunman in front of me and hurled them to the vacant rooftop of the building across the alley. He was now out cold and unarmed. Even if he woke up, he wouldn't pose any further threat.

Satisfied that I'd done everything I could there, I rushed back to the roof hatch. To save time, I didn't bother descending on the rungs, but instead jumped down to the concrete floor inside. It was only about three meters, a feat I was able to accomplish without injuring myself.

Another round of gunshots echoed through the air as I raced down the stairs. I wondered how many other people had been shot or already killed. There'd been too much chaos for me to make much sense of the damage that had been done. I thought about the police officers I'd witnessed as they went from shooting victims to murder victims; how they'd been lying helpless on the street, already struck down, when the gunman finished them off in cold blood.

Understanding how someone could do such a thing was beyond me.

But slaughtering strangers wasn't something most people could understand.

My left hand ached from where the gunman had slashed me, and I realized the bleeding from the wide slash had increased due to my heightened pulse rate from running. Pausing my descent on the third-floor landing, I tore off the left sleeve of the hoodie and wrapped it around my left palm, tightening and knotting it enough to stop the flow of blood. As I wrapped my wound, the sound of gunfire stopped. It began again less than a minute later as I finished with the makeshift bandage and continued my rush down the stairs.

As I reached the bottom of the stairs and pushed my way out the fire door, the proximity of at least three distinct sets of sirens told me that help had arrived.

I briefly considered making a sharp turn right when I got to the adjacent street. I could run over to Penn Station, get my hairy butt to Newark airport, then to Gail. Best to just leave things to the more-than-capable professionals who had now arrived. But I reminded myself of the circular logic I'd already played back in my head a few moments earlier.

Deal with this quickly, then get to Gail. You can't let anyone else die from your inaction.

Some days I really wished I didn't take that Spider-Man *great power, great responsibility* mantra so seriously all the time.

I raced east down the street in time to see an ambulance pulling up onto the wide expanse of sidewalk in the front of Madison Square Garden, where the two dead officers lay prone. I didn't need to focus on whether they had heartbeats; I already knew they were gone.

But I marveled at the paramedics who, despite the continued gunfire, rushed out of the vehicle, crouched low, and made their way to the fallen bodies. Across the street a NYPD cruiser screeched to a stop at the curb. Another siren echoed from a nearby adjacent street, indicating another cruiser was approaching.

This city, this country, this world, had seen so much violence, so much tragedy. There'd been so many horrific actions of terrorists and madmen hell-bent on destruction and chaos. It somehow seemed the norm since 9/11. But that wasn't enough to put a damper on the conviction of those who put themselves in harm's way on the front line every day.

They did this constantly. Rushing into dangerous situations.

I only did it when the incidents found me.

But they could use my help.

The gunman's window in the hotel across the street would normally have a clear view of where I was, but the billowing tear gas provided some visual cover. I kept low and as tight to the building on my left as I could as I ran toward 7th Avenue.

As I was rushing closer to the cruiser that had just pulled up, the two officers inside leapt out of it and took cover on my side of the car, crouched up against the vehicle facing the hotel across the street with their guns drawn.

The shooter was aiming in this direction, and I heard the zing of a couple of bullets as they whizzed past me just a few feet to my right. The next few shots struck the opposite side of the cruiser the officers were crouching behind.

The female officer shared details of what they were able to see into the radio attached to her left shoulder. I could, of course, hear her clearly from more than thirty feet away.

"We've drawn their fire. There appears to be at least one active shooter on the west side of Hotel Pennsylvania. On the fifth floor. Three rooms in from the north side of the building."

Crouching lower, I inched my way closer to them. I figured I needed to let them know about the other decommissioned shooter on top of the K-Mart building. He was unconscious and unarmed; but some official authority really needed to take care of cuffing and securing him before he escaped. And the more they knew about what had already gone down here, the better.

As I was scuttling up towards them, the male police officer of the pair spotted me out of the corner of his eye and turned.

I waved. But the burst of shock and apprehension coming off him matched the sudden wide-eyed look he threw at me.

"Officer," I said. "There's—"

But he spun his body all the way around, and turned his gun, in a two-handed grip, in my direction. "Freeze!" he yelled.

"But I'm—" I began to say, still walking forward in a slightly crouched position and raising my hands palm up in that universal *I'm unarmed* gesture to show I didn't mean either of them any harm.

The female officer also turned her head to look, but kept her gun trained on the hotel across the street.

"I said stop!" the male officer commanded. "Stand down. Or I'll shoot."

I realized how stupid it had been to sneak up on a pair of police officers in the middle of a tense active shooter situation in a hoodie, a pair of swim goggles, and a bandana that covered my face. Of course they would assume I was one of the perpetrators.

Freezing in place as I realized this, I also understood that I wasn't about to take the goggles and bandana off my face and reveal who I was to them.

"On your knees. Now!"

"Listen," I said, kneeling with my hands still raised, "I know what this looks like but if you contact Detective Wa—" I stopped in mid sentence. I'd been about to suggest that they reach out to Detective Wagner, because he knew me. But that wouldn't help with anything. Because, though Wagner knew Michael Andrews was a good guy who had, along with a motley crew of his friends, participated in supporting and helping the NYPD, and could certainly vouch for me, that would do no good in this particular situation. Wagner had no idea of my own paranormal abilities; and I wasn't about to reveal my identity beneath this silly getup. And Wagner definitely wasn't about to vouch for some anonymous guy in a stupid identity-hiding outfit who was demonstrating supernatural abilities.

The rapid-fire sounds of gunfire picked up again, but this time the gunfire was not aimed in our direction. The shooter aimed down the street. I heard the ricochet of bullets off pavement as well as the sound of them hitting the metal of one or more vehicles. I wondered if it was a different squad car that had arrived, or perhaps the ambulance.

I needed to get back to my feet, leap over these two police officers without harming them—and, just as importantly, without them shooting me. But that didn't seem likely in my current position. I could easily leap over the cruiser from a standing position. But I wasn't all that adept at jumping when on my knees.

"Cover him," The male officer said as he shuffled around the one side of me. "I'm going to move around and cuff him." The female officer spun to train her gun on me as her partner continued to swing around, grabbing my right arm. I let him twist it around my back.

The gunfire echoing out from the hotel across the street stopped as the gunman was likely again reloading his weapon.

"Listen, officer, I can explain. It's not what it looks like." I said. But he wasn't listening. The metal of a handcuff came around my right wrist. A moment later, just before he grabbed my left arm, I smelled a brief indication that he'd hesitated for a split second before grabbing it.

He'd noticed the blood dripping down my left arm.

"Whose blood is that?" he said, twisting my left arm behind me and cuffing my arms together. Like before, I could have easily prevented him from doing that, but I went along with it, not wanting to give him or his partner any reason to shoot me. "What did you do? How many people did you kill?"

"None! I'm trying to hel—"

I'd wanted to say *I'm trying to help*, but he placed a hand on the back of my head and shoved me forward hard, slamming me onto my face to the pavement.

Keeping his hand on the back of my head, he pressed a knee hard into my shoulder blades.

The pressure on my back and head suddenly released, followed immediately after by the sound of gunfire as the officer above me grunted in a combination of shock and pain. I then heard him fall to the pavement beside me.

He'd been hit.

And the strike had been deadly, as I could no longer hear the sound of his heartbeat.

Chapter Ten: The velvet blood comes off this bloody iron fist

New York

MICHAEL
12:19 p.m.

"Wallings!" the female officer shouted.

A split second later she was speaking into her radio again. "Officer down. My partner's been shot. Repeat, Officer Wallings is down."

I felt an uncontrollable rage burning from somewhere deep within.

Wallings, the police officer who'd been cuffing me, was dead.

He wouldn't be dead if I hadn't snuck up on the two officers and surprised them wearing this stupid outfit. He wouldn't be dead if I didn't look like some deranged lunatic, likely involved in the multiple shooter action that was going down. He would not be dead had he not considered me a threat that needed to be dealt with immediately and left the protected position he'd taken up behind the side of the cruiser. He wouldn't be dead if he hadn't focused his attention on me to put me down on the ground and handcuff me.

It was my fault.

The bitter regret over my stupidity grew and spun inside me. But as a new burst of gunfire from the hotel across the street sent shots ricocheting off the cruiser and the building to my left, I realized something important, and a very concrete resolution emerged.

Sure, I was to blame, and would wear that guilt. But ultimately, Wallings wouldn't be dead if it weren't for the homicidal gunman still shooting from the fifth floor of the Hotel Pennsylvania.

I was practically seeing red as I pushed myself hastily to my feet.

The female officer, still in a defensive crouch behind her cruiser, re-trained her gun back on me. "Get back down," she yelled.

"No!" My voice was filled with a gravely resonance that sounded like a growl deep from within me. I immediately smelled the change in emotion off the officer. She was taken aback, and her previously offensive manner stood down just a little.

Of course, I was almost as shocked by my voice and response to her as she was.

"I'm going into that hotel. And I'm going to take out that guy up there who just killed your partner."

She looked at me and slowly lowered her weapon. That action came with a simultaneous scent of her realization I wasn't a threat. Ironic, considering the hostility and anger in my voice. But I think she understood, very clearly, that I was going to exact vengeance for what happened to her partner.

"Do it," she whispered, covering her body mic with one hand. "Get the bastard."

I then took two strides forward and jumped over both her and the police cruiser, leaping headfirst into the air, then flipping just before landing on the ground on my feet and hands. Then I bolted straight across the street toward the hotel.

As I was performing these actions, I wasn't consciously aware of how I was controlling my movements until I was in the middle of doing them. It was like my body had gone on some sort of reflexive autopilot. Sometimes, in the heat of a fight, an instinct kicked in, allowing me to dodge punches, kicks, knives and bullets. This was like that, but somehow faster, and buried beneath utter fury.

There was no question I wanted to stop this guy from shooting, hurting, and killing more people. But something inside me was burning with an intent like no other to get into that building and make him hurt.

A howl escaped my throat as I reached the hotel lobby and pushed my way inside.

A half-dozen people cowered up against the walls and behind furniture in the lobby area. Hearing the medley of their rapid heartbeats, their breathing and sobbing, and smelling their terror—unlike the emotions flowing around outside, as there was less wind and airflow to dissipate the scents in here—angered me even further.

I know that the term "seeing red" is just an expression, but while my other senses remained clear and strong, my vision took on an odd pinkish filter. It was almost as if someone had slipped a large pair of novelty pink-tinted Elton John-style glasses onto my face.

On top of however many people these two clowns had already killed, there would be countless others who would suffer from PTSD. For years they might wake up in a cold sweat horrified that they or a loved one was about to be gunned down in cold blood by some random gun-toting psychopath.

My rush to the nearest stairwell and up the several flights of stairs was mostly a blur. All I kept thinking was that I was going to take this guy down as quickly as possible, then get my ass to Newark airport and on the next flight to New Orleans to be with Gail.

Following the sound of gunfire, I exited on the floor where the gunman was.

A tall, stocky, bald white guy wearing a navy-blue blazer with the word SECURITY printed across the back was on the other side of the fire door, peering around the hallway toward the room where the gunman was. I figured he was a hotel security guard. He started to turn my way when I opened the fire door with a loud squeal.

"You need to stay off this flo—" he said as he turned. But he stopped when he saw the getup I was wearing, and immediately went into fight-or-flight mode, likely assuming I was a bad guy trying to sneak up on him.

He rushed toward me, swinging what looked like a nightstick.

There was no time to reason with him. Not that my instinctual reaction even let me do that. The pink-tinted hue in my eyes became a little darker.

I thrust my left hand out to knock his arm back against the wall, and he dropped the black nightstick to the ground. I then grabbed him by the shirt collar with my right hand, lifted him up off his feet, and threw him backward across the hall. The plaster where he hit the wall cracked from the impact of his shoulder and his head, and he grunted and crumpled to the floor.

Moving past him, I made my way down the hallway toward the sound of the gunfire.

Behind me, I heard the guard getting back to his feet, the rise in his heartbeat as he prepared to launch himself at me.

"I don't have time for this," I said as he leapt at me. While he was trying to stop me, other people might be shot and killed. There was not another second to waste.

I ducked down, grabbed the arm he'd attempted to throw around my neck, flipped him over my back, and slammed him down hard onto the carpeted floor.

The impact knocked the wind and consciousness out of him.

He wouldn't be getting up any time soon.

Stepping over his body, I proceeded down the hall toward the room the gunman was in.

The sound of rapid gunfire stopped momentarily as I reached the door.

I kicked the door in, easily smashing the part of the wall the securing the door lock. The door flew open, and I could see the gunman about twenty feet in front of me standing at the open window and in the process of slapping a new cartridge of ammo into his gun. The body of what looked like another security guard was lying in the middle of the room in a pool of blood.

The gunman turned at the sound of the door crashing open.

My vision shifted to an even darker and thicker shade of red.

"You're done!" I growled, thrusting a finger at him, before rushing forward and launching myself across the room. I struck him hard in the chest, causing him to drop the gun as he flew back against the wall beside the window. He hit it and the wall buckled inward from the impact.

He was still on his feet, and he shook his head and glared at me.

That's when I saw the thin dark snake-like blackness swim across the white of his left eye. It was the same thing I'd seen in the other gunman's eyes.

What the hell was infecting these guys?

My left hand throbbed and pulsed as I was looking at his eyes.

Letting out a primal scream, he reached for a knife on his belt.

I reacted before I was even aware, grabbing his forearm and squeezing his hand hard enough that the bones shattered beneath his flesh. I squeezed harder.

He let out another yell, this time a scream of pain, and as his eyes widened, the dark tendrils of ink in his eyes exploded into smaller lines, squirming madly across the entire surface of both of his eyes. I recalled the large metal tank my dad stored minnows in when I was a kid.

Whenever you lifted the lid off the tank, the minnows scrambled away from the light in a dozen different directions at once.

I continued to squeeze his arm tighter, feeling a sickly bolt of pleasure knowing that I was causing him pain. And the crimson hued lens I looked at the world through got thicker, darker than before.

He fell to his knees and howled.

The dark red in my eyes intensified as I let out my own guttural howl of triumph at his pain.

I reared my right arm back, intent on hitting him with as much force as I could. As my punch connected with his nose—something I experienced in a painfully sick slow motion—and just as I was relishing the deliciously satisfying crunch of bone beneath his skin, the dark-crimson filter on my eyes thickened and darkened until I couldn't see anything at all.

And that's when everything went black.

Chapter Eleven: Gail Sommers and the order of the Irish Exit

New Orleans

GAIL

The Boudreaux mansion filled with people almost the moment my mother finished her grand "You're a Wizard, Harry" speech. She insisted I *be polite* and *get dressed* and *stop fidgeting*. Isabeau's parents, Daniel and Marla, had been the first to show up, embracing my mother like long-lost siblings. Other family arrived—cousins, aunts, and uncles—as well as friends and neighbors.

Darina introduced me to everyone, but their names immediately disappeared into my mushy brain. Before I could catch my breath, the house was full, and large glasses of wine and bowls of savory stew were passed around. The people crowded in the kitchen seemed to be holding a vigil of sorts for Finn Hayes—the mood was somber, but occasional laughter punctuated their tears. Conversations tended to hush when I entered rooms.

"It's so nice to finally meet Darina Sommers' daughter," I heard over and over again.

I couldn't reply in kind, because it wasn't nice to meet any of these people. I had never even known of them before today. After about an hour, I pulled an Irish exit. I doubted anyone would even notice, including my mom. In any case, I had a perfect excuse. I had been slashed by a Druid blade. Not that I knew exactly what a Druid blade was, but I knew that my back hurt like hell. Maybe being slashed by a Druid blade was a common occurrence in witch circles, but it was a new experience for me, and I wanted to go to sleep.

I tiptoed around the house, looking for a phone, but Mrs. Boudreaux didn't seem to have a landline. I even snuck into Iz's room and looked for her phone. No honor among thieves, I figured. She lied to me for a decade; I was entitled to steal her phone.

She woke up as I was poking through her dresser drawer.

"Hey," she murmured.

"Hey back," I said. "How are you?"

She shrugged and closed her eyes. For a moment I thought she might keep talking, but then her breath went slow and even, and I backed out of the room.

Just before I shut the door, I heard her voice again. "You won't find a phone."

I peeked my head back into the room. "What?"

"You heard me."

I stepped into the room and snapped on the light. To hell with her recovery. "You may remember that I have a business to run. I have an important meeting tomorrow. You can't stop me from making work phone calls."

"It won't happen." She sighed. "Everyone knows you'll try to find Michael. The shop will survive without you. Instead of trying to sneak around, you should get some rest."

Her eyes remained closed, as if she was talking in her sleep. Every argument bubbling up in my throat disappeared, because in the sudden bright light I could see once again how tired and ill she looked.

I snapped off the light and went to my room, where I tossed and turned for the rest of the night, only faking sleep when my mother came in to check on me.

*　　*　　*

"None?"

"None."

"Not one?"

The depot agent shook her head at me, with a what-can-I-tell-you kind of helpless shrug, and then gestured to the man in line behind me to move forward.

I held my hand up to stop him. "Hang on. I'm not finished. So, there are no trains to New York. Not one. Even though there are supposed to be four departures daily."

"That seems to be the case."

"Are you aware that there are no flights to New York? Or anywhere near it?"

"Are you sure?"

"I was at the airport this morning. Couldn't get a single flight to anywhere on the Eastern Seaboard."

"It is strange," she admitted.

"Ya think?" I said, my voice rising. As a person who works in retail, I knew full well that anyone who sniped at service workers when they didn't get their way was the lowest form of humanity.

But also, I was also starting to lose my cool.

"Did I miss a major event in New York? Maybe a hurricane or something?"

I couldn't see her computer screen, but I watched her eyes furrow as she scanned the screen. "It doesn't look like it," she said. "There was a mass shooting near Madison Square Garden yesterday. But I don't think it shut down the city. I guess lots of people are going there for summer vacation."

I took a deep breath. "Can you get me anywhere near New York? Pennsylvania, maybe? Massachusetts? Vermont?"

Clickety, clickety, click. Her fingers flew as she tapped her keyboard, searching for available train tickets.

"You could have saved yourself a trip down here and done this all from home, you know," she said. "We have an excellent website. You can plan your own trip, upgrade to a sleeper cabin, even arrange room service in advance."

"Yes, I'm sure your website is lovely," I said, through clenched teeth. "But I can't find my phone, and no one will let me use a computer. That's why I'm here, trying to get help from a human."

She cocked an eyebrow but didn't reply. "Well, I can't find anything in Vermont. Should I try another one?"

I massaged my temples. Nothing about this day made any sense.

"How about this," I said, a flash of inspiration lifting my ugly mood. "Get me a ticket to California."

"Where in California?"

"Literally anywhere. I don't care. The second I arrive there I'll get a flight to New York."

"Alright, then," she said. "I have a train leaving for San Diego in about an hour. You'll arrive in, let's see, about 66 hours."

"Fuck's *sake!*"

Her eyebrows went all the way up and she fixed me with a stare that told me quite clearly that she was tired of me.

"Shall I book the ticket, or not?"

"Yes, please." I slid over my credit card. I'd lost my phone somewhere along the Portal to Hell, but my wallet had remained in my pajama pocket. Small mercies, I guess.

"Declined."

"What? No, that's not right. Try again."

"I've tried three times. That's the max I'm allowed to try it. Do you have another card?"

"No. Let me try, sometimes it gets wonky. You have to really jam it in there so it reads the little chippy."

"Lady, when you find some cash, or another card, or a real destination, come talk to me."

"But you don't underst—"

"I understand that you don't know where you want to go, and even if you did you don't have any money. I'm gonna need you to step aside for paying customers. Next!"

Bewildered, I didn't move from my spot in front of her window when the man behind me in line asked for a ticket to Nashville like it was the easiest thing in the world. I hadn't even moved when the next person in line walked up.

The ticket agent addressed me again. "Now, you're not gonna make me call security, are you? Go deal with your life, and then come see me again when you have it figured out. Next!"

I turned and walked from her window to an empty bench in the terminal. Every train was full. I couldn't call anyone. My money no longer worked. What the hell was going on?

I rubbed my eyes with the palms of my hands, itchy from lack of sleep. Mrs. Boudreaux had come into my room early this morning and rubbed more of the ointment on my back and changed the bandages. The pain had diminished, but I was strangely aware of it. My heartbeat pulsed along the edges of the gash.

There didn't seem to be any other options for me. No flights, no trains. I couldn't afford a taxi all the way to New York, even if my cards did work. I studied my hands, and then had an inspiration.

I stood up from the bench, only to find myself face to face with Isabeau. She still looked pale, and was much thinner than I remembered, but at least she was on her feet.

"That's a really stupid idea," she said.

"What is?"

"Hitchhiking."

"I don't know what you're talking about."

She sighed and sat down on the bench where I had just been. I crossed my arms and stared down at her. Iz's face remained placid, and it slowly dawned on me what had happened.

"You did this." It was suddenly so obvious. "You maxed out my credit cards. You booked all the flights and trains."

"That's strange. Everyone else is buying tickets with no problem." She waved her hands at the ticket counter, which was not backed up for miles the way it would have been if there really was a travel standstill. "And I don't have that much power."

"Ah. My mother did it."

She shrugged. "I'm sure several of the elders were involved."

"You've made it impossible for me to leave, and now you're here to lecture me about wanting to hitch a ride?"

"You're desperate, so you think you can walk right out there and stick your thumb out and some nice person will to give you a lift all the way to Manhattan. What are the chances they'll be serial killers? Wait, let me guess. You think because you are dating a werewolf, and you're the daughter of a witch, and you went through a portal without losing your breakfast, that you can handle a run-of-the-mill murderer. Am I right?"

She was, but I was damned if I would give her the satisfaction of admitting it.

"How did you find me?" I asked, slumping into the seat next to her.

At this, she actually laughed. "Let's just say, you're not exactly subtle. I know," she said, putting her hand up to stop me exactly the way my mother had done the night before, "you think you are. One day you will be very good at moving around without being detected. But for now, you're the absolute worst. It was like tracking a blue whale on land."

"But I'm part witch. I should be as sneaky as all the rest of you, right?"

"It doesn't just happen, Gail. It takes training. A lifetime of learning, for most of us. And there is no such thing as 'part witch.' You aren't a sausage."

She kept her eyes on the other passengers making their way through the terminal in various states of hurry, but I could tell she was acutely aware of me and my next move.

"I need to get to Michael," I finally said.

She didn't even look at me. "Not gonna happen."

"Everyone in the world knows what's best for me."

At this, she turned and looked directly at me. "Yes. You finally understand. Everyone knows what's best, except you. If you don't believe me, look around. In the short time we've been sitting here, I've spotted three witches from Tír Uaighe, two wolves, and a demon."

Startled, I looked at the people milling around the train station. Sure, it was a huge variety of people, some scarier looking than others, but they were no worse than the people I saw every day in New York.

"Isn't that a normal number of freaks for a train station?"

"They're called Paranormals, and you're one of them, so mind your manners. And, no. It's not a normal number of them among the Mundanes, ever, in any location. I used to go years at a time without seeing other Paranormals outside of my own family. The rules have changed, Gail. They've grown bolder. They are seeking you out, even if they don't entirely understand why. That's why we're trying to keep you hidden. For once in your life, you have to listen to people who are smarter, and wiser, and want you to live."

"Michael wants me to live."

"That may be true, but Michael doesn't have a clue what he is, or where he comes from, or what it means to be involved with you. In many ways, he's even more dangerous than you are, because he's just as ignorant, but with uncontrolled Paranormal powers. Plus, he has nothing to lose."

"What about my work? You, of all people, know how I feel about the shop."

She seemed to waver, so I pressed on. "I'm having staff problems right now, Iz. My manager can barely hold it together. And she says it's been full of strange customers lately. She said she's been scared of some of them." I couldn't remember if Jaya had actually used the word *scared*. I suspected it had been more along the lines of *confused*. But I needed to make a point.

"Where's she from?" she asked.

"Arizona."

"No, dummy, I mean, where is she from? How'd she find you and the job?"

"Just walked in one day, and we started talking. She really knew her stuff, said she was new in town and needed a job. You had just left me high and dry, so I hired her on the spot. Never even checked her references. She's been a godsend. But even she can't do it alone."

Iz quirked an eyebrow, and I held my breath. Bringing up Iz leaving the shop was pushing my luck.

"Dammit," she finally said. "I told them we should have shut down the store when I left town."

My jaw dropped. "While you were at it, you should have burned down my apartment and stabbed me in the gut. Because who cares if I have a life or a career?"

"Stop being dramatic. We only did what was best for you. At the time, we had enough of our kind checking in on you that we thought you were safe. But now…well. Word has obviously gotten out. Other Paranormals are trying to get close."

"To me?"

"Partially, yes."

Her eyes dropped to my arm, where I was absentmindedly slipping my fingers in and out of the wretched cast, trying to scratch the unbearable itchiness.

"Take that off," she said. When I protested, she leveled me with a gaze. "Please."

I removed the brace and she took my forearm in both hands, wrist up, the way an athlete would hold up a baseball bat in front of their body, testing its balance. I flinched in anticipation, but she held firmly and I realized that despite weeks of pain, her touch didn't hurt me at all. She closed her eyes, and a warm, liquid heat fill my arm. It moved slowly from my wrist up to my elbow, growing hotter deep in my flesh. My skin tingled and I swear I could feel the blood moving inside my veins and the bones knitting themselves back together. Her grip loosened, and the hot honey sensation dissipated through my body.

"Fixed," she said, and she picked up my brace with the edges of her long nails and tossed it into a nearby trashcan.

Without an x-ray, I had no way of knowing for sure that she'd healed me, but I could tell it was different. My arm loosened. In fact, my whole body felt lubricated, as if I'd just had a great massage. My exhaustion from the night before seemed to have disappeared, too.

"Can you do that to my back?"

"I wish. A Druid blade leaves a different kind of wound."

"So, you're a healer."

"Most of us are, to some extent," she said. "But Healing is my talent."

"What is mine?"

She gazed at me for a long time before answering. "We won't really know for a while. But it has always been suspected that you are a Seer."

"Very funny."

She didn't laugh, and I realized she was serious. It was ridiculous, obviously. If I was a seer, I doubt I'd be so confused about what was going on in this witch-filled world.

But then I thought back to all the times people had called me some variety of "perceptive" or "observant." Michael used to tell me I had a Spidey sense, but comic book nerds always love telling their dates they reminded them of their favorite superhero. It would have been dorky coming from most guys, but was pretty adorable coming from him.

"I wish you would have told me this years ago," I said. This time, I saw her flinch at my words.

"I had very strict instructions," she finally said.

"But we were best friends."

"We still are," she said. "But that didn't change the fact that I was sent to New York to do a job."

"If we're friends, then you already know what I'm going to do. No matter how hard you work, no matter what it is you are doing to public transportation or my credit cards, I'm going to keep trying to get home."

"We're stronger than you."

"I'll keep trying until I die of exhaustion."

"You don't know what's waiting for you out there. You'll be killed very easily."

"Then someone can come with me to New York. A bodyguard. But either way, I'm going back to my shop, Iz. I have a life. You can come with me, if you want."

"I will die before I let you see Michael again, Gail. Know that right now." She paused, and then spoke her next words slowly. "But I do agree that you deserve a chance to keep the life you have built there. It's fairly unique to be totally independent of the coven. You're something of a unicorn."

"Are you telling me unicorns are real, too?"

She smirked, but I could see that she was pondering my idea.

"Think about it, Iz. We could take a road trip, like the old days. We could eat greasy diner food and drink Slurpees until our brains freeze and sing really loud car karaoke."

"I wouldn't mind meeting this Jaya person. She seems to have slipped under our radar. It's unusual."

She chewed her lip, but she hadn't said no, so I kept at it.

"Plus, if you come with me, we could talk." Yes, it was underhanded, but I wasn't above using cheap shots to get what I wanted. If she meant it when she said she thought of me as her best friend, then I was going for the emotional jugular vein. "I mean really talk, Iz. The way we used to. You could tell me about everything." I swept my hand in front of me, indicating the train depot. "You can tell me about all of these demons, and how to kick their asses."

She laughed nervously, and her eyes darted around the room. "There aren't any in here right now."

"Are you sure?" I nodded toward a rail-thin, icy blond man in a light grey suit. "That guy for sure wants to suck your blood out."

She dropped her head into her hands. "I am going to get in so much trouble."

I almost danced. "If we take turns driving, we don't have to stop. We can make it home by tomorrow. Let's go pick up your travel bag and hit the road."

She stood up, her face grim. "No to both. I don't have a death wish. We'll stop at motels along the way. And we are not going back to the house. Gran will know what I'm up to the second I walk in the door."

"So, we're going right now?" I asked, hardly daring to believe it.

"You're the Seer. You tell me."

She strode toward the exit, and I followed, in spite of the circumstances, happy to be in her wake once more.

Monday, July 31, 2017

Chapter Twelve: Yes, Gail, there is a Virginia revelation

Staffordsville, Virginia

GAIL

I'm safe. I'm coming home.

I hit send, thought for a second, and then chanced another message.

I love you.

As anyone with half a brain could have guessed, Iz caught me before I could send the second one.

She took a long pull of her coffee and regarded me for a second before saying anything.

"Are you kidding me?" she asked.

She took the phone from my hand and dropped it on the ground. She stomped on it with the heel of her Doc Martens, picked up the shards, and tossed them in the nearby bin. She then raised her cup at me in mock salute.

"I'm not going to stop trying."

"Then you're going to waste a lot of money on burner phones."

To be fair, this was the third one she'd confiscated in the twenty-four hours we'd been on the road. Even Iz has to use the ladies' room occasionally, and I used those moments to ask the cashiers at every single gas station, rest stop, and fast-food joint we stopped at. I hadn't even been able to activate the SIM card on the first two—she got to me before I even got them out of the package. But I'd purchased this one at a Walmart, where we'd stopped to buy a change of clothes.

Walmarts are big enough that I slipped from her gaze, claiming I needed to try on some shorts. I hit the changing room and locked the door behind me. I'd waited until the next rest stop to actually try to text Michael, but hadn't been fast enough.

Iz leaned against the car and looked out across the expansive vistas of Virginia. I took the pump out of the gas tank and replaced it. Iz was far more comfortable with stillness than I was; the sedentary hours in the car were seriously testing my nerves. I paced around, jogged in place a bit, and locked my arms behind my back to stretch my chest up to the sun. When I'd gotten most of the impatience out of my system, I joined her at the car. She pointed with her cup-holding hand toward the tallest point of the wilderness.

"That's Big Walker Lookout," she said. "You can see five states from their observation deck."

"Yes, charming," I said. "God bless America."

She turned cold eyes on me. "Gail Sommers, do you know why I'm with you right now?"

"To protect me?"

"Correct. From what?"

"Bad guys. Witches with tacky tattoos."

"I'm protecting you from the mutts."

"Mutts? Do you mean Michael?"

"I mean his kind, yes."

"Wow," I said. "Nice."

"Don't you dare get high and mighty with me. I've given up a lot of my adult life, including my own love life, to watch over your ignorant ass. Don't call me out about subjects you don't know anything about."

"It's not my fault if no one will tell me anything about Paranormals."

"Get in the car," she snapped.

I slipped into the passenger seat and let her take a turn at the wheel. When we were back on the highway, she spoke again. "Don't talk out in the open like that."

"No one was around."

"Just because *you* didn't see them doesn't mean they weren't there. I already told you that Paranormals aren't acting right lately."

I turned my back on her and stared balefully out the passenger window. The undulating greens of the Jefferson Forest sped by me.

After my irritation diminished, I turned to face her again. "Please tell me."

Her eyes didn't leave the road, but she inhaled deeply before she answered. "Witches and wolves have existed since the dawn of time. In the beginning, of course, everyone got along well enough. The wolves didn't eat the people, and the people protected wolves. Each had powers, each had weaknesses. And then, two of them mated."

This took me a minute to digest. "Wait—what? A human and a wolf? Sickos."

She glanced over at me. "It's not that different than what you are doing right now."

I burst out laughing. "Very funny. I don't actually have sex with animals, in case you didn't notice."

"Neither did our ancestors. Remember, these were ancient times. People and animals were able to communicate and take on each other's forms. It's not as crazy as you might think. Their union produced a—well, a crossbreed. Most of our clan uses worse language, and the werewolves have their own slurs against us. But for our intents and purposes, we'll call Michael's type a cross-breed."

"Mutts."

She had the decency to flush. "I'm sorry I said that. I know you care about him. I know you think he's a nice man. But the rest of us have centuries of mistrust to overcome."

"So, we hate the werewolves because they are crossbreeds?"

"*Interspecies* cross breeds. And we were able to stay civil to one another for many centuries—wolves, and witches, and other were-creatures."

"Jesus. There are other were-creatures?"

"Unfortunately, humans don't seem to have any self-control when it comes to falling in love. Or lust."

I whistled. "Imagine fucking an octopus."

She laughed, and for a moment, just a heartbeat, it felt like the old days, when Iz was trying to work and I was bored and antsy and I cracked joke after joke. Her laugh sounded like diamonds bouncing off a sea cave. I held my breath, wishing with everything inside me that we could be transported back to those days, and I could make her laugh all day, just for the joy of hearing that sound.

If we could take one of those stupid portals back in time, I'd still have Iz.

But not Michael.

The thought took my breath away.

She continued. "Almost all Paranormals functioned well alongside each other. We lived many ages in relative peace. And then it happened again. Only by this time, the wolves and the witches had evolved. We fought each other for land and dominance. Then Aisling Sommers, of your clan," she said with a glance in my direction, "fell in love with Connal Murphy, of the Breathnatch wolf clan. They produced a child, and the clans went to war to claim her. Battles erupted. A whole bunch on both sides died. Eventually, the elders agreed to a binding contract: that any descendants of either clan who loves a member of the others would be subject to death. And when a certain witch fell in love with a particular wolf, it would cause destruction that would rend the world to pieces."

I stared at her for a long time, trying to digest it. "But I didn't even know I was a witch. And Michael wasn't born a werewolf. So, there is no such thing as his 'clan.'"

"The curse very specifically points to you and Michael. The witch was the younger twin of a non-magic boy. The wolf was a storyteller from the north. No one ever really understood that reference, since the pact was formalized in what's now Ireland, and all of the wolves in Iceland, to the north, had been extinct for centuries. But, as our clans spread and met other clans, we understood that it could have been anywhere."

"Iz, pull over."

She asked no questions, just smoothly steered to the right and stopped the car.

I jumped out of my seat and slammed the door. She was out of the car and at my side in a second. I balled my fists and leaned my head back and screamed, screamed, screamed into the sky. I screamed until my voice gave out and my throat was scraped as raw as smashed glass.

Finally, when I was finished and collapsed on my knees in the spiky gravel, I felt her arms around me.

"I know," she said.

"No you don't," I whispered. "No you fucking don't. This isn't fair."

"That's what I know," she said. "It's never been fair. That's why we all hate it. I think that's why your mom kept it from you. But fair or not, we have no choice. We have to handle what's in front of us."

"Needless to say," my voice croaked. "I'm going to need some help."

"I know. This time, I got you."

Chapter Thirteen: And that's when the evil stung me, and I had a feverish dream

New York

MICHAEL

I was trapped in a bizarre feverish nightmarish haze where I was spinning uncontrollably while kicking and punching at eerie goblin-faced specters launching themselves at me from the darkness in a never-ending assault.

Their demonic faces laughed and cackled as they came at me. And when I struck them, they let out agonizing howls of pain.

Sick satisfaction filled me with every single blow I landed.

"Michael!" I heard a male voice calling to me from somewhere beneath the thick cackles and screams of the twirling ghost-like monsters.

I tried to focus on the voice, knowing it had come from someone familiar to me, but for the life of me, I couldn't place who it was. Nor could I place where he was in the darkness that surrounded me; not with the maniac chants of the gruesome faces that continued to rain their attacks on me.

"Wake up, Wolfman," the voice said. There was something else about it too, the vague familiar notion I knew someone who called me by that nickname.

I just couldn't place it. There was too much noise, too much chaos swirling around.

Some time later, I was running through a dark and musty tunnel. I couldn't see in the pitch darkness, but all my other senses kept me from slamming into the walls of the twisting and curving tunnel as I ran. Unlike the previous nightmarish vision, there were no monsters attacking me. But I was chasing something. And something else was chasing me. I was caught between those two desires—to flee from something terrible; but also, to keep going and catch whatever it was I so desperately sought.

I wasn't sure who or what I was, but my throat burned as I called out the name "Michael!"

Was that who I was chasing? Who was Michael? And who was I?

My fists were bloodied and raw, but I kept punching at the brick wall in front of me. The wall screamed with each punch that send chunks of mortar and clay into the air. And the screams, in turn, caused a deep roaring laughter from my gut. As I kept punching, the brick wall morphed into flesh, and each impact of my fists came with the satisfaction of puncturing flesh and cracking bones. I laughed even harder, realizing that the blood on my fists was not my own, but was coming from whoever, or whatever, I was punching.

Darkness. Utter darkness. No movement. No noise. Nothingness.

"Michael," a male voice, calm and assuring, spoke to me.

That's me, I thought. *I'm Michael.*

Then the sound faded, and I slipped, again, into the unrelenting darkness.

My head throbbed as if Bill "Bojangles" Robinson was tap-dancing on the top of my head to a beat that Ringo Starr was banging on the inside of my skull.

I opened my eyes to a bright, blinding light that acted like someone had just slipped the two musicians an injection of Red Bull.

"Bright light! Bright light!" I called out, clamping my eyes shut again, much to the chagrin of my dry, burning throat.

"Let me close these blinds," a male voice said. I recognized that voice, and the smell of this guy. He was someone I knew, but I wasn't able to place him in my foggy haze.

Keeping my eyes closed tightly, I let the sounds and smells around me tell me where I was. I took a breath.

I'm in my apartment. At the Algonquin.

My name is Michael Andrews. I'm a writer. And a werewolf.

And…something had just happened recently. Something important. I needed to be somewhere, didn't I?

Gail!

She's in danger!

I couldn't remember what the danger was, or where she was, but something told me I needed to get to Gail.

"Gail!" I yelled, sitting up and opening my eyes.

I was on my couch in the living room area of my hotel apartment. It wasn't as bright as it had been before, because the blinds had been closed, but the act of sitting up and opening my eyes sent a marching band down the middle of my forehead.

"She's on her way here," the male voice said. And I realized whose voice it was. Someone I hadn't spoken to in years.

Gail's brother Ben.

But he hates me.

What was he doing in my apartment? How did he even know where I lived? No, wait, maybe I had recently spoken with Ben. I had a fleeting memory of him barging through my apartment door.

"Andrews, we need to talk!"

Talk about what? What the hell did Ben have to talk with me about?

"Just lay back," Ben said, his hands on my back and shoulders, gently pressing me back into the couch.

I blacked out again.

2:34 p.m.

"Hey Michael," a male voice said. I instantly recognized it as Ben. "Your breathing has changed. Does that mean you're finally back in the land of the living?"

Opening my eyes, I sat up slowly. Ben was sitting in the chair beside my sofa. It was brighter in the room, despite the blinds still being closed. Ben lifted a glass of water from the coffee table and thrust it in my direction.

"Here. Take a drink."

I grabbed the glass and drank the entire thing down, relishing the cool sensation on my parched throat.

"Ben?" I asked. "What's going on?"

Ben put out his hands. "Slow down. Tell me how much you remember."

"Uhh," I thought back to the latest things I could recall. "Fighting with goblins and some sort of demons. But that wasn't real, was it?"

"I don't think so. You've been in and out of consciousness and running a high fever since shortly after I found you and brought you back here this morning."

I looked at him as I thought about spending the entire morning laying on my couch. Images of the wicked, flashing, grotesque faces swirled around me. A sudden barrage of other memories spiraled in my head. Of fighting supernatural bad guys, the PFA, in an underground tunnel alongside Gail and Lex, and Carl. Of Carl being killed. Of Lex falling down the depths of some dark hole, of me wanting to throw myself down that same hole. Of an endless series of days and nights lying in bed and moping around in a feverish daze. Of Gail taking care of me, sitting with me, comforting me the whole time.

Of what happened next between Gail and me.

And of Ben and Isabeau showing up at my apartment.

Then it all came back to me. Everything that had happened since then.

Well, almost everything.

"Okay," I said, putting a hand up to my head to ward off the dizziness. "It's coming back to me now. I was heading to Newark, to get to New Orleans. Shit, you said it's the next day? It's Sunday? I missed my flight!"

"It's actually Monday."

"What?" I stood up from the couch but was hit with a wave of nausea and vertigo. I let myself fall back onto the cushions.

"I need to get to Gail. She needs my help."

"No," Ben said. "She doesn't."

"But her text message."

"That wasn't her."

"Of course it was. I received a text from her cell phone. She needs my help."

"Michael, listen." He stood up from the chair and walked over to the kitchen counter. "That wasn't Gail."

"How do you know?"

Ben returned to the chair, holding a cell phone in his hand. Gail's cell phone.

I stared at it.

"She must have dropped it when she went through the portal," Ben said. "I found it on the floor under the couch. She had the ringer and notifications turned off. That's why we didn't hear it ring when you tried to call her."

Gently taking the phone from Ben, I turned it over in my hands. "Then who sent that text?"

"I suspect it was some sort of interference spell."

"Interference spell?"

"Some warlocks and witches have the ability to influence gremlins that can interact with different technologies. Some can cause lights to turn on and off, some can infiltrate entire computer systems, and some can highjack various radio waves, such as the electronic ones that bounce between cell phones."

"Are you saying that gremlins in the machines are a real thing?"

"My Irish ancestors called them gruaimín. That translates to 'gloomy little person.'"

"Okay, so that wasn't Gail who texted me. It was a *gloomy man*. But you said they were on their way here. Have you heard from her?"

"I received word from Iz," Ben said. "They are on their way back to New York."

"Good," I said, sinking back into the couch, relieved I didn't need to rush to the airport. "We can sort out all of this when they get back. When does their flight get in?"

"They're not flying; they're driving."

"What?" Why on earth would they be driving when they could be back here in a matter of hours by catching a flight? I suddenly remembered what had happened to distract me when I was on my way to Newark. I looked down at the t-shirt I was wearing. The last thing I remembered wearing on top of this shirt was the *I* ♥ *New York* hoodie.

"Ben, you said it's Monday, right?"

"Right."

"The last thing I can remember was the shooting near Madison Square Garden. There were two shooters. I took one down, and the other, I was fighting when everything went black."

"Everything went black?"

"Well, dark red, actually. I was seeing red. I was losing control. Fighting on auto-pilot." I thought about the security guard I'd tossed around like a ragdoll. And the delight I'd felt as I was hitting the gunman in the face as hard as I could. I was out of my mind with rage. Then there was nothing. I scanned my memories, but only kept coming back to the swirling, laughing goblin faces I'd kept punching in my feverish dreams. "Ben, I think I hurt someone."

His face went solemn and the scent coming off him told me I'd done more than that.

"I didn't." I said under my breath. "I couldn't."

"The reports of what exactly happened are unclear. There were seven people, in total, killed by the two shooters. Three of them were police officers. There were also more than a dozen injuries, mostly people cut by shattering glass, or with side-effects from inhaling the tear gas. A security guard whose arm was broken described being attacked by a guy in the hoodie, with a bandana around his face and a pair of swim goggles, who had stormed his way into the room where the second gunman was holed up. The same outfit you were wearing when I found you. That second gunman..." he stopped, looked to one side, and took a deep breath before he continued, "...was found bludgeoned to death."

My heart flip-flopped, and I raced back through my memories, coming up with nothing but a deep crimson darkness.

I couldn't have killed that gunman.

But I honestly couldn't remember.

A cold chill ran through me.

When I first started dealing with the lost time of turning into a wolf all those years ago, one of my biggest fears had been not having control of myself—even in wolf form—and causing harm.

As time went on, I learned more about the nature of wolves. Based on that, the snippets of memory that came to me in brief flashes, and reports of my behavior as a wolf, my lupine self had never harmed a single innocent person.

But that fear had never truly left me. And now it came back in spades.

What the heck had I been doing from the time I blacked out in the Hotel Pennsylvania to when I woke up back here in my apartment?

Chapter Fourteen: Feel or feel not. There is no joke

Jordan Springs, Virginia

GAIL

"**A**bra Cadabra!"

I threw my hands out in front of me, dramatically lunging into Iz and stretching my face into a wide grimace. Not a single hair on her head moved.

She didn't flinch, only blinked at me slowly. "You wanna take this seriously?"

I wiped the sweat off my forehead and sat down. The wild grass in the surrounding field rustled in the light breeze, and the dim evening light dulled my thoughts. We'd been at this so long that I barely knew up from down anymore.

In her attempts to train me in witchcraft, she'd thrown just about everything on earth at me—rocks, sticks, even clods of earth itself. Every one of the missiles struck me, despite my attempts to dodge them. When I got mad and threw things back at her, she batted them away with a flick of her finger.

"Trust me, Iz," I panted, "No one is taking the curse against my love life more seriously than me. But we're a million hours in and I'm no closer to magic."

Her face softened, and she plopped down next to me with a sigh. "Every time you try to be cute, you are telling me you think this whole thing is a joke."

"You, of all people, know damn well that's not true. I would give a limb to have all of this over with."

We sat in silence. My stomach growled loudly. We had been here for so long, and she didn't show any signs of letting up yet. If I brought up a dinner break, she might hex me all the way back to New Orleans.

"It's all just…" I searched for the right words. "A little much."

She nodded slowly. "I guess it would be a lot to absorb in a very short time."

"I make stupid jokes when I'm nervous. Or pissed. Or worried."

"Or all of the above," she said, putting her hand on mine. "I do know this about you."

"Well, does any witch actually say 'abra cadabra'? Isn't every legend based in some reality?"

"Ye-e-es," she said slowly. "Sometimes they are. But usually, the legends the Mundanes repeat have nothing to do with us, and what they ignore completely is witchcraft, right in front of them."

"Like what?"

She shrugged. "Could be a lot of things. You buy a jar of jam from a woman at a farmer's market and the next day you meet the love of your life. A person considering ending their life meets one of us and suddenly decides to live another day, just to see what happens. A doctor is surprised that someone healed so fast from an injury, and attributes it to modern medicine." She looked pointedly at my arm.

"So there's no such thing as science? Or luck?"

"Of course there is. But not always. Sometimes things happen because of the influence of a witch. One of the main reasons we are still able to go undetected is because most of the modern world is looking for logical answers. We think our methods are the most logical ones, but Mundanes can't even imagine our skills. They will use any excuse to explain our nature away."

I thought about that for a while, absorbing this new detail into some of the madness I'd witnessed over the last forty-eight hours.

"Nombeko," I said. "She's your cousin?"

"Second cousin, yeah."

"She was doing some light saber shit. I saw these fire beams come straight out of her palms. There is no way that went undetected by normal people."

Her chin went up a degree. "Please don't use that word. *We* are normal. People without magic are Mundanes. And Nombeko is a special case. She can gather vast amounts of solar energy and send it out of her body. She rarely has to work in front of Mundanes, but when she does, she is able to shield herself from their vision."

"She turns invisible?"

"Not exactly. Any Mundane who was watching yesterday would have seen her leaning out of the car window, raising her hands in the air. But they would have thought she was a reckless teenager acting foolishly. They wouldn't have seen the firebolts. It's important to understand how extraordinary it is to have such highly visible talents and to be able shield it. Few witches are born with both powers."

She paused, considered her words, and then continued. "Actually, that's not right. We're all born with a lot of the same powers, and we learn our strengths early in life and focus on developing them. Very few can harness two forces of energy projections at the same time as skillfully as Nombeko can. She has trained very hard to do that. If you have that skill, it will take years to master. Maybe decades. But she has weaknesses, like all of us."

"What are your weaknesses?"

Iz sighed and plucked at the grass at her feet. "I have no sense of Divination, so I usually have to rely on the wisdom of others for guidance. I'm a strong witch, and I'm more gifted than most at moving undetected in the modern world. But my power comes in bursts and then takes a long time to return. That's one of the reasons they sent me to fetch you. I am one of the few who could conjure that portal, but it took a lot out of me. In a combat situation, that's more than just a weakness. It could mean my death."

"What are my weaknesses?"

"Tall, broad-shouldered Canadian men," she said. "Get up."

I stood up to face her.

Iz held her hands in front of her, palms facing each other, and stared into the space between them. "I need you to stop thinking about objects. Understand that you are a very small part of the world. You cannot create magic; you *are* magic. And you can learn to harness the power of the earth's magic if you stop thinking about it and start listening to it. Every animal, every star, every blade of grass and drop of water. All life. All death. All of it is connected, and all of it is magic. The witch can manipulate that energy. Right now, I want you to just try to *sense* it."

I mimicked her movement, holding my palms in front of me.

"Now, close your eyes, and trust yourself."

I did as she told me, and I heard her step closer to me. The sound of the summer cicadas dulled, and her breathing was steady and even. She stood so close to me that I could practically hear her heart beating. She placed a ball in my hands, about the size of a volleyball. Warm to the touch, it had a gelatinous quality, and when I tried to push my palms together it resisted and then bounced back softly.

Whatever she had handed me buzzed in my ears, but that wasn't the only sound I heard. I could hear the wind now, moving gently through the wild grasses that Iz had just been plucking. I had always thought wind was a monolithic sound, solid and dull. But now I could hear the tendrils of air weaving between every blade of grass on the field. The wind was so fine I suspected that if I held my hand out, it would pour through my fingers like sand. It braided into strands between the grass and melded into a huge tapestry that covered all of us. As the understanding of how wind worked dawned on me, I realized the ball had expanded in my hands; my palms were now stretched out past my shoulders.

"Gail. Look."

Without fear, I slowly opened my eyes. The ball in my hand wasn't there. At least, no one else would have seen it. But it wasn't invisible to me. It was as if someone had slipped heat glasses over my eyes and given me a new kind of sight. I could see a pulsing, liquid orb, shimmering softly around the edges. Nothing showed through it, and yet it wasn't opaque. My fingers sank into the surface of the ball.

It was like holding a beating heart.

"Look down."

I gazed down past the ball and saw that the grass around me had erupted in a pale blue fire. It formed a perfect circle with me in the epicenter, and the blaze rose high over my head. But it did not spread, and it did not burn.

I looked up, and the blue blaze dimmed where I looked. To my surprise, Iz was all the way across the field. I laughed out loud, and could see her beautiful smile in response.

"Did you run over there?"

Even from the distance, I could see her chiseled eyebrow raise, and I laughed again.

"In a manner of speaking," she said. "Why aren't you afraid?"

I didn't know what, if anything, Iz could see in my hands. But somehow, I knew that nothing surrounding me at this moment would hurt me; that even though I was holding something I'd never seen before, it wanted to protect me.

"Should I be afraid?"

"Being engulfed in flames seems like something that would scare most people."

"How did you do this?"

"I didn't."

I did.

I held the energy of the wind in my hands, and I conjured blue fire.

My life was suddenly very, very cool.

"Catch!" I hollered, and threw the ball to her.

I laughed again as the blue flames parted, and I watched the orb soar through the air. But Iz stood still, watching me carefully. The ball arced over the field between us, landing directly on her head. It was like she was showered with glitter that instantly absorbed into her body. For an instant, the edges of her skin shimmered, and I thought she was about to transform the way Mrs. Boudreaux had. I realized that, like her grandmother and my mother, Iz had another, wilder form inside her.

But the shimmering stopped, and her face broke into a wide smile. "You catch."

She threw another rock across the field, and it landed on my shoe. This time I did not try to duck away from it. I remained still, as she had, and willed it to absorb into my skin.

Instead, it landed hard on my foot, and I yelped. The fire flickered around me, but didn't dim.

"Gail!" She groaned. "Stop thinking."

She bent over again and flung something toward me. The next moment reminded me of the seconds between a flash of lightning and the crash of thunder. This was that exact instant, fat with potential, when I knew what was coming but didn't quite know what it would be. Iz did not move, but in the split second after she said those words—*stop thinking*—a tidal wave approached me from where she stood.

Whatever she had thrown thundered silently across the grass. I fought my body's instinct to hold my breath, and instead, I exhaled. Time slowed. Iz remained across the field, but she was also so close that I felt her warm breath against my ear and saw straight through to the depths of her dark irises, into the very nerves of her brain. Even as I watched her so closely, I could also see the waves roaring across the expanse of grass between us, bearing toward me. I put my hands up in front of me and put one knee on the ground, certain I was about to be swallowed whole, but not bowing my head from the onslaught.

Instead of fear, I felt strong and immovable; a boulder blocking a tiny stream. Whatever she had thrown parted around me. My hair blew back in its gentle wake, but otherwise nothing touched me.

The air had gone quiet. I couldn't hear the cicadas, or that woven-together wind, or the buzz of the invisible ball. I stood up, a little shaky, took in a deep breath, and my lungs expanded in the silence. My weird little blue fire remained around me, its flames dancing gently toward the sky, and then it simmered down again, as if I'd turned off the energy source.

The sounds of the field came back again—birds, bugs, rustling leaves. Iz's footsteps as she jogged back to me.

She tilted her head to gauge my reaction. "You okay?"

"I think so?" I held up my hands, but they just looked like my regular old hands once again. Chipped black nail polish. The scar from the one time I tried to bone a fish. No fuzzy clear ball. "Was that…normal?"

She chewed her lip. "Not for a beginner. Not for your clan."

"Can we try again?"

"Do you want to?"

"What did you throw?"

"The same thing I've been throwing at you all day. Energy."

"No. This one was different. This was some kind of tsunami."

She smiled, and for the first time it was a shy smile, not the one she gave me when I was trying to make her laugh. The one she gave when she learned something new, or when she thought I wasn't looking. A smile of hope.

"You Saw," she said.

"Obviously. You threw a giant wave at me. How could I miss it?"

"You missed it the first hundred times I threw it. You bitched about rocks hitting you."

I pulled up my t-shirt. My stomach, breasts, and neck were pockmarked with bruises. "I bitched because the rocks you threw hurt me."

"Why would I throw rocks at you? That's just crazy talk. And would it kill you to wear a bra?"

I yanked my shirt down again, huffing in irritation. "I didn't witchcraft these bruises on to my own skin."

"No, but you were thinking like a Mundane. You saw what made sense to you until you were ready to see what was really happening."

I stared at her for a long time. I could See. This was a fact I didn't entirely understand, but suddenly knew, down to the marrow of my bones.

I am a Seer.

"Can we do it again?"

Iz replied with a laugh, and jogged back across the field. "If you do it again, I'll buy you a bra," she called back. "From Paris."

I breathed deeply again; the electricity in the air filled my lungs. The grass around me, green once again, shimmered in the waning evening light.

"Let's go."

Chapter Fifteen: Just another Apatetic Monday

New York

MICHAEL
2:52 p.m.

"You said it's Monday," I finally said, after about a minute of sitting in silence with my head reeling from learning I'd killed a man. Sure, he was a bad man, and had killed a cop. But I'd killed him? Why couldn't I remember doing that?

"Yeah," Ben replied.

"And you brought me here to my apartment?"

"I did."

"When?"

"Early this morning. Around 4 a.m."

"Jesus, Ben. I can't remember anything from after I stormed into that hotel room and attacked the gunman. Tell me what happened."

"Well," Ben said. "After you left, when I woke up, that's when I saw Gail's phone under the couch. I grabbed it and rushed out of your apartment to find you, to show you it wasn't Gail who texted you. But you were long gone. I needed to stop you from getting on that flight, so I took a cab to Penn Station.

"But by then the shooting had started, so that whole area had been blocked off. I couldn't even get within a couple of blocks. So, I had the cab take me directly to Newark. But that was a waste of time, because you weren't there.

"By that time, the news was reporting details about the two shooters, and this odd third character whose face was obscured with goggles, a bandana, and a hoodie. How he'd leapt impossibly high into the air, growled like a wild animal, charged into the Hotel Pennsylvania, and attacked a security guard on his way to the gunman.

"This vigilante then escaped the police, who wanted to question him about the dead gunman. The news wasn't sure if he was some sort of accomplice to the attack, or someone completely unrelated.

"I figured, since you seemed to disappear on the way to Penn Station, and the incredible feats this person displayed, that you might have been the vigilante they were looking for. I am, after all, familiar with your penchant for sticking your nose into police business."

Ben stood up from the chair and pointed at my empty glass. "Do you need a refill?"

I shook my head.

He walked over to the kitchen and filled a second glass with water from the sink which he drank on his way back to the chair across from the couch.

"I kept wandering the city, looking for any sign of you. There had been scattered reports of the bug-eyed vigilante spotted in various places through Midtown."

"Damn," I said. "It's all completely black. Did I hurt anyone else?"

"No. Not that I'm aware of. At least nothing serious. There were a few reports of lightning-quick attacks by a figure matching your odd guise who strikes at random, then runs away, screaming incoherently. Sightings of you only lasted for the first half day after you disappeared from the Hotel Pennsylvania. All I know is you didn't get on that plane. And nobody knew where the hell you were. I spent most of the day going to places I knew you regularly went to. Your agent's office. Gail's store. A few nearby restaurants and cafes."

"You seem to know a heck of a lot about me."

"Isabeau and I have been watching you for years. Ever since you came into my sister's life."

"So how did you find me?"

Ben shrugged, and a sheepish look crossed his face. The air also filled with the smell of his embarrassment.

"I didn't. At least, not on my own. Late Saturday night, I went back to your apartment, in case you'd returned. But you hadn't. And I couldn't get back into your place. So, I got myself a room at a nearby Holiday Inn, and kept checking the television and news on my phone to see if there were any other sightings of the mysterious vigilante. I spent most of yesterday continuing to search for you. And also continued the research about where we might locate the artifact that is hidden here in the city.

"But it was this morning, around 3 a.m., when I suddenly woke up in my hotel room. I'd heard something outside in the hall. I leapt out of bed and raced to the door. There was a sheet of paper that someone had just slid underneath it. Usually on check-out day, they slip your receipt under the door in the middle of the night. But I knew it wasn't that, because I'd checked in for a full week.

"There was nobody in the hallway when I looked out.

"And the paper slipped into my room wasn't, as I suspected, the receipt for my stay. It was a hand-written note."

"What'd it say?"

Ben stood up again, this time reaching into his front jeans pocket and pulling out a white sheet of lined eight and a half by eleven paper that had been folded twice. He handed it to me.

I unfolded the paper and saw, in hand-written black block letters, the following:

YOU'LL FIND WOLFMAN NORTH OF BOW BRIDGE IN CENTRAL PARK.

I had a sudden flash back to one of the voices I'd heard and recognized during my feverish haze.

"Wake up, Wolfman."

There was only one person who called me that. Someone who jokingly referred to me by the name; but who had no idea I was actually a werewolf. *Or did he?*

Buddy J. Samuels.

The guy whose nick-of-time arrival in his car saved my life during that wolf attack in upstate New York all those years ago that led to my affliction. The longest friendship I'd had since moving to The Big Apple.

The man who constantly showed up at just the right time to save my skin.

"Buddy," I whispered.

"What?" Ben asked.

"Buddy, my traveling salesman friend. He's the only one I know who calls me 'Wolfman.' I have a vague memory of him talking to me somewhere in that confusing mess of goblin-infused memories of the past day or so. Buddy must have been with me at some point. He had to be the one who wrote you this note."

My head was spinning.

"Buddy?" Ben's eyebrows went up in surprise. "Who the hell is that?" His body had gone tant, ready to spring on this tantalizing new bit of information. An odor of confusion underlined his physical reaction. Ben had no idea who Buddy was. Hadn't he been following and spying on me all these years? How could he *not* have known who Buddy was?

I shook my head. "Buddy's an old friend. Never mind that. So, is that where you found me? In Central Park?"

"Yeah. You were there. You were lying on the dirt in this alcove between an outcropping of rocks facing a little island in the lake there. It was pretty well hidden. You were there, stunned and barely conscious."

"That's one of my usual spots for when I change between human and wolf. I must have gone there out of instinct. But I don't know why Buddy would have known I was there."

"This Buddy, this friend you were telling me about, does he know about your Paranormal nature?"

"No. Not that I'm aware, anyway. And you never noticed, in all these years you were spying on me, that I've met with him on a regular basis?"

"Watching."

"What?"

"We weren't spying on you. We were watching you."

"Toe-may-toe. Tah-mah-toe."

Ben ignored me. "No, this traveling salesman guy was never on our radar."

I thought about that for a second, and the enigma of Buddy that kept growing, particularly in the last several years, grew three sizes that day, like the Grinch's heart. But I didn't have time to worry about that now.

"So you found me. And brought me home?"

"Yeah. But not before removing the hoodie, the bandana, the swim goggles. They were looking for someone matching that description, so I knew enough to get rid of that stuff."

"Was I conscious? Speaking?"

"Somewhat. It was as if you were drunk. A little spaced out. You knew who I was, but you had this lack of energy. Like something had tapped you out. And occasionally, you freaked out and reacted oddly to some strangers we'd pass, as if regular people were trying to attack you."

"The goblins. The laughing demons," I muttered, thinking about the maniacal grins that haunted those feverish dreams.

"But I got you back here, and that took up all the rest of your energy, because you passed out, and were in and out of consciousness for hours."

"I don't understand," I said, getting up from the couch and walking over the kitchen to lean on the counter. "What the hell is wrong with me?"

As I was standing there, the anger grew in me, and the room turned an odd pink hue. An intense hatred and fear overwhelmed me.

Ben moved around to the other side of the counter to face me. I tilted my head to look up at him, about to yell at him to get out of my face. And that's when his face went white, and the scent of fear shot out of him like a cork escaping the clutches of the top of a bottle of champagne.

"What?" I asked. "What's wrong?"

"Y-your eyes."

I turned to look at my reflection in the glass of the microwave door, but I couldn't make out more than a vague shape. I ran to the washroom to look at myself in the bathroom mirror.

Dark minnows of inky blackness swam through the whites of my eyes, dancing about and flickering back and forth.

They looked exactly like the eyes of the two gunmen I had taken down.

Ben was at the door, standing there, taking deep breaths.

"What the hell is in my eyes, Ben?"

"It's an Apatetic Spirit."

Chapter Sixteen: May the evil spirits fly from the Funky Cold Medina

New York

MICHAEL
3:04 p.m.

"A Pathetic Spirit?"

"No, not pathetic. Apatetic."

"Tom-may-toe, toe-mah-toe. Whatever it's called, what the hell is it?"

"It's a manifestation of darkness and hatred and evil that can inhabit a person's body—control their actions. If a Wraith gets too close to a human, it can affect them in this way."

"If a *what* gets too close?"

"A Wraith. They are evil spirits that take on a solid form." Ben paused, stroking his chin. "Yes, this all makes sense."

"No. None of it does. None of this makes *any* sense. When the hell did I walk onto the set of *Supernatural*?"

"About fourteen years ago when you let that wolf bite you."

"It scratched me; it didn't bite me. And I didn't *let* it. It's not like I had any choice in the matter. Can we get back to the pathetic wrath thing inside me?"

"Apatetic Spirit. It's impossible to have a Wraith inside of you."

"Okay, so whatever it's called, what is it doing there?"

"It has been controlling you."

"Controlling me? Ben, what the hell?"

I turned from Ben to look back at my reflection in the mirror. The black shapes were fluttering about with an intensity that matched the racing of my pulse. My reflection turned a dark red.

Ben's hand came down on my shoulder. "Michael, listen to me. Take a deep breath."

His voice was steady, very calming.

I focused on him, the soothing vibes he was giving off, and did as he instructed. My pulse slowed down and the red hue I was seeing through started to fade.

I took another breath. A deeper one. And the color filter dissipated even more.

"That's good," he said, then guided me back to the living room where he sat me down on the couch. "Slow, steady, deep breaths. That's it."

"What's happening to me, Ben? I'm just like the gunmen."

"What?"

"The two gunmen I confronted. Their eyes looked the same as mine. They had these same things swimming around in the whites of their eyes."

Ben nodded. "Those men were also possessed by APs."

"APs?"

"Apatetic Spirits. When you fought with them, did either of them bite you?"

"No," I said. I remembered the knife wound on my left hand and the black tendril that reached out toward my hand when I'd punched the gunman. And the stinging sensation I'd felt. "But this," I held up my left hand, showing Ben the scabbed over wound on the side of my left hand. "This knife wound. I thought I saw one of those black tendrils launch itself from the first guy's eye toward the blood."

"And that's how you got infected. Humans carrying an Apatetic Spirit can spread it to another human. Wraiths can also infect humans, but I'm sure you would have noticed if the men you were fighting weren't human."

My head was swimming with a dizzying amount of new information.

"What the hell are Wraiths, again?"

"They're usually summoned or conjured by a lower-level demon or sorcerer." Ben said. "They are evil incarnate. They are drawn to and feed on negative emotions like hate, in order to manifest into physical form."

"And Wraiths can inject these apa—these APs into humans?"

"Yes. And APs usually can't live long in a host. It depends on how severe the emotions of the host are. The stronger their hatred, the longer they stick around. When a person is possessed, the AP usually pokes at negative energy—anything with a raw and powerful intensity. They work at removing inhibitions, playing upon existing prejudices, long-buried desires."

Ben paused, closed his eyes, and I could smell the fact he'd come to some sort of revelation before he again spoke. "That would explain the much higher incidents of domestic violence and racist attacks in the city."

"The PFA inspired that kind of hatred already."

"Not exactly," Ben said. "The Proud Fighters for America inspired copycats; people dressed up in bizarre costumes going out and terrorizing neighborhoods, mob-like behavior that often happened after dark.

"These APs control people, getting them to act out upon their darkest internal demons. Things the hosts think and feel, but often would never say or do, or act upon. Everyone has some darkness inside them. But the APs are typically drawn more to those whose fury is much closer to the surface. Because they flourish on that. And they thrive much longer in a host that remains enraged for a longer time. They multiply quickly and are able to infect others either from proximity, or the same way a virus is transmitted. Respiratory secretions. Contact through mucous membranes. The way a cold can spread when you rub your eye after coming in contact with a virus.

"They're fickle though. When a host is injured, or it looks like they might die, the Apatetic Spirit slips away, tries to escape. But they can't survive very long outside of a host."

I thought about the black tendrils I saw escaping from that first gunman's eyes and floating off into the sky. That spirit must have died. Only, before that, it split itself off and got inside of me.

"It's been two days since this spirit infected me, Ben. You said they usually didn't stay very long inside a single host. But I've been carrying it since Saturday afternoon. It's almost forty-eight hours later, and it's still inside me."

As my sense of panic rose, the red hue returned.

Ben gave off a sense of alarm. He could likely see the black tendrils manically dancing in my eyes again. "Deep breaths," he said. "Take long, deep breaths."

I closed my eyes and pulled in a long, full breath. With my eyes closed I'd swear I could feel the little dark shapes swimming around beneath my eyelids. But I tried to ignore them and focus on the breathing.

In and out. In and out.

A minute later I opened my eyes and my vision seemed normal again.

"It's probably sticking around because you're not like other humans. You're Paranormal. You're strong. You're powerful," Ben said. "But also, you're not like the other werewolves. Most of the werewolf clans I'm aware of have full control over the change between human and wolf. And they maintain a consistent single consciousness. The same mind transcends either form.

"You don't have that. There's an alter-ego living inside of you. Those dual natures you walk around with must bring a consistent and ongoing conflict between man and beast into play deep beneath your consciousness. As a man, you're aware of the wolf blood coursing through you. And that knowledge you carry around leads to an ongoing subconscious conflict that the Apatetic Spirit is drawn to."

"I thought you were an anthropologist, not a psychologist."

Ben shook his head and scowled at me. "You're so damn much like my sister. Stubborn and trying to joke when you shouldn't."

I pressed my lips together. This wasn't the time for being a smart ass; but it was me default reaction to dealing with something so startling. "Yes," I agreed. "I have flashing memories of my time as a wolf. So I'm aware there's an alter ego inside of me."

"And when the wolf is in control, it must be somehow aware of the human blood flowing through it."

I nodded. In those occasional brief snippets of wolf memory, my alter ego had at least a bit of an understanding of where it was, of its need to remain hidden from people. And it also appeared to know who my—the human's—trusted friends and allies were.

"Neither of you has any control, any true sense of understanding or consciousness when the other is in charge. That duality, that internal frustration of both man and beast, must be what continues to feed the evil spirit lurking in you right now. It's likely enough of an energy source to keep the AP fed, despite the fact you're not seething with rage all the time."

"How the hell do I get rid of it?"

Ben was quiet for a long time while he seemed to be searching through some archives in his head. "You have a bathtub, right?"

"Yeah."

"Do you have any Epsom salt?"

"No."

"What about in your kitchen? Any sea salt?"

"I have kosher salt."

"Good. That'll work." Ben jumped up and ran to the bathroom.

"Work for what?" I asked, following him.

He bent over the tub and turned on the water. "I'm filling this bathtub with lukewarm water. Go grab that salt. Add as much kosher salt to this water as you can. Dump in the whole box."

I headed back to the kitchen.

"Do you have any lemons?" he called out. "Rosemary? Any sort of fresh mint?"

I flashed through a quick mental inventory of things that were in the fridge and cupboards. There wasn't much left. My kitchen's current status gave Mother Hubbard a run for her money. There were some leftover lemon peels in my compost container from the tea Gail had made the other day. But there were no sprigs of anything fresh left in the kitchen at all.

"There might be some lemon peels. That's about all."

"Okay. Bring those."

I retrieved the peels from the composter, grabbed the box of salt, and returned to the bathroom with both.

Ben grabbed the peels and tossed them into the water. He also dumped the entire box of salt into the bath. "Okay. Now take off all your clothes and get into the tub. I'm going to run out."

"Where are you going?"

"Water is one of the natural ways that people can reset their energy, cleanse their spirit. But we need to enhance the water with elements that help draw out the tension, draw out the anxiety. It'll help calm you.

"While you're doing that, I'm going to head over to Gail's store and grab some of the other things we can use with the water, to try to exorcise the Apatetic Spirit from your body. I need to find some crystals. Obsidian, Clear Quartz, Spirit Quartz, Turquoise, Amethyst, Tiger's Eye. These are the crystals that serve to ward off evil spirits. They can draw it out of you. There are other items I need, too. There's a ritual we can perform involving those and a few other items. I'm sure I can get them all at Enchanting Magic."

I stood, bewildered, in front of the tub, staring at him.

"What are you waiting for?" Ben said. "Get in that tub and stay there until I get back."

"Okay," Ben called out when he came back into the apartment. "I've got everything on my list."

He didn't need to announce his presence, as I could hear him coming the moment he got off the elevator, and his scent preceded him into the apartment before he even opened the door.

I was still soaking in the tub, just like he had directed, having occasionally drained some of the water and added fresh warm water. Ben was right, soaking in the water calmed me. Well, not initially. Because when I first got into the water—after Ben had left—I'd thought about being in this tub with Gail all those years ago the morning after our first night together. Those memories aroused me. I mean, how *couldn't* they? And, after all this time, Gail was back in my life again. Only, she wasn't.

The combination of arousal and disappointment at being separated from Gail set my emotions into overdrive, and the Apatetic Spirit within me began to take hold. As my vision started to blur with that now-familiar red filter, I took deep breaths and focused on the warmth of the water. I laid my head back against the edge of the tub, my feet resting on the other side, with the rest of my body submerged. It had been decades since I'd been able to fit my entire body inside most bathtubs, so this was as relaxed as I could get.

But it had worked. And I'd remained in that calmed state until I heard Ben return.

As he made his way through the apartment, I sat up in the tub, leaning forward a little and raising my knees up in an attempt to keep my private parts as hidden as possible given the situation.

"That took a long time." I said.

"The person at Gail's shop was extremely unhelpful." He brought a small box and two large paper bags into the bathroom and set them on the counter. "I also had to stop at a grocery store."

"I see."

"Okay." He gave off an odor of seriousness like he was a surgeon about to perform brain surgery. "First things first. Let's add some fresh hot water to the tub, and then sprinkle in these crushed crystals." He walked over to the tub and opened what looked like a sandwich bag of black powder into the water. Then he followed that with a baggie of something that looked more like sea salt with a purplish hue. "I also picked up a few herbs." He plucked sprigs of rosemary and spearmint leaves from one of the bags and handed them to me. "Here. Tear these into little pieces and drop them into the water."

I did as he said. He turned back to the bag and pulled out what looked and smelled like a large charcoal pencil.

"Okay," he said. "Turn to face the wall so I can draw on your back."

"I'd like you to draw me a boat," I said. "No, maybe make a nice house, with a white picket fence and some hedges. And when do we get to the part where we paint one another's nails?"

My attempt at humor almost worked. I could sense part of him softening up, appreciating my desire to defuse a bit of the tension in the room. But then that serious surgeon manner he'd had took over again.

His response was one that chose to ignore my quip. "I'm drawing a series of conjoined circles," he said, as the pencil pressed into my back.

"Why?"

"They are usually used on a door or a wall to prevent evil spirits from entering a location. I know the spirit is already inside of you, but this should make it uncomfortable. We need to give it as many reasons to leave as possible. This is one.

"Once I finish this, I'm going to the kitchen to cook some ingredients together for a ritual. It's one I've seen Isabeau's grandmother perform to exorcise an evil spirit. Stay here, keep soaking. Try to remain as relaxed as you can be."

"As relaxed as a man can be when another man is mucking about in his kitchen."

Again, my awkward joke barely affected him. He was a man on a mission and wasn't going to acknowledge my vain attempts at humorous banter.

I remembered how hard I worked to make him like me that one time we'd met all those years ago, during a Fourth of July picnic. It didn't matter what I said, or what I did, Ben's vitriol towards me was thicker in the air than that day's gunpowder from all the celebratory explosives.

He went into the kitchen with one of the bags and the box. I decided to remain quiet while he moved about, opening and closing drawers, cooking something that gave off the odor of wet socks and onions.

It must have been close to an hour before he returned with a large mixing bowl and a mug that he set on the bathroom counter. He closed the door to the bathroom and pulled what looked like a giant novelty joint out of the bag. It smelled woodsy and astringent. With a contemplative look on his face, he held it at a forty-five-degree angle then lit it on fire, letting it burn for a few seconds before blowing out the flame. Embers continued to smolder, and he walked around the bathroom, circling the smoking sage over top of my head, before placing it on the edge of the counter.

He then pulled a bunch of thick red and black candles out of the bag, placed them along the edge of the bathtub and lit them. Then, he turned the bathroom lights off.

I remained silent the entire time. Sure, I was tempted to offer up some sort of smart-ass quip, but he was so serious, concentrating so hard, that I knew better than to try to disturb his flow.

"Okay," he said, handing me the mug. "I need you to drink this."

The mug smelled of cinnamon, cloves, salt and something really dank that I couldn't place.

"What the hell is this Funky Cold Medina, anyway?"

He didn't catch my Tone Lōc reference. "It's meant to help entice evil spirits to leave your body," he said.

I immediately regretted trying to be a smart ass. Ben was working hard at this, and I didn't want to screw up the energy he was establishing.

As I cradled the mug and lifted it to my mouth, he walked over to me with the mixing bowl in his hand. The smell coming off the liquid in it was a combination of nasty odors. The boiled socks, the rotten eggs, and some sort of menthol-type scents overpowered even the smell of the burning sage in the room.

Is he going to pour that shit into the bathtub?

I paused, with the mug against my lips, and looked up at him.

"Drink," he said.

I nodded and tipped the mug up. The taste wasn't so bad. It was more like a strong tea.

"Keep drinking it. Don't stop. Swallow it all."

I closed my eyes as I tilted all the way back to drink down every last drop.

And that's when the putrid liquid splashed over my head.

What the hell?

He'd dumped that mixture of foul liquid on my head. I felt like Carrie at the damn prom.

As I sputtered in shock and disgust, I heard Ben reciting something under his breath while making a noise that sounded like he was rapping his knuckles on a piece of wood in time to the beat of his chant.

"Evil spirit residing here, who plays upon our darkest fear.

"Feel the grace and feel the love. Retreat from the light that shines above.

"We reject now your endless night and return to hell your evil plight."

I dropped the mug into the water and tried to wipe away the liquid that was burning my eyes and nostrils.

"No, don't wipe it off!"

I kept my eyes closed but could tell he was swirling the burning sage around my head again.

"Return to hell your evil plight," he chanted while he was doing this. *"Be gone now from our sight."*

I remained sitting in the tub, quiet, as he returned the burning sage to the counter.

We were both quiet for a few moments. Ben was breathing hard, as if performing the ritual was as exhausting as running a 200-meter dash.

He flicked the light on.

"Okay," he said. "Open your eyes. Look at me."

I did as he instructed, despite the burning from the concoction he'd poured over my head.

He stared at my eyes for a few moments, a hopeful scent coming off him.

The scent suddenly switched to a powerful sense of disappointment. "Dammit!" he shouted, storming out of the bathroom. "It's still there."

"I'm sorry. I shouldn't have said what I said. Interrupted your flow. Let's try it again."

"No," he yelled. "It wasn't you. It's me. I should have known. I'm not magic. It doesn't matter how much I've studied and learned. I shouldn't have wasted time trying to perform a spell I'm not capable of doing. I should have just found a witch to cure you."

The odor of bitter defeat that drifted in from Ben in the other room was far more powerful than all the smells that infused the entire bathroom.

Tuesday August 1, 2017

Chapter Seventeen: Guess who's back. Back again. Gail is back. Tell a friend.

New York

GAIL

It's Gail.
I'm home.
Call me quick, before she takes the phone away.

I slipped the new burner back into my pocket and glanced around. Iz wasn't behind me, not that I could see, anyway, but given what I now knew about her tracking abilities, I fully expected her to show up suddenly and yank it out of my hands.

My brain still reeled from my altered vision, and the energy gymnastics we'd performed on that field, but at least I wasn't sick anymore.

We'd spent the night in a motel in Virginia afterward, despite my protestations. Iz had been firm that I needed to rest.

The phone buzzed.

Can't call. Ben is here.

Are you safe?

My heart quickened when I saw that Michael had texted me back, and I ducked into an alley and made certain I was alone before I answered.

I'm safe. Heading toward your place. Can you meet me?

This time I didn't put the phone away, but kept it in my hand so I could respond faster, and kept walking.

Naturally, Iz hadn't been wrong that I needed rest. I had passed out almost the second we got to our motel. Part of it was the dizzying side effects of my new Seeing ability.

"You'll learn to turn it off," Iz said, resting her hand on my back when I put my head between my knees to keep from throwing up.

"How?"

There was a long pause before she answered. "I don't know," she finally said. "Most of us don't have it. From what I have heard from the elders, you have to train yourself to switch between the visions."

Unable to turn it off, I'd pulled a pillow over my head and squeezed my eyes shut until I fell asleep, fully dressed, on top of the disgusting flowered comforter. I stirred a few times during the night, vaguely aware of Iz moving around the room—taking a pizza delivery, watching the muted television in the dark room, and eventually, dozing next to me. She didn't sleep well. I could tell because every time I moved, her eyes popped open to watch me.

If Ben finds out he'll kill both of us.

So will Iz.
I don't care.

The nausea hadn't diminished when we woke up and left that cheap motel—everything was moving, even the things that were supposed to be still. Cars careened through swirling eddies of air, buildings pulsed with people inside them, trees vibrated with more colors than I even knew existed. I kept my eyes closed for most of the drive. Iz had gotten us back to Manhattan before nightfall, as she'd promised, and ushered me up to her apartment, where she'd fed me and put me to bed again.

I was half wondering if I'd be the type of witch who stayed in bed all day and hexed people from her pillow. It didn't sound like a half-bad life, come to think of it.

Gail. How is this happening to us?

I snorted out a laugh at his response. *Fucked if I know, man... You're the wolf. You tell me.*

But I couldn't answer him with my usual sarcasm. It wasn't fair to Michael.

No matter what else was happening, one thing I knew for sure was that he was as scared as I was. Maybe even more scared. Michael could handle a lot, but seeing someone he loved in danger would be tearing him up.

He needed me to be strong.

We can't catch a break, can we?

I had been surprised to discover that Iz had kept her tiny Manhattan apartment, the same one she'd had when we worked together at the shop all those years ago. It was bare of all but the most basic furniture now, because, as she explained, she only slept there occasionally while on missions to watch me. I was too nauseated to be gratified by the slightly sheepish tone in her voice. I had snuck out when Iz was still sleeping this morning. Poor thing hadn't had a proper night's rest since we left on our road trip, thanks to me. Even before our trip, come to think of it. The one night we'd spent at her grandmother's house, she'd been so sick I was afraid for her life. I'd never seen that level of exhaustion on a person—hollow-eyed, heavy-limbed. I wondered if she envied that I could use magic without wasting away.

No doubt she was getting bombarded with furious messages from her grandmother, and probably my mother, and most likely everyone else who had been at that party at the Boudreaux mansion. I didn't know how covens punished rogue members, but I suspected she was in for some trouble.

When I slipped out of her apartment, it had taken me all of ten minutes to get a burner phone and send a message to Michael. I needed to get to him, but figured it wasn't safe to risk public transport. Anyway, the thought of a train station terrified me—enclosed, underground, packed with morning commuters. Even I wasn't stupid enough to think I'd be safe from Paranormals down there. The thought of getting into a cab made me sick again—no way was I going to chance all those swirling colors going by.

Walking was my only option. I could slow my pace to keep my nausea at bay, and I could keep close to the buildings and stay relatively undetected. It was a three-mile walk to Michael's place from Iz's apartment in NoHo. If she slept late and I hightailed it, I might even make it back before she woke up.

There was no way that was true, but I told myself it was.

Knowing you're okay makes me feel a little better.

I laughed out loud at this one. *Bless your soul,* I wanted to text back, if only I could figure out how to say it with Mrs. Boudreaux's gentle accent.

Michael was being held captive by my brother, just as I'd been under Iz's watchful gaze. I'd gotten that much from her, at least. I didn't know how much Michael knew about me and my family. About this damned-to-hell curse. One thing I could count on with him, though: he was always kind. Hearing from me would soothe him, even as hearing from him drove me insane.

I was not going to give up what we'd just gotten back. Not a chance.

Bless his soul.

Did creatures like Michael even have souls?

Come to think of it, did I?

I won't be okay until I can see you again.

I had no business abusing Iz's trust this way, but there was no way I was not going to see him. No matter what was happening with me, I had to be with him. This stupid curse could kiss my ass; Michael and I would handle it like we'd handled everything else.

I never wanted any of this to happen.

New York had changed in the days since I'd left. Not in any tangible way—the street signs were in the same places; the buildings hadn't moved. But what I saw was different. I suppose it was more accurate to say that I was different.

Iz had been right, as usual. My eyesight was slowly adjusting. It was as though all of Manhattan was one of those giant Magic Eye pictures that used to be so popular, and my eyeballs kept slipping from one reality to another, even as I stared at single images. I paused in front of Bryant Park, and the calm green of the trees was a respite from the oscillating energy coming off every being in the city. I took a deep breath and tried to quell the motion sickness in my belly. I focused on a tree and watched the oxygen drift up and meld into the surrounding atmosphere. The heat of the day was already pulsing off the ground, and now I could see it bubbling up like a thick stew, spewing onto every surface around it. The birds, the bugs, the dogs on walks with their owners—all of them vibrated the air around them.

With an almighty effort, I focused instead on the objects, and the energy forces disappeared. I had to learn to focus my eyes on what I had been seeing all my life. What were those hidden picture things called? Some kind of glasses-free 3-D.

Autostereoscope, I suddenly remembered. My now-daily reality. A word Michael probably already knew, and kept in reserve for the Sunday Times Crossword. He could complete the puzzles in ink, and didn't even think it was a big deal. "Anyone can do it if they just have patience," he'd say with a modest shrug. As if I hadn't tried to help him and gotten pissed off after one mistake and thrown my pen across the room. He loved stuffing his brain with complex words, collecting them like stamps and filing them away to think about again and again.

As soon as I got control of this personal autostereoscope, I planned to turn it off forever. Even if it meant not completing a crossword with Michael.

I wanted to see like a Mundane again. I wanted to *live* like a Mundane, with my Mostly Mundane boyfriend who just happened to be a werewolf every now and then. Other than that, our lives were going to be regular. I would disavow everyone—my family, Iz, all of them—if I could be with him and live my life undisturbed. I didn't give a shit about the curse. If we ignored it, it wouldn't bother us.

I'm almost to your place. Can you get out?

Slowly, the park slipped back into its usual shapes. The graceful tree branches ringed the neatly trimmed lawn, and the fountain slipped from noisy, tumbling glass to a gentle shower of water. I took a deep breath.

I can control this.

There was no answer from Michael, so I kept walking, trying to quell the sudden fear in my gut.

It would be so easy to turn down his street and bound up to his apartment. I wanted to look for him, and if I couldn't see him, I wanted to drink in the Algonquin and burn every inch of it into my brain. It was where everything had happened for us, and now he was so close to me that it almost physically hurt. But I passed 44th, barely glancing as I went by. My brother was there with him, and I wasn't entirely sure what types of Paranormal skills he did have. For all I knew, he and Iz had put some kind of tracking device on me, and right this minute he was at the front door, ready to tackle me.

No matter. I could still outrun him.

I knew then where I could go. The site of our first date was only another block up and over. I'd wait for Michael there.

Too risky if Ben's there. I'll wait for you at our place.

Granted, "our place" could mean any number of New York spots. We called every park, bar, and restaurant "our place" if it had even the slightest meaning to us. But Michael would know what I meant. It was our favorite of "our places." The bookstore café where we'd had our first date-that-wasn't-supposed-to-be-a-date. I ran up the stairs, ordered a coffee, and stood by the windows overlooking 5th, scanning every person on the street for his familiar loping walk.

An hour passed. No sign of Iz yet, which either meant that I had eluded her, or her exhaustion was so great that she was still asleep.

Something had happened.

I had long ago finished my coffee and then chewed the edge of the cup into a pulp. Disgusted with myself, I threw it into the trash and paced in front of the window.

Ben must have gotten to Michael's phone?

That was the only thing that could have happened. Nothing else would prevent Michael from seeing me. Maybe he was waiting for Ben to leave the apartment, or use the bathroom. But eventually, I knew he'd get to me.

I just needed to wait.

As long as Iz didn't show up, I could stay here all day. I had nowhere else to be.

I put my hands on the back of my neck and rolled my head into my fingers, stretching out the kinks my terrible hunching posture had given me. When I looked back out the window, my vision had slipped back into the LSD trip that was my new sight. I took a deep breath and pushed my sight back to Mundane vision.

Not this time, Spooky Magic Eyeballs, I thought. I hummed our song—Smooth, by Santana—and the smile disappeared from my face immediately.

A man engulfed in a black cloud was walking on the opposite side of the street.

That sight was crazy even for New York. Why was no one giving this guy a wide berth?

I cocked my head and looked closely. No one else saw what I was seeing, I realized. The blackness throbbed off him as he walked, obscuring his face and swirling into the surrounding air. His stride was slow and determined, and when he swung his arm forward, the sleeve of his blazer lifted and I saw that his skin was a pebbly, fleshy red, like the wattle of a giant rooster, or the neck of a vulture.

He seemed lost, and I watched him pace along the block several times, turning his head as if he'd dropped something nearby and couldn't figure out how to find it.

When he reached the far end of the block, I scanned the rest of the street. I couldn't See anyone else who looked unusual, even when I tried to focus on their energy and not just their Mundane form. This must have been what Iz meant when she said that the Paranormals weren't acting right lately. No one on the street even noticed this vulture man.

Out of the corner of my eye, I saw unusual movement on the other end of the block, and I whipped my head around to see what was happening.

Michael.

He had changed drastically in the four days since I'd seen him last.

He was taller, almost hulking. He wore a shirt I recognized, but I didn't understand how it fit over him now. His hair had grown longer, and it curled over his neck. He had a thick, dark beard, and his vulpine body moved differently, almost straining forward as if he wanted to put his hands on the street and leap over the cars and pedestrians.

How could everyone just walk past him so easily? How could they not see what he was? He practically vibrated.

He moved fast, glancing up at the window of the café. My heart hammered in my chest, and to my own surprise, I pulled back behind the blinds so he wouldn't spot me. He continued up the sidewalk, his heavy brow dark with determination, and I moved so I could peek out again.

He was terrifying.

And fascinating.

I saw him smile at a passerby who greeted him, and his white-hot fangs glinted in the bright morning sunlight. Why she didn't run screaming from him, I'll never know.

I whipped my head back to the stranger in the black cloud and saw that he had stopped in his tracks. He wasn't looking at Michael, but he seemed to sense that something on the street had changed. His head swiveled on his neck, and his hands jiggled in nervous anticipation.

I glanced back at Michael. To my relief, I could see him normally again. Still tall and imposing, still handsome as hell, but no longer the walking wolfman who had terrified me only a minute ago. I glanced at the vulture man again and saw him in his Mundane form. He was just a dumpy-looking middle-aged businessman in a cheap suit, looking befuddled by the snarl of pedestrian traffic on 5th.

Michael had stopped in front of the bookstore and was looking up, scanning the windows for me again. I ducked below the windowsill and shot off a text as fast as my fingers would fly.

Not safe for you.
Leave.
NOW.

I knew what would happen if he spotted me. I could See it. An electricity would run up and down the street, and the fleshy crimson-skinned businessman would sense it. I didn't know if his kind could See the way I could, but I knew that my form and Michael's form were attracting him somehow. And if we saw each other, it would pull him to us like a magnetic force.

I held my breath for an eternity, and then stood up to peek out the window again.

Michael was gone, but the vulture man was out there, still befuddled, turning circles at the corner, and looking up at the buildings like a lost tourist. But he had less energy now, as if he recognized that the thing he wanted had disappeared. After an interminable amount of time, he finally left.

I looked down at my hands and saw that I'd gripped the phone so tightly it had left a welt in my palm. There was another text from Michael.

I love you Gail.

My eyes burned with tears, and I went into the bathroom and threw up the coffee I'd sucked down earlier.

Chapter Eighteen: Scary demon walkin' down the street

New York

MICHAEL
11:18 a.m.

"Where the hell did you go?" Ben's voice filled the silence before I even had the door halfway open.

He was livid as he came to the door, spittle flying from his lips, the smell of sour whisky from last night's over-indulgence strong on his breath. His eyes were a bloodshot, road-map havoc, and he thrust his finger in my face. His heart was beating a mile-a-minute, and along with the fear, he continued to exude more of the chagrin at his previous day's shortcomings.

I pushed through the door and closed it behind me, remembering to take deep and steady breaths to keep myself calm. I'd also been walking around with turquoise and quartz crystals in my pockets.

I wasn't about to admit to Ben that I had slipped out in an attempt to rendezvous with Gail. But I did have something to share with him.

"I needed some air, so I went on a bit of a walk to help clear my head, remain calm. But I saw—"

Ben interrupted me. "I thought the AP had taken you over again, that you were off wreaking more havoc, and this time without your stupid identity-concealing getup. Do you have *any* idea how worried I was?"

Wow. I hadn't been chastised like this since I was a teenager and my father yelled at me about how staying out hours past my curfew had sent my mom into a tailspin. If felt strange having Ben playing that same type of parental guilt card with me. Particularly when I was the older one here.

I tried to imagine what those arguments between Ben and Gail must have been like when Gail and I had first met and started dating.

I took another deep breath.

"Ben, listen," I replied in a loud, stern tone. "I didn't slip back into the spirit-controlled state." That was a bit of a lie, but I wasn't about to share that either. "But I think I found someone. Some sort of demon, or sorcerer, or whatever. Maybe it was one of the Wraiths responsible for spreading the APs."

"Where?"

"Just around the corner on Fifth Avenue."

I lied and shared with him that I'd gone out to walk around the block and to get some air, and that's when I spotted him. It was best for me to leave out the fact I'd first encountered him after Gail had texted me this morning and I'd slipped out while Ben was still passed out in a drunken stupor.

After the failed ritual he'd performed, he sank into a dark funk. There was no getting him out of it. I could smell from the emotions he was giving off that he was frustrated and exhausted. Part of that exasperation likely came from being stuck baby-sitting me. And I wondered if he might also be upset at being the first of multiple generations of the Sommers family to be without any magic abilities.

I considered telling him that his twin sister was in the same boat as he was—that at least they were both in it together and could lean on one another—but I didn't bother. Particularly after I remembered how Gail had been able to follow some magic recipe she'd found to create a magic-detecting orb. Maybe, as a life-long scholar of the occult, she'd been better attuned to following recipes and making them work. Knowing that wouldn't help the depressive mood he'd been in. Especially since I knew how competitive Gail had always been with her brother; and how much that infuriated him.

He didn't talk much the rest of the evening. By the time I'd gotten out of the bathtub—most of my body wrinkled like I'd be joining the California Raisins to accompany them in singing "I Heard It Through the Grapevine," —he'd already been several inches deep into the bottle of eighteen-year-old The Macallan scotch. Along with Gail's apparent prowess at following ancient magic recipes, I also didn't share that the bottle he was swigging like it was one of those large plastic bottles of Pabst Blue Ribbon was one that set me back two hundred and fifty dollars. I kept one of those bottles on hand to drink from—quite conservatively, I might add— whenever I got to the end of a manuscript. It was a ritual I'd enjoyed ever since first reading how Neil Peart, the drummer and lyricist from the rock band Rush, enjoyed a cigarette and a glass of The Macallan after an exceptional day of riding on his motorcycle.

Ben drank straight from the bottle and rambled on about not having his own life; how he was the only male in the family, and was tasked with being an errand boy, focused for most of his adult years on protecting his sister. He mumbled a lot of other things as he continued to drink from the bottle, but I did hear him say one thing very clearly. "And for what? None of all that time I spent trying to protect Gail—my entire wasted life—made an ounce of difference."

I sat in silence and nodded sympathetically, not bothering to break his long-winded and meandering monologue where he conjured up every single failure he'd ever had in his life. It's a good thing I'd had plenty of practice being on the receiving end of such verbosity. Buddy had trained me well in that over the years.

So, I nodded appropriately whenever he glanced over in my direction, until he finally passed out on the couch, with three quarters of the bottle emptied. I spent the rest of the evening scrolling through the news feed of the heightened incidents of domestic violence, vandalization and property damage.

He was still sleeping it off this morning when I received Gail's text.

I slipped outside and headed to the Barnes and Noble where she said she would be. I must have let the heightened anticipation of seeing her reign strong, because during the walk, the Apatetic Spirit emerged and started to take control. I continued to walk as the red hue filter came over my eyes, and there were moments I was partially not aware of—where the AP might have been in control.

My consciousness faded in and out as I got closer to the Barnes and Noble on Fifth Avenue just across the street. In the middle of struggling with the spirit infection—concentrating while taking long, deep breaths—I smelled two things simultaneously.

Gail's scent—she'd passed by recently—and a most powerful combination of what I can only describe as malevolence and sulfur combined with cucumber and rotten eggs coming from about a block ahead. All I could make out at the next corner where I'd sensed that dark presence, was a group of normal-looking pedestrians. One of them had to be exuding that scent; but I couldn't tell which one.

I stood in front of the bookstore, torn between my desire to see Gail and wanting to understand what the hell that thing which reeked of evil was up ahead at the next corner.

That's when Gail texted me to leave, and with it I caught a scent of urgent fear, and also picked up the panicked beat of her heart from up on the second floor where the café was.

Simultaneously, I picked up the odor that whatever that creature was up ahead was aware of my presence. It felt almost as if it could detect the dark spirit presence within me.

The idea that this horribly evil presence I'd scented might get at Gail through me sent a shiver down my spine. I bolted across the street and around the corner of West 46th Street.

If this evil beast, or whatever it was, was on to me, I wanted it to follow me, and to stay far from Gail.

I hurried down West 46th and all the way to the end of the block, before heading south two more blocks and then doubling back to 5th Avenue. The creature didn't appear to be following me, so I wanted to see if I could sneak up on it from the south.

As I returned to 5th Avenue, I picked up its scent, tracking it down to West 42nd Street where it disappeared down into the subway station adjacent to Bryant Park. The trail ended at the edge of a train where the man or woman who'd been giving off that sulfurous scent had disappeared on a subway car that had left minutes before I got there.

Skipping the details related to Gail, I relayed my discovery of this evil entity that seemed to sense my presence, and how I tracked it.

"That's exactly why you shouldn't have gone without me," Ben said in a scolding tone.

"You were a little busy getting over your love affair with that bottle."

I couldn't resist snapping back at him, and immediately regretted doing it, particularly when he turned, walked back into the living room and stood in front of the coffee table considering the mostly empty bottle of scotch.

"That was one of the demons," he finally said. "Likely conjured by the same Paranormal responsible for infecting the city with Wraiths."

"So, what do we do now?"

"We call Iz," Ben said, dropping down onto the couch, still staring at the bottle. "We need Iz and her power in order to defeat this AP inside you."

Chapter Nineteen: The bitter frustration of a bridge too far

New York

GAIL

Iz stood at the door, one hand on her hip, her phone at her ear, her face murderous.

If I thought Angry Iz was scary, that was nothing compared to Not Speaking To Me Iz. Her fury knocked the wind out of me.

She didn't let me in the apartment, but stood blocking the door, wilting my insides with her rage. Without looking down, she grabbed her keys from the side table in the foyer.

"Yeah, I've got her," she barked into the phone. "I'll see you there in an hour."

She held out her hand. "Give it to me."

"Let me text Jaya and tell her I'll be out a few more days," I said. "Please."

Her eyes narrowed as she considered this request. "You have sixty seconds."

My hands were shaking as I tapped out a message, to the person I now realized should have been my first call with this contraband phone.

It's Gail. Had a family emergency and lost my phone. I'll be out a few more days. Will be in touch soon. Thanks for holding it together.

I hit send and handed the phone back to Iz. She hurled it onto the hardwood floor so hard that it smashed into bits. Without looking back, she slammed her apartment door, locked it, and strode to the stairwell. I followed without question.

When we reached the lobby, she glanced around to make sure we were alone, and then spoke in a low voice.

"We are going to my car. Do not say a word. Do not make eye contact with anyone. Do not wander even one inch away from my side. Are we clear?"

I nodded.

I could hardly keep up with her as she marched to the parking garage. Heeding her instruction, I didn't look at other passersby on the street, but noticed that they veered around her as she took up all the space on the sidewalk.

Once we were in the car, doors locked and seatbelts fastened, I took a deep breath and tried to explain.

"Nothing *happened*," I whined. But she fixed me with such a look that I immediately shut up. I kept my mouth closed while she navigated out of the city and on to the freeway. Once I tried to turn on music, and she actually slapped my hand away from the volume.

Finally, she spoke.

"I don't care that you don't value your own life. That's your business," she began. I opened my mouth to protest, but she raised one finger. "Gail. Shut. Your. Mouth. I'm not going to tell you again."

I shrunk away from her into my seat. My little walk through Midtown was no joke.

"I care even less about Michael. He doesn't value his life. Or yours. That is his business." She paused, merged into the traffic, and took a deep breath. "What I care about is me. My life. You know who else I care about? My family. The coven in New Orleans and the covens in Africa. Thousands of them who I haven't even met yet. I care about most of the Mundanes. All of these people I care about are in danger every single time you disobey the very clear, very simple instructions you have been given. Why can't you understand that?"

I waited a beat and then realized that this time she actually wanted me to answer. "I just wanted to see him."

"You really think you are smart enough to outwit a centuries-old curse? You are that arrogant?"

That accusation startled me. "It's not arrogance, Iz! It just doesn't make sense that two people who have no previous contact with all this Paranormal shit have to bear the brunt of everyone's survival. Michael and I have been through a lot together. I thought we could figure it out. I thought if I could just see him, it would be okay. Maybe we could—I don't know. Leave? Can we just go away together and leave the rest of you to fight it out?"

"You want to go live in a little beachside cottage with your crush and raise his babies and grow your own food?" She cackled loudly, almost madly.

"Where are we going?"

She took one hand off the steering wheel and rubbed her eyes, which weren't quite as darkly shadowed as before. The sleep had done her some good, anyway.

"We're meeting Ben at High Bridge. It's the least crowded outdoor spot I could think of. There are too many people in the city and the noise is messing up my tracking. Central Park has too many hiding places."

"Why can't Ben just come to your place?"

"No one trusts you or Michael to be alone, even for a few minutes. We're trading, but we must keep you apart when we do it. Ben is taking you; I'm taking Michael. He's been infected."

My heart raced. "He's sick?"

She sighed. "Not physically. He was attacked by an Apatetic Spirit. It lives in him now and it's clouding his vision. Ben can't get it out without my help. But we can't just meet at one of our apartments because you two can't be near each other." She glanced at me.

"I saw him today and it was fine." I realized my error when I saw her hands tighten on the steering wheel. "I mean, I didn't see him up close or anything. I was inside a building, and he was outside on the street. Pretty far away. I'm not even really sure it was him."

"Is that so?" Her voice dripped with sarcasm. "Fine little outing? Cheerful day? Everyone in Manhattan wearing their haute couture?"

"No." My voice was small. I didn't want to tell the truth. "There was a sort of weird guy."

"Sort of weird? Like maybe one of those guys on drugs you see in alleys?"

"Not exactly. More like he had a big black cloud around him and his skin was red and drippy."

"Cool. So your vision lets you see actual demons walking the streets of the city and you still think you can handle this on your own?"

I had no reply.

"How do you like being almost forty years old and your babysitter has to quit because you're so much damn trouble?"

We drove in silence for the remainder of the trip. I gazed listlessly at the passing scenery, overwhelmed by how fast everything had changed. I had too much to think about, and I wished I could turn my brain off. I was eager to talk to Michael in person, worried about this strange virus he had caught, and relieved that I would finally have eyeballs on my brother.

Iz parked on the street adjacent to High Bridge Park, put her hand on my lap to stop me from moving, and peered around her slowly to check the area. Eventually, she must have decided it was safe enough, because she turned to me.

"Here's what's going to happen," she said, her voice deadly serious. "The bridge is basically empty this time of day. Less chance of any of us being seen. That does not mean you get to act up. We are entering this side, Ben and Michael will go in the Bronx side. You and Michael will wait at the opposite ends. You hear me? I will meet Ben in the middle. Without you. We will talk for one minute. Maybe two. Then I will take Michael home and Ben gets to deal with you. You have no say in any of it. You will not interact with a single other being, Mundane or Paranormal. You will not try to walk away from where I leave you. You will not make eye contact with Michael, or anyone else. You will *not* fuck this up. Am I making myself absolutely, completely, crystal clear?"

I nodded.

"That's not good enough," she said. "I need you to say the words out loud. Say it. You will stay in one spot. You will not move. You will not try to talk to Michael. You will not disobey me."

"I will not disobey you. But if Michael is wearing that tight blue shirt, all bets are off."

"God *dammit*, Gail!" She pounded both fists on the steering wheel and buried her face into her forearms. Her shoulders shook and, to my horror, I realized she was sobbing.

In all our years together, I had never seen Iz cry.

"Hey," I put my hand on her back. "Iz. Babe. I'm sorry. I was making a joke. A really bad joke. I'm sorry."

I continued the soothing words, patting and rubbing her back until her breath steadied.

Finally, she lifted her head and wiped her eyes angrily with the back of her hands. "I just don't know what to do anymore. I don't know how to get through to you. You won't listen to anyone. If you were the only one in danger, I'd leave you be. I'd be sad to lose you, but I'd let you ruin your own life. But I can't make you see that this is so much bigger than you. It involves..." She waved her hand vaguely in the air, and I glanced at the people outside, living their beautifully mundane lives. "It involves everyone, Gail. Everyone."

"I know," I said solemnly. "I know. I won't move. I promise, Iz."

She studied me, nodded curtly, and then unbuckled her seat belt. I followed her.

"How does Ben know where to meet us?" I couldn't even bring myself to say Michael's name in front of her.

She snorted out a laugh. "Ben and I have been talking nonstop. He's basically the only one still talking to me."

"Your family is mad?"

She stopped walking and faced me directly. "I ran away from home with my best friend, the popular but dimwitted cheerleader who happens to be screwing the high school delinquent, and we've put everyone we know in danger and potentially brought about the end of the world," she said. "Yeah. I'd say they're pretty mad."

I pressed my lips together hard to keep from smiling.

"I won't let anything bad happen to you out there," I said.

She shook her head and rolled her eyes. "Girl, you don't know your ass from a magic wand right now. But I appreciate the sentiment."

She turned quickly, the ends of her long braids whipping past my face. "Let's do this."

Chapter Twenty: And on a bridge over Harlem River, bad shit will go down

New York

GAIL

Iz parked me on a bench at the Manhattan side of the bridge and strode across it to meet Ben in the middle. If everything were different, I would have pretended to be in a Soviet-era spy swap, keeping my eyes peeled for rogue KGB agents and double-crossing CIA moles. But alas, this was an everyday, run of the mill, witch-versus-werewolf negotiation meeting, and I had no real part in the action. I busied myself reading plaques, gazing at the water tower, contemplating the drop to the Harlem River below. I avoided watching Iz walk away, and didn't bother trying to see the other end of the path, in case I spotted Michael and lost my cool.

Seeing Iz cry had knocked some sense into me, not that she would ever believe that. I was determined to earn her trust back.

Humming to myself, I stood up, leaned over the railing of the bridge and gazed out over the water. The solitude of the moment enveloped me, and I closed my eyes and tilted my head toward the hot sun. It was a glorious, sparkling afternoon, and the heat lulled me almost into a state of relaxation.

Almost.

Goosebumps formed on my arms and the hairs on the back of my neck stood up. Someone was watching me. I resisted the urge to whip around and hit the intruder with the pepper spray jammed in my pocket. I remembered Iz's words and kept still. *Don't make eye contact with anyone*, she had said. For once, I decided, I would pause before reacting.

Look at me, Iz. I'm listening to your instructions and not causing trouble!

I sensed the person—or whatever it was—approaching me. My hands rested on the concrete railing and sweat beaded on my back, but I remained perfectly still. I smelled the familiar and comforting scent of musk and forest, and all at once my breathing steadied and my heart rate slowed.

I was not in danger.

"Michael?" I whispered his name.

"Shhhh," I heard him breathe. I could feel him behind me now, but I didn't turn around.

"How did you get away?"

I heard his shirt rustle and imagined the shrug he gave, though I still hadn't seen him. "They don't know everything about me," he said. "I moved fast. And climbed. And jumped."

I took a deep breath and glanced toward the middle of the bridge. Iz and Ben stood deep in conversation, and neither of them had noticed I was talking to Michael. At least this time it wasn't my fault. He came to me. I wasn't a strong enough witch to control a Canadian. Not yet.

His arms came across my waist, slowly at first, and then his grip tightened. I leaned back against him, my back resting on his firm chest, and let my head rest on him.

"I miss you," I murmured. "Everything is so shitty."

"I know," he whispered back. He kissed the top of my shoulder and nuzzled his face into my neck. "We'll fix it."

"What if we can't?"

"We will." He stood up straight, and I turned to face him. It had only been three days, but it felt like years. I put my hand up to his cheek and ran my thumb along the tiny lines at the corner of his eye.

He smiled at the familiar caress, took my hand in his, and kissed my palm. "We have to be patient."

"I just got you back." My voice caught in my throat. "And now all this."

He leaned in to kiss me.

I pulled back. "We really shouldn't. Iz will lose her mind."

The corner of his mouth twitched. "Ben, too."

Suddenly he laughed quietly, and the sound was so comforting, so delicious, so *Michael*, that I couldn't help but grin. We tried to hold it in, but the harder we tried to suppress it, the worse it became. Our hysterics erupted out of us and within seconds we were howling. He put his fingers over my lips to quiet me and the sensation of his skin on my mouth was too much—I pulled him close and pressed my lips against his.

The sensation was immediately electric; my whole body turned molten in his arms. But almost instantly, I sensed the change around us. A stillness had settled over the bridge, a heavy quiet.

We pulled back and looked at each other, and I could see fear in his eyes. Without speaking, we turned our heads toward the dense vegetation that lined the river, and to my astonishment, a large, white-tailed deer walked onto the bridge. Both Michael and I held our breath and watched the magnificent creature lift her hoofs daintily and step toward us. Erect, she stood a solid four feet, and looked to be an easy 300 pounds. Fierce and beautiful.

She was magnificent.

Michael's arms were still around my waist, and now his palms spread wide across my back. Whether that was to communicate his awe or to stop me from trying to pet her, I will never know, because the deer lowered her head and charged forward.

A woman pushing a stroller had noticed the deer and was just squatting next to her toddler and pointing it out when it head butted her so hard she flew backward, knocked out cold against the walkway.

"My god!" I gasped.

Her baby screamed in terror but the deer ran to the next pedestrian, a jogger with neon yellow shorts and expensive headphones, oblivious to the gasps and yells of others on the bridge. He was rammed in the back and sent sprawling forward onto his arms and legs, leaving bloody smears on the ground.

"What the f—" the man yelled when he sat up, but his eyes widened in shock when he looked back at us. Everyone on the bridge, we saw, had turned to face me and Michael, but they were looking past us with mouths agape.

Michael released me, and we turned slowly.

Dozens of deer, even larger than the doe who had attacked the young mother, gathered at the entrance of the bridge. Several large bucks stood at the front of the pack, pawing the ground and shaking their massive antlers aggressively.

"Holy shit," Michael whispered. "Where did they come from?"

He moved to stand in front of me.

I felt a rustle near my foot, glanced down, and froze in horror at what I saw.

A rat sat on my shoe, gazing up at me placidly. My whole body trembled as I saw more coming up from the arches onto the bridge, climbing over each other and swarming the path.

Michael's hands had gone behind him, grasping my hips to hold me safe, but I broke away. Kicking rats as I ran, I bolted toward Ben and Iz. I could hear Michael running behind me, but I didn't look back. A fox streaked past me, and then a coyote, its lips pulled back and its teeth bared. From the other side, I saw more coming toward us. Squirrels, raccoons, even cockroaches, all hoarding to the center of the bridge.

I spotted Iz and Ben facing each other, and wondered how they could remain so oblivious to Noah's ark descending upon them.

Neither of them moved a muscle, and when I leapt over a waddling skunk, I saw why. Artair, the tattooed snake man from New Orleans, was behind Ben, a knife at his throat.

"Ben!"

Artair looked up when I screamed, and when he spotted me, his face broke into a grin. He shoved Ben to the ground and pointed his knife in my direction. "'The ceaseless labor of my life is to build the house of death.' How about that one, girlie?"

Without waiting for a response, he charged toward me, the animals amassed around him like an army.

Michael vaulted over the swarming animals with astonishing speed, and landed on Artair, knocking him to the ground.

Iz spread her hands out, cruciform, and a surge of energy pushed all of the animals back toward the bridge entrances. But her force didn't stop the people now running toward us—dozens from either end of the bridge. Some had the shabby, ripped clothes and snake tattoos of Artair, and others had the bubbled red flesh of the demons.

The deafening screams of the remaining tourists on the bridge drowned out the pounding hoofs and whooping warriors. I tried to copy Iz's moves. I held my hands in front of my face and squeezed my eyes shut, attempting to concentrate on the energy sources around me. With all my might, I tried to hold it in my hands again—a volleyball, I remembered, a beating heart. But nothing appeared.

The first snake man to reach me barreled headfirst into my chest, much the way the deer had done to the woman. I flew backward, breaking my fall with my arms so my head didn't hit the ground. I rolled over and jumped into a crouch.

Ben had grabbed a metal sign that warned people not to climb on the railing, and used it to knock the attackers over the bridge. Rats jumped up his legs, and I saw him flinch in pain at their bites, but he kept swinging wildly. Iz warded them off with her energy waves, but her strength waned; each defense was weaker than the last.

Michael was on top of Artair now, bloodied and drenched in sweat. Artair took swings at him, but Michael managed to pin down his arms. He reared his head back, opened his mouth, and to my horror, I saw his fangs. I screamed his name just as he was about to plunge his mouth onto Artair's neck. Michael hesitated, and then looked up at me. For an instant, in all the chaos of the animals and the fighting, I saw Michael's eyes.

A tendril of a thin black snake shape slipped past the whites.

His eyes focused, the snake disappeared, and he looked down at Artair, who used the split second of distraction to punch Michael in the face.

Hordes of animals piled on Ben, and Iz's most recent energy waves were barely a ripple; the snake men advanced through her spell like it was a cool breeze.

Michael hollered my name, and I saw one of the snake men coming at me. Artair had flipped Michael over, straddled him, and was now lifting the blade over his head, ready to impale.

I closed my eyes, took a deep breath, and put my hands in front of me, forming a triangle with my thumbs and forefingers. With an almighty effort, I slammed my fists down to the ground and felt all of the life forces around me join the energy I harnessed. A tidal wave of pure light emanated outward in a rippling circle, knocking over every living being in the vicinity.

I looked back at Michael, and his eyes were round with horror.

"What the hell *was* that?" He had lost the wolfish fangs, and he appeared meek and almost broken under Artair, whose unconscious body was now crumpled on top of him. I kicked the Druid blade into the river and shoved his inert body off Michael. I knew Artair only looked dead, and I recoiled from both of them.

Whatever was infecting Michael gave him squirming, dark worms in his eyes. He'd been about to eat the man who attacked him.

I could see the same terrified confusion in his face.

Neither of us knew exactly who we were looking at.

"Oh, no," I heard Iz moan. "Gail, no."

I ran to her side. She clutched her middle and writhed in pain.

"Iz? Can you walk?"

"No," she moaned again. "No, this is bad, Gail. Shit, this is so, so bad."

I looked over at Ben, slumped against a concrete bench. His eyes were unfocused, but he was breathing.

"Get up!" I yelled. "All of you. Let's get off this bridge."

"Gail." Michael's voice cut through the din in my head. I looked over at him and saw that he was once again staring at the side of the bridge.

More attackers were coming. They advanced on us slowly this time, almost in lockstep, each holding blades, each with a murderous glint in their eyes. The ones already on the ground stirred, shaking their heads. Some got to their feet.

I screamed again. "We have to run!"

Iz couldn't move. My brother was unconscious.

Michael was at my side again, and he put his fists up in front of him like a prize fighter ready to take on Manhattan.

I moved quickly behind him, facing the Bronx entrance, and put my hands in triangle formation again. This time, when I slammed my fists toward the ground, nothing happened.

The first snake man had reached me, his fist up high, blade glinting in the waning sun, when an explosion landed next to me, knocking me to the ground.

A portal opened, and Darina Sommers stepped out.

In the space of a second, her eyes took in the scene. Ben slumped over, Iz curled into a ball. In a smooth, balletic motion, she spun on her toes, drifting her hands gracefully outward. She looked like a twirling fuchsia flower, but plumes of smoke emanated from her, and the snake men turned and ran for their lives, screaming as if their skin burned. The animals didn't look harmed by her action, but they watched her closely, and then slowly, carefully, turned back to the bridge entrances and disappeared into the trees.

Michael remained tensed in front of me, fists up, as if he wanted to spar with my mother. Her face was dark with fury, her heavy eyebrows knitted together over her nose and her jaw clenched. She turned her attention to me, her palms at her side. Before I could say a word she flicked a hand, and another portal opened up. It sucked Michael in, and he didn't even have time to gasp before he disappeared into its inky blackness and it closed up behind him.

"Mom?" I whispered.

Her eyes narrowed. "Get Ben."

I stood up, every bone in my body searing through my flesh.

"They're coming back," Iz moaned.

My mother and I looked up, and the snake men were returning. Slowly, clearly wary of my mother, but advancing nonetheless.

"How did you find us?"

"Your brother had the decency to call me and inform me of this inane plan. You owe him your life."

I hobbled over to him and pulled his arm around my neck. I hadn't even stood upright before my mother was at my side, cradling Iz in her arms as gently as if she held a tiny baby. Her head erect, her posture as majestic as a Greek goddess, my mother jerked her chin. Another portal opened up, and she stepped in calmly, as if she was entering a day spa. She turned to look at me, and the fury in her eyes had not dimmed.

So much for earning Iz's trust back.

I stepped in after her and once again, my body screamed through the roller coaster ride, while I held my brother tightly and dreaded the landing.

Chapter Twenty-One: Hello darkness my old friend, I've come to drown in you again

New York

MICHAEL
2:58 p.m.

"*S*tay *away from my daughter.*"

The authoritative female voice echoed in my head as I tumbled through a giant round funnel of light and dark rings.

I'd never heard her voice before, but I knew it was Darina Sommers, Gail's mother, whose voice continued to spiral with me down the long, twisting tunnel.

Stay.

Away.

From.

My.

Daughter.

The scene on the bridge was definitely not the best way to make a good impression on the mother of the woman you loved and wanted to spend the rest of your life with. And the scent of hatred and fear the woman gave off were almost as powerful as the magic powers she so effortless demonstrated.

Stay Away!

From!

My daughter!

I continued to spin and fall, but not in any particular direction. At times, I was dropping, other times I was falling upward, or sideways. That alone was as dizzying as the stripes of bright light and dark void that rushed past me.

"The wolfman and the witch cannot abide together."

Everything went black as the circular lightshow ended and my back slammed into something hard.

As I lay there on a cold concrete surface in the darkness, the breath knocked out of me, the air around me filled with a fragrance of some funky moldy scent, Darina's words were steel spikes jabbed into my brain. They were all I could focus on.

I had no idea where I was, or if I was still alive. Or, if I was alive, if I was still on Earth or in some strange paranormal plane.

What had happened with Gail? And Ben? And Isabeau?

Were they still on the bridge? And still in danger?

I tried to sit up, but a sharp pain shot through my back and side. Gasping, I tried to inhale, but instead of rich, nurturing oxygen, it felt more like I was sucking back a mouthful of glass chips.

My inability to move allowed me to reason things through.

Gail's mother had appeared out of nowhere, and done something that sent the army of creepy goons running. The confidence and assuredness with which she'd handled herself was thick in the air.

But I'd also immediately smelled the anger she'd been directing toward me.

I thought for sure I was next.

But she didn't attack me. She sucked me into whatever the hell this place was. And through some sort of telepathic voice in my head, made her intentions very clear. But that final, very specific statement from Darina about the wolfman and the witch filled me with conviction. I realized how wrong I'd been to disobey Ben's direction.

How wrong I'd been about everything.

There was so much I didn't know.

Including where the hell I was right now.

I needed to find that out.

Taking thin, shallow breaths, I was eventually able to get more oxygen back into my lungs. I didn't try to move right away; I just lay there and focused on what I could smell and hear around me.

My nostrils took in a damp and musty odor. And the taste of the air itself was stale. A drip of water echoed somewhere in the distance. Nearby, there was a powerful rush of something thrumming through a nearby chamber. Forced air? Water? I couldn't be sure.

Focusing beyond the room I was in, I heard the familiar sounds of New York City traffic. But it was muffled, and coming from far above. The musty smell and the stale air suggested I was deep underground in some cavernous location beneath the city.

I moved my right arm, tapped my fingers against the concrete floor I was lying on. That was good. No pain, so far.

Reaching into my front pocket, I grabbed my cell phone and triggered the screen to come on. There were no signal bars—an indicator of just how deep beneath Manhattan I was—but the light my screen gave off helped me see a little of my surroundings.

I was in a large concrete chamber that had a rounded ceiling a good twenty feet or more above me.

Rolling onto my side sent a sliver up my body, and I let out a gasp of pain. I wasn't sure if it was the landing that had damaged my ribs, or if it had been from my tussle with that bald tattooed guy on the bridge. My quick yelp echoed through the cavernous space. As I aimed the soft light of my cell phone around to see more of my surroundings, I spotted a gigantic pipeline that bisected the far end of the room. And I knew that was where the rushing sound of water was coming from.

It somehow seemed familiar.

As I continued to turn, I also saw broken bits of the concrete floor in large slabs and shattered pieces, and left of that, what looked like a huge opening in the floor surrounded by a twisted metal steel railing.

No!

I knew exactly where I was.

This was that underground chamber where we had faced Marco and a bunch of his PFA goons. Where we'd stopped them from poisoning the city's water supply.

Where Lex had died.

As I stared at the hole in the floor that Lex had plummeted down—where she'd sacrificed herself to save Gail's life—my breath caught in my throat, and I couldn't get any oxygen into my lungs. It was worse than having the air knocked out of me just a few minutes earlier.

I let go of my phone and the room plunged back into complete darkness.

The entire room spun and as my breath came back to me, I pounded my fists against the concrete and cried at the top of my voice. I called out for Alexandria, for Gail. And also for Irwin, another friend we'd lost that day. My anguished screams filled the darkened chamber, and I felt myself swirling into the nightmare of despair I'd been buried in for the weeks following that loss.

Even in the thick blackness, that familiar red hue came over my eyes, softly burning as if it were some sort of onion-skin layer. The Apatetic Spirit inside of me was taking hold; and this time I was too weak to fight it off.

I blacked out.

When I regained consciousness, some undeterminable time later, I could tell that I was in the same underground chamber. Things were still pitch black around me.

The remnants of spent and dusty tears caked on my cheeks like the crusty, dried blood on my knuckles.

I'd succumbed to the evil spirit inside of me and beat the concrete with my fists. Thank goodness I was trapped in this subterranean chamber with nobody to harm when it happened.

The thought of harming another person triggered the memory of Darina's voice echoing through my head.

Stay away from my daughter.

She had sent me here. After saving us all from the attack on the bridge.

An attack that happened because of me.

When Ben walked across the bridge to meet up with Iz, I'd been overcome with a desire to see Gail.

I'd rushed around down a grassy knoll along the side of the bridge, across half a dozen lanes of traffic, leapt onto the steel girder archway on the underside of the bridge and made my way across to the other side.

All I'd wanted was to let Gail know, in person, face to face, that it would be okay; that we would get through this.

But what the hell did I really know? About any of this?

And what the hell did I know about Gail?

I'd seen what she had done.

Gail had created some sort of shock wave in the air that knocked the small army of snake-men, including the one who'd been about to stab me, off their feet.

And her mother was obviously some sort of sorceress who waltzed in and effortlessly saved all our asses.

Gail's mother was a witch. An extremely powerful witch.

From what I witnessed Gail do, she must also be a witch.

How could she have kept it from me for all these years?

Particularly after she'd told me that she didn't believe in the paranormal and occult wares she was hawking in her store. And especially considering how pissed off at me she had been that I kept my werewolf nature from her.

No, wait. I would have been able to sense if Gail had been lying about that.

Gail couldn't have known she was a witch until just recently. When Iz whisked her off to New Orleans.

She must have only learned about it.

But it made sense now.

Ben had failed at the ritual magic he'd been trying to perform to rid my body of the Apatetic Spirit because he wasn't magic. But when Gail had followed some recipe procedure to create that melon-sized magic detection orb, it had worked. Because, underneath it all, she possessed witch power and abilities.

Gail was a witch. And I was a wolf.

The wolfman and the witch cannot abide together.

Stay away from my daughter.

Darina's only words to me. What her voice in my head said, as she'd banished me here.

Here, to this specific location.

On purpose.

She had to have known.

It was a message.

She was trying to tell me something. Remind me of something.

I thought of the hole, and of seeing Lex and Gail both hanging on for their lives in front of me while I was lying under a huge slab of concrete, helpless to save either of them.

Darina sent me back here, to face this place.

To face that horrid truth.

That the women I loved were destined for this type of fate.

Chapter Twenty-Two: Whoa, whoa, momma, tell me 'bout the good old days

Upstate New

York GAIL

"Iz?" I sat up with a jerk and then clutched my head in my hands. When the pounding stopped, I looked around and tried to get my bearings.

"Mom? Ben?"

I heard a low moan from across the room and saw my brother lying on the guest bed of my childhood home in upstate. I'd been deposited on the couch with a scratchy blanket draped over my midsection. I stood up, wobbly at first, and went to his side. He was still out of it, but breathing evenly. I pushed his dark hair off of his forehead.

"You okay, Ben?" I whispered. "Can you hear me?"

"Come away from him."

I jumped at the sound of my mother's voice, and turned to face her. She stood in the doorway of the bedroom, in a fresh set of long, flowing skirts and scarves, her steel grey hair pulled into a top knot. The severity of her expression had not changed since I last looked at her at the edge of that portal.

Portals. The damn portals again.

Without another word, she turned away and walked down the hall.

"Wait a minute, Mom."

She didn't look back at me.

"Mom. I said wait!"

The sound stopped her in tracks, and she turned around slowly. "I beg your pardon," she said, her voice dripping like lava oozing out of a volcano. "Do you wish to say something to me?"

"Yes, I do. Let's start with you telling me what the hell is happening."

"I will not." She turned and marched away again, opening the door to my old room, and slipping inside.

I followed her and pushed the door open. She didn't even flinch when it slammed against the bedroom wall. It was still painted black from my goth phase in high school. She'd hated that, which, let's be honest, was probably fifty percent why I did it. I would have thought that was the first thing she would've changed when I moved out, but it had been twenty years since I'd lived at home and here it was, bleak and spooky. Just like I was pretending to be at seventeen.

Mom was bent over Isabeau, asleep in my bed. She looked more peaceful than when I'd seen her last, crumpled in a fetal position on that bridge. Almost too peaceful, once I really looked at her. She had a glowing, serene expression on her beautiful face, and her arms were clasped over her chest. On the nightstand next to the bed, I saw an array of bottles and jars.

"How is she?" I whispered.

"She will be fine, eventually." Mom paused for a moment, but then couldn't help herself. "No thanks to you."

I knew she wouldn't miss an opportunity to needle me.

"No thanks to *me*?" My voice rose to a screech.

Before I could take another breath, my mother had my arm firmly in her grasp and she pulled me out to the living room.

"You will not put her at risk." The quaver in her voice startled me, but only for a second.

"I would love to not put her at risk, if only I knew what the fuck was going on—"

"What's going on is that your actions have set a calamity in motion. Your actions and those of that ridiculous mutt you claim to love. You were warned. Both of you, and repeatedly. But you chose to ignore everyone around you, because you thought you were smarter than everyone around you. Like always."

She turned and went into the kitchen, but I followed close at her heels. For once, I would not back down during a fight with Darina Sommers.

"Did it ever occur to you that I thought I knew best because no one told me anything else? Maybe if someone had told me, oh, I don't know, that there was such a thing as witches, maybe, *maybe* I would have been more careful?"

"You have been told. By me and Madame Boudreaux. Then you promptly took advantage of her hospitality and ran away like a child, only to cause chaos amongst Mundanes and put everyone at risk by using magic you are wildly unqualified to use. You are like a child with a box of matches, Gail, and you are exhausting everyone. Especially me. Sit." She pointed to a counter stool, and I sat.

The kettle on the stove whistled loudly, and my mother turned and shut it off. She poured the water over a concoction of herbs in a small bowl, and then strained the liquid into a pile of linen bandages.

"I'm taking these to Isabeau. Stay here." She raised one eyebrow, as if she knew that what she had instructed was impossible, but then she turned and left.

My gaze drifted across the kitchen. It looked just as it had when I was a kid, though a lot cleaner now that Ben and I didn't live here anymore. Every surface gleamed, every spice, utensil, and plate set neatly in its designated spot. I stood up and wandered to the fridge, changed my mind, and ran my finger along the counter. Dust free, like everything in Darina Sommers' house.

I'd spent my entire life thinking my mother was an intimidating, but slightly kooky, 70s hippie. Stern and uncommunicative, yet constantly brewing "teas" and tinctures for all of us. Large bundles of drying flowers lined the walls, and powders, trinkets, and charms had their place in a small, locked chest on the counter. She used to tell me she used all that stuff for magic; I had never once believed her. I thought maybe she smoked too much pot in college, and it made her mean and dippy in her old age.

I picked up the little jar of dirt that lived next to a large pillar candle. She dropped a pinch of this dirt on the candle every day, and yet I'd never questioned why it never ran out. The soil inside was black and oily smelling, nothing at all like the rich loam she cultivated in our back yard.

Holding it against my chest, I leaned against the counter and gazed through the kitchen window past our back fence, across the neighbor's field, to the town cemetery.

The realization of what I held in my hand dawned on me, and I dropped the jar on the counter. I heard her coming down the hallway again, and scurried back to my seat.

She entered the kitchen carrying a tea tray filled with spent teacups and jars of ointment. She set it next to the sink, and before she looked back at me, her eyes caught the jar of graveyard dirt. I had dropped it only a couple of inches from where it normally lived, but she moved it into place automatically. If Precision was a witch talent, I'd guess she was the high priestess of it.

"How is Ben?"

"He has a mild concussion. Doctor Evans has been here and seen both of them."

I smiled at the thought of our childhood pediatrician Doc Evans, with her delicate red curls and softly lined face. Then I looked at Mom quizzically.

"She's both kinds of doctor, so I trust her diagnoses of both of them." A smug smile went across her face. "We have doctors, Gail. We have lawyers. We have chefs. Witches are everywhere."

"Where is Michael?"

"The only way to keep both of you safe is to keep you apart."

We stared at each other for a long time before she finally spoke again.

"Imagine being me," she said. "Imagine knowing that there is an existential threat so massive that everyone you know—every one of our kind in the world, in fact—is afraid of it. Imagine then giving birth to a child, a quiet, gentle boy, and then moments later to a screaming girl, just like the curse predicted. Imagine pushing away your fears because that girl is a fierce, beautiful, devil of a daughter, and together these children are exactly what you had wished for since you were a child. One of each, exactly as you wanted, intelligent and creative, exactly as you wanted."

"If I was exactly what you wanted, why were you always so goddamn mean to me?"

There was a long silence. My mother smiled, and her voice trembled when she spoke again. "For years I told myself it was coincidence. Twins were born all the time; it wasn't any more likely to be you than anyone else.

"But then you grew up to be you. All through your teenage years, you did exactly what I told you not to do, just to spite me. You fought with me. You mocked my work."

"Maybe I wouldn't have if you had just told me what was going on."

"That's what I wished for, too. But you contradicted me every step of the way. This is the part I most want you to imagine: the defiant daughter who battled every perceived injustice so fiercely was also turning into a wildly inventive, creative, competitive woman. A woman I admired, and wished I was more like. A woman who I knew would have a wonderful life if I stayed out of her way.

"But suppose I had told that little girl? Knowing her," a pause, "*particular* personality, what do you think would have happened? She would have gone even more wild and reckless. She would have intentionally sought out the very thing she was warned against. Or, perhaps worse, she would have been dimmed. Her spirit, her ferocity. Her light. I would have broken the very part of her that I loved best about her."

"Maybe we could have just talked about it. You didn't even try. Maybe we could have been teammates, instead of enemies."

"I suppose we'll never know," she said, without conviction. "Instead, I chose to do what I thought was best: I kept it from you, and protected you with silence. You laughed when you caught me doing spell work, so I let you laugh, and didn't hide it. I relied on your arrogance, and it never once let me down."

Good one, Mom. Even when trying to explain away childhood trauma, she managed to get a jab in.

"Is everyone a witch? All your sisters, all my cousins?"

She nodded.

"Ben?"

Her eyes closed for a moment. "Ben is a Messenger. They do not have any paranormal abilities, but they are vital to the community."

"How long has he known?"

"Since middle school. He figured it out on his own. And he kept it secret from you because I told him about the curse."

"You told a twelve-year-old that everyone would die if his sister fell in love with a wolf?"

My mother put her hands in front of her, hands together as if she was cradling something fragile. "Our kind is accustomed to legends, Gail."

I took a deep breath. "So, I'm the curse. But we both know it can't be with Michael. He wasn't bitten until he was an adult. He's not even a *real* werewolf. He's more like a refugee."

"Given what we've been through, you will never believe this, but I wish that was true. Unfortunately, no one is half anything. You either are or you aren't; there is no equivocating. Paranormal isn't part of you. It *is* you. The second he was bitten, Michael Andrews became Paranormal in every cell of his body. Forever. There has never been a reversal."

"I don't understand how we could cause this kind of destruction if we didn't know. We didn't have any of that shit." I jerked my hand toward her spices. "We didn't do spells. We just fell in love. Then were best friends. Then, we took care of each other. None of that is bad."

She held her hands in a triangle formation, the same one I had used on the bridge.

"Sexual ritual. Community Ritual. Service Ritual. Three of the most powerful rituals we know, combined into one. It sounds like perfect happiness. But since it was codified in the curse, it is corrupted when it happens between a witch and a werewolf, even if they don't know what they are doing."

I snorted a laugh. *Cool, cool,* I thought. *If only all those abstinence-only lectures I'd gotten as a kid in Catholic school had worked, we wouldn't be in this position.*

Undoubtedly knowing what I was thinking, she continued without comment.

"Around the end of 2003, we got word that a new werewolf was wandering around Manhattan, where you lived. They keep track of us," she added quickly, seeing my expression, "and we keep track of them. Trust me, it's for the best if we know where everyone is, so we can avoid each other. It's civil.

"But this new werewolf didn't belong to anyone. He didn't seem at all... governable. Which happens now and then. But this time, as you know," she said, her eyes drifting over my shoulder, and out the little bay window. "You were there."

And I met Michael.

"If you had told me," I began.

"Yes, I know, you would have avoided all of this. I'm working very hard at being honest with you, Gail, so I'd ask that you do the same. If I had walked into your store and told you that you were a witch and I didn't want you to fall in love with a werewolf and ruin civilization, what would you have done?"

I lowered my eyes. "I would have had you locked up."

"Precisely." She poured two cups of tea and sat down across from me. "Everyone was watching out for you, but you kept circling closer to this man. We knew he was writing a book about the occult. We knew he'd at least hear of you. It was only a matter of time before you encountered each other. The coven had finally decided that you needed to know. Everyone agreed that Ben should be the one to talk to you, since you are closest to him. But we were too late."

I had been so angry when Ben was rude to him at that picnic.

"By not telling me, you set me up for failure."

"Yes."

"And now I did magic wrong and caused something awful to happen."

"You and Michael re-ignited the curse. The moment your lips met on that bridge, you invited all Paranormals to war. And the magic you used in defense was unskilled and caused tremendous damage. Several Mundanes were injured, and the bridge is now closed for structural repairs. But the magic you used, though amateurish, was far more sophisticated than anything we were aware you possessed."

"And now everyone in all of the covens around the world hates me."

She sighed. "Hate is strong. But we are not popular."

I took a big gulp of the now lukewarm tea and stood up.

"Well, great, Mom. Thanks for everything. Always super fun to visit you. I'm really happy with how my life turned out thanks to the family heritage."

Halfway down the hall, I heard her speak, and turned around again. "What did you say?"

She came to the kitchen door. Her eyes were glassy, but she held her head high. "I kept secrets to keep you alive. Remember what I asked you to imagine? That young woman who wanted a daughter so desperately? All she ever wanted was *you*. Alive. At any cost."

I swallowed over the lump in my throat and then went into Iz's room. I crawled into the bed beside her, entwined my arm with hers, and fell asleep.

Chapter Twenty-Three: Step-by-step, ooh baby, as I fight my way out

New York

MICHAEL
7:03 p.m.

I'm not sure how long I lay there in the dark letting Darina's less-than-subtle message sink in. Ben shared natural disasters that kicked off when the two of us first met and fell in love. And when I went to her on the bridge, some magnificent and bizarre shit went down.

But when I was finished stewing in the darkness, I resolved to get the hell out of here—to distance myself from this very last place in the city I ever wanted to see again. And, of course, to maintain my distance from Gail.

Plus ça change, plus c'est la même chose.

Though I was Canadian, and we're supposed to be a bilingual country, I couldn't speak French fluently. But I had picked up tidbits of it over the years. And that particular phrase is one I learned from a Rush song called "Circumstances."

Plus ça change, plus c'est la même chose.

The more things change, the more they stay the same.

After all we'd been through, all we fought, we finally found ourselves together again—only to be faced with this forced separation.

This wasn't the time to be hung up on that. I'd have plenty of time to mope and bemoan my fate later. At the moment, all I wanted was to get home.

I was able to find my cell phone—which I must have dropped when I was being controlled by the Apatetic Spirit—easily enough in the dark. The oils from my hands combined with the metal and glass of the device left a very distinctive scent on it. There was still no signal, but its main screen informed me how many hours had passed since I'd been banished down into this cavern.

It was a few minutes after seven. The sun would set in a little over an hour. I was always keenly aware of the day and time, when sunset occurred and, of course, the phases of the moon. It was the 2nd of August. The moon was at 77.3%. Tomorrow the moon would be at 84.8%. And I usually turned into my wolf self whenever the moon was at 80% or more.

Finding my way out of here with the light of my cell phone would be easy enough. Based on my last time here, I knew it would take at least half an hour to make my way out of this labyrinth.

I paused at the entrance to the tunnel that led out of this cavernous room and, with the help of the glow from my cellphone, took one last look at the gaping hole in the floor on the far side of the room.

It was far smaller than the gaping hole in my heart from the loss of Lex.

"Well done, Darina," I said in a low voice that echoed back to me through the chamber. "Message received. In spades. I will stay away from your daughter."

I'd made it most of the way back through the combination of tunnels, ladders, and doorways and was just starting my way up a part of the route I distinctly remembered—a twenty-floor circular metal staircase—when my phone battery decided to die on me.

"Of course," I mumbled, slipping the phone back into my pocket.

I would have to rely on a combination of my other senses plus my memory of this place, which I'd only been through twice before. Once in, and once out. Heading up this extremely tall circular staircase in the dark would be easy enough. And there weren't that many tunnels and stairways to ascend after this. I'd be fine; just moving a little slower than originally planned.

The only sounds as I slowly ascended the stairs were my breathing and the sound of my feet on the steps. The echoes of those sounds as they bounced back off the top and bottom of this tunnel gave me a bit of an idea of how much further I still had to climb. The experience made me wonder if that was how echolocation worked for bats.

That set my mind racing off to think about Batman, and the fact he had no supernatural powers at all. Not like Spider-Man, who incorporated the proportional strength, speed, and agility of the spider that bit him. Not to mention his spider-sense. If Batman had been bitten by a radioactive bat, he'd likely have that bat radar sense. But Batman didn't have any superpowers. He was rich and had a plethora of gadgets and a utility belt that seemed to always have whatever he needed. Particularly in the campy late 1960s television series starring Adam West and Burt Ward. The funniest thing on his utility belt, of course, was the bat repellent spray he used to get an attacking shark off his leg when he was hanging from a helicopter on a rope ladder.

If only I had my hands on some sort of *Fast Ascension Spray* or maybe even *Phone Battery Enhancement Spray.*

Of course, getting my hands on an *Ancient Witch-Wolf Curse Nullification Spray* would be ideal in this situation.

But I wasn't Batman. And this wasn't a campy television series. This was the pathetic tale of a ruminating Canadian author who—

The sounds of dozens of feet slapping on the concrete from somewhere beyond the top of this staircase interrupted my thoughts.

And with that sound came a scent that was oddly familiar.

The strange combination of sulfur and cucumber-meets-rotten egg smell I remembered coming off that guy I'd tracked from in front of Barnes and Noble. I'd also detected it on a number of the soldiers in that small army who'd attacked us on the bridge. These must be the Wraiths Ben had told me about. They were heading my way.

As if to confirm that thought, I heard the echoes of the clanging of their shoes striking the upper part of the metal staircase as the group rushed down to meet me.

I was in no mood for this; but I took a deep breath, hoping to keep the Apatetic Spirit inside of me at bay. I wanted the satisfaction of being fully aware when I gave these assholes a little taste of just how pissed off I was at this entire situation.

"Come and get me you Slytherin thugs!" I yelled up at them as I rushed forward.

I couldn't see anything in the pitch darkness, but I could smell a stronger rotten-egg odor of response to my voice. They were now perhaps forty feet away. I considered the narrow width of the staircase and figured it would be an advantage. They couldn't really attack more than one or two at a time. Which meant they couldn't surround and swarm me. And while deciphering the distinct smells and sounds of the footfalls was difficult, I estimated I was dealing with at least a dozen attackers.

"Okay," I said, more to myself than to them, since none of the approaching Wraiths gave off any indication they were even aware I'd tried to taunt them. "Let's go."

When the first one reached me, I grabbed it by the shoulders and turned to throw him down the stairs behind me. As I was doing this, another one jumped onto my back, and I twisted to throw him down on top of the first Wraith.

Neither one of them even grunted in pain as they tumbled down the metal stairs.

A punch from the next one in line connected with the side of my head as I was turning back to face the oncomers. I grabbed that one by the throat with my right hand and punched him square in the face with my left hand. It stung to punch him, because my knuckles were raw and bloody. The blow knocked him unconscious and he collapsed. I stepped over his body and grabbed the next one by the front of his shirt and pulled him forward and on top of the first guy.

Then I took another step upwards as the next Wraith threw himself at me.

I twisted, grabbing his arms, and threw him down.

The next one got in a punch to my ribs, and that hurt, sending me back down a few steps. After leaning against the railing for a quick second to catch my breath, I barreled headfirst into that Wraith's stomach, knocking him onto his back on the stairs. I could hear the next two behind him fall on top of him. As they fell, I struck one of them with my left elbow in the back of the head.

As I struck the next one in line, I could hear a few of the Wraiths I'd thrown down the stairs. They'd gotten back to their feet and were coming at me from behind. I grabbed the one in front of me by the shirt and threw him down, knocking at least two other Wraiths, from the sounds of it, backwards.

I turned, taking another step forward, and repeated that same movement.

Then another step, a punch, a toss. Then another step. Then another punch. Another toss. Wash, rinse, repeat. Except with pain. Pain in my knuckles; pain from the blows they got in.

The progress was a slow step-by-step action.

For an obscure moment I was tempted to sing that old New Kids on the Block classic; to keep from freaking out at fighting this hoard in the dark, as well as to distract and confuse them.

But there was no indication they were more than zombie-like attackers. They were giving off no emotive scents. They weren't human. They couldn't be taunted.

That idea was initially disappointing, but it also empowered me further.

If they weren't human, then I didn't need to pull my punches.

I threw a jab with everything in me at the next one in front of me.

My fist struck the side of his head with such force that I heard the bones of his skull crack.

And then there was a faint flash of light, accompanied by his body instantly disintegrating into fine dust-like particles that glowed briefly as they fell.

"That's what I'm talking about!" I yelled. I normally had to concentrate to pull my punches when fighting other humans. But I had to admit, letting loose with all I had felt damn good.

If I had at them with full strength, I could destroy them.

And it appeared that a good solid blow to the head did the trick.

A Wraith coming back up the stairs behind me grabbed my legs, while the next one from above tackled me. I punched the face of the one on top of me hard enough to make him disintegrate in a flash of pixie dust;

and I shifted, falling onto the stairs, to grab the one holding my legs by the head and slamming his head hard against the metal railing. He too disintegrated.

The two quick flashes of light revealed there were at least six more Wraiths coming back up the stairs at me, and maybe ten more in front.

Still laying back on the stairs, I lifted both legs and kicked hard at the two scrambling to jump on top of me. My right foot hit the closer one dead in the face, breaking his neck, and he vaporized into the bright sparkly dust. The one that I struck in the chest tumbled backwards and into the next Wraith behind him. I heard the clatter of them falling back onto the stairs.

As I was getting to my feet, the next one coming down got a quick one-two punch into the side of my head and chest. I drove my fist straight through his forehead, and he pixilated.

I kept fighting my way upward, absorbing random kicks, punches, slaps, and sloppy tackles along the way. Most of the time when they tackled me, I was able to use their momentum to throw them back down the stairs, and either knock them or the one they were being thrown into to dust, or at least prevent the ones coming back up the stairs from getting too close.

The repeated strikes from the attacking Wraiths, plus the pain from hitting them with my raw knuckles, sent spasms of agony through my body. At one point, as I sensed the AP inside me trying to take control, I took a few deep breaths and then actually started to sing the old New Kids on the Block classic aloud.

I didn't really know or remember most of the lyrics, but that didn't stop me from making something up and calling out the words at the top of my lungs as I fought.

"Hey Wraith, in your eyes.

"I see the hatred you have all the time.

"And Wraith, it makes me smile.

"Hitting you with full force drives me wild.

"Step-by-step, ooh Wraithy.

"Gonna get through you aaaaall."

Focusing on that song seemed to act in a similar way to Ben's suggested deep breathing exercises. It allowed me to concentrate on something else.

And it worked brilliantly in two regards. I managed to keep the Apatetic Spirit at bay and distract myself from the pain.

When I finished massacring the New Kids song, I moved on to a more fitting song. "Sixteen Tons" was a song that was popular in the small mid-northern Ontario mining town where I grew up. My parents had an album from Lorne Green where the Canadian actor—whose look and pose reminded me of The Friendly Giant on the album cover—had covered the coal mining classic.

A guy's got to amuse himself while fighting his way through a small army of Wraiths.

"Another day older," I sang, grabbing the next guy in front of me and tossing him down the stairs to knock several of his buddies down, "and deeper in Wraiths."

They kept getting in enough punches that my body and face ached from them; but I was making progress, slowly.

By the time I neared the end of the song, where fittingly, the lyricist says he has fists made of iron and steel, and that if the right didn't get you, the left one would, I realized I was finally down to three final adversaries. One above me, and two below.

"Good thing for you guys," I called, out of breath, "because I was about to sing one of my favorite Rush songs. And my attempt at hitting the same notes as Geddy Lee might have burst your poor eardrums."

Of course, the Wraiths didn't respond to that. Just like they didn't respond to any of the parody versions of the songs I'd just butchered.

Too often my most excellent humor is lost on others.

As the final Wraith dissipated into that fine sparkly dust, I let out a huge breath and collapsed onto the stairs.

"Woah, that was one hell of a workout. Richard Simmons, eat your heart out."

It took me a few minutes to catch my breath and gather the strength to continue up the stairs on my trek out of that dark labyrinth. But I finally made my way—a lot more slowly than I had been moving before—up through the series of tunnels and ladders until I made it to the maintenance tunnel that deposited me on the subway tracks near the Columbus Circle station.

I strategically waited for the trains to pass, and there to be very few people around as I pulled myself up from the tracks to the subway station platform, and then walked up and out, onto the street.

It was later than I expected; the sun was already low behind the towers in the west, long dark shadows of the buildings seeming to reach toward me.

A number of sensations overcame me simultaneously.

The first was a palpable fear drifting about the city. It was a bitter scent of fear that reminded me of the worst days of when the PFA had inspired night-time attacks throughout Manhattan. And in the distance were cries of anger and fury from what sounded like a half-dozen fights or skirmishes coming from numerous directions.

A dude carrying a guitar was rushing along the sidewalk closest to Central Park and muttering under his breath. "The whole damn city is going crazy," he said. "People are attacking strangers at random."

The second thing I felt, as I was processing a mini hell-on-earth, was a familiar aura.

Startled, I looked over to the west, towards the setting sun, despite the fact I couldn't actually see the orb in the sky.

The tingling and buzzing sensation rippling in my head was one I associated with the lycanthropic change that came over me.

But it's only August 2nd.

I shouldn't be changing until tomorrow night.

"Dammit," I yelled, and bolted toward the entrance to Central Park, hoping I could make it in time.

Thursday August 3, 2017

Chapter Twenty-Four: A morning meeting with my hairy wolf mother

New York

MICHAEL
5:57 a.m.

I woke to find myself on my back and staring up at the leaves of an elm tree through a light layer of fog. The dirt I was lying on was moist and cool, which was easy to detect because I was, as I'd become accustomed to over the years, entirely naked.

Momentary panic set in when I thought back to the last thing I could remember from the night before.

Rushing into Central Park, feeling the aura of the change coming on, a day earlier than I'd expected.

That was it.

And now here I was in a familiar spot. One I regularly returned to when in wolf form, likely sensing something indicating the change was going to happen. Of course, I had no idea what my wolf self actually thought or experienced, or even knew about my condition. The best I ever had were the occasional fleeting memories—glimpses, smells, sounds—of things experienced when in wolf form. The wolf must, similarly, pick up snippets of things from my time in human form.

I doubt I'd ever truly know.

Something else I didn't know was what the heck I'd done with my clothes, my cell phone, and my wallet. Not that the cell phone was useful. It had died. But I also had my wallet on me. I normally never prepared for a change with anything but throwaway clothes. And I had no idea where I'd stashed any of my things last night. Or even if I'd had a chance to stash my clothes somewhere before making the change.

I sat up and trawled my memory of the night before. The best I could conjure up was running into the park near Columbus Circle and feeling that all-too-familiar aura indicating I was about to change into wolf form. But there was something else there too; the Apatetic Spirit inside me was fighting against it, trying to keep the transformation into animal form at bay. That slowed me down as I ran, moving nowhere nearly as quickly as I was normally capable. The last thing I could remember was racing down the flat green of the softball diamonds of Heckscher Fields.

Then nothing.

Not even the briefest snippet of wolf memory.

"The sun's up," a familiar voice came to me from somewhere at least a few dozen yards to my south. "You must be back in human form."

I knew the voice. And the scent that drifted in on the northerly breeze. The person speaking to me in a quiet voice from a good thirty or so meters away was likely standing on or near Bow Bridge.

Buddy?

"Your clothes are tucked under that rock outcropping on the other side of the dirt path," Buddy said in that same low voice. "I've got your wallet and your phone."

"Buddy?" I whispered in response. "Can you hear me?"

There was no response, and no indication he could hear me. So, he didn't have superpowered hearing, like I did. But, as I had long suspected, he knew about my condition. And he had to have some sort of special abilities. Because if I had a nickel for every time Buddy showed up at just the right moment to save my ass, I wouldn't have to write another book to earn my living.

I shuffled out of the wooded area and across the packed dirt path to my clothes, which I could now detect by scent; the clothes had the sour smell of my sweat and the metallic odor of my blood from yesterday's subterranean battle. Sure enough, they were tucked under the outcropping of a large rock formation like he'd said. I pulled them out and dressed.

"I trust," Buddy whispered, and I could hear his footsteps as he was moving closer. "That you'll be fully decent by the time I get over there. I've already got enough of a complex about the shape of my body compared to yours, not to mention other endowments I couldn't help but notice when I had to nurse you back to health in the City of Angels."

"Yeah," I replied, louder, so my voice would carry over to his normal human ears. "Getting dressed now."

As I was pulling my jeans back on, I could now see him walking along the path toward me.

"I suppose," he said, a gigantic grin spreading to fill his entire face as he got closer, "that you have more questions than Libby's has beans."

6:41 a.m.

"The way I've always seen it," Buddy said, "you're not cursed with this condition. You're blessed with it. It's a gift. One that has come in handy numerous times in both your career and your extracurricular need to help other people; and one that is going to be necessary to put a stop to all this shit that's been going down."

I was sitting across from Buddy in a corner booth of a diner on East 70th Street. We were relatively secluded, with three empty booths between us and the nearest other customers.

I'd just polished off the last bite of my three-egg steak and cheese omelet with a side of hash browns, sausage and toast, and had eyed the plate of bacon and eggs in front of Buddy that he'd barely touched.

He noticed my longing stare and pushed his plate across the table after picking up one slice and chewing on it.

It had been days since I'd had anything solid to eat. And that was the breakfast I'd prepared on Saturday. All

I'd had was a cereal bar here, a chocolate bar there, an apple or a banana I'd grabbed when passing by a bodega. I doubt I'd taken the time to eat when I'd been in Apatetic Spirit black-out mode. And maybe my wolf self had found a small animal or two while roaming about the park last night. But I was making up for that lack of food intake now. The transformation between human and wolf consumed a boatload of calories. And who knew what effect running around under control of the Wraith had on me.

"I've always been amazed at just how much food you can pack in at a single sitting," Buddy grinned. "I mean, I know where it's going, but it's still a pretty spectacular sight to behold."

The waitress returned to the table to refill our coffee cups and while she was filling mine, my right arm brushed my coffee cup to the side and scalding hot coffee splashed onto my right forearm.

"Oh my God, I'm so sorry!" the waitress said.

"No, it's okay. That was entirely my fault. I'm sorry."

I prepared for the sudden shock of pain to bring that now-familiar red misty glaze over my eyes, but my vision remained normal. Yes, my arm stung from the burn, but I was still me; no dark internal presence was struggling to take over my consciousness.

"So sorry," she repeated, dabbing at my arm with a napkin.

"You'd better not keep apologizing," Buddy quipped. "He's Canadian. He needs to get in the last apology. Or else."

I laughed to show her I was okay. "It's fine. And I am sorry. It was my fault. I knocked the cup."

"See?" Buddy said. "He's fine. Especially now that he got in the last 'sorry.' But since you're here, can we please have a second omelet plate for my ravenous friend? And just an order of toast for me."

"Are you sure?" she said, eying us both skeptically, but then taking in the empty plate beside me and the dish of Buddy's food that I was shoveling into my mouth. I smelled her vague disgust.

"Yeah, I'm sure. My pal here is an ultra marathon runner. He'll find room for more."

As she turned to head back to the kitchen, Buddy took a sip of his freshly filled coffee.

I finished chewing the food in my mouth long enough to talk. "It must be gone."

"What must be gone?"

"The Apatetic Spirit. When that coffee burned my arm that should have triggered the infection to rise up inside of me. Usually, I start seeing red. But there was nothing."

Buddy pursed his lips together. "You said that when you change between man and wolf it often comes with significantly advanced healing."

"Yeah. I've always figured that the biological change acts something like when you give a quick shake to an Etch A Sketch. The particles reset. I mean, look at my fists. Look at my face! I took a beating yesterday, and they're practically back to normal."

"So maybe the spirit that possessed you couldn't handle the transition. Maybe it couldn't attach itself to the

Canis lupus host. Perhaps the transformation kicked it out."

I nodded.

"Yeah," he said. "That makes sense."

"It does." I nodded again, then took a sip of my coffee and gently set the cup back down. "You know, you still haven't explained who or what you are."

"No. I haven't. Like I told you, there's no time for that. Not now. It's too complicated to get into, or to explain. Partially because I barely understand it myself." He lifted his left arm up and glanced at his watch. "But also, because I have some place I need to be soon."

All Buddy had shared with me at that point was a confirmation of a few of the things I'd already suspected.

He knew I was a werewolf. He'd known almost from the beginning.

It was too difficult to explain how he often showed up at the right time or with the right sort of hint to help me out—it was just something, a compulsion that he barely understood, for him to be in a particular place at a specific time. It was the same internal drive that was telling him he needed to be in Jackson Heights by 8 a.m.

He had indeed been the one to provide Ben the clue as to where to find me. Because Buddy had, himself, found me by following a suggestion that came to him in a way he wasn't sure he could explain.

"Of course you do," I said. "You materialize in and out of my life like The Great Gazoo."

Buddy grinned. "Naw, that was the Flintstones equivalent of jumping the shark. The show was widely criticized for introducing him in their sixth season. They called him absurd, and like something from The Jetsons rather than showing up in Bedrock. And yet, despite this, he was a recurring character in the comic books, merchandise, video games, and even the commercials for Fruity and Cocoa Pebbles. You know that guy was voiced by Harvey Korman? The now late actor once said that he continued to be asked to utter common phrases spoken by The Great Gazoo at conventions and—"

My fork dropping onto the now empty plate in front of me interrupted him.

"You don't have time to explain things, and yet you launch into Encyclopedia Brown mode about a character on The Flintstones?"

"Sorry. Old habit. But unlike The Great Gazoo, I definitely didn't crash here on a spaceship, exiled from some other planet. And I think I've been useful to you. That little green guy was a play on the Trickster God trope. He caused more havoc than anything in the lives of Fred and Barney."

"But, only *children and dum-dums* could see him. Isn't that like Ben and Isabeau not being aware of you?"

"I honestly have no idea why that is. But I'm no Trickster God. I'm a mortal. Like you. My job as a salesman is real. People see me. That waitress, she spoke to me. I think you've interacted with me enough over the years to realize I'm flesh and blood. I just happen to get these odd compulsions that help me find you and others like you. Things come into my head that I share with you. But I don't understand how or why."

"But that makes you appear out of nowhere. And often it's at the right time. You're like some sort of fairy godmother to me."

"More like a hairy wolf mother," Buddy laughed and took another drink of his coffee. "Like I said, there's no time to get into this right now. I have to leave for Jackson Heights in less than half an hour."

"What are you going to do when you get there?"

"I don't know. I have an image in my head of a Denny's on the corner of Northern Boulevard and 87th Street. I can see myself walking inside. The rest of it usually comes as I'm already crossing that bridge, you might say. My life feels like I'm an improv actor performing based on a live pitch from some unseen audience."

"What happens when you don't follow one of those random anonymous compulsions? What if you don't make it to Jackson Heights in time?"

He said nothing; he just stared at me quietly. And his face went so instantly pale that I didn't need my ability to smell the cold and bitter fear he exuded thinking about the unspoken answer to that question.

He slowly shook his head.

"Okay then, that means you have a limited time to wave that magic wand, turn my pumpkin into a carriage and get my hairy ass to the ball."

"You know I don't have magic abilities. Just this bizarre intuition that instructs me where to be, tells me things, or suggests I relay a particular piece of information to you or one of my other protégés."

His other proteges?

"Your other protégés," I said. "Are there any others like me? Are there any nearby?"

Again, Buddy quietly stared across the table at me, a blank look on his face. This was one of those times where I could not get a bead on his scent.

We stared at one another for several beats.

This might have been the longest I'd ever sat across from him without him launching into some type of extended lecture about some random trivial tidbit.

"Your meeting in Jackson Heights? Is that with someone like me? A werewolf?"

Buddy remained silent, stern-faced.

"You're not going to tell me, are you?"

There was a long pause before he spoke. "I can't," he finally said.

"You *won't* or you *can't*?"

"The latter." This last statement came with an odor of regret.

"This isn't just about me, you know." I gestured to the copy of the Daily News on the side of our table that had been here when we arrived. "The entire city is going to shit. And it's worse than the after-dark terrors the PFA were inspiring. People are attacking one another at random. Those gunmen the other day near Madison Square Garden; they were people infected with Apatetic Spirits. Those two shooters were already survivalist nutjobs with a hate-on. But the virus can spread. It got to me. And I'm pretty sure that's what's causing so many other normal citizens to act out. And there are more inexplicable paranormal creatures, like that crimson demon army I told you about that attacked me below the subway. The combination of clone snake-men and those demons on the High Bridge."

I stopped talking when I heard the waitress moving in our direction with the second round of our food order. I shook my head and stared at Buddy, who was looking back at me with a tight-lipped expression on his face.

Buddy thanked the waitress and waited until she left until he spoke. "Speaking of the High Bridge, did you know it's not only the oldest bridge in the entire city, but it was originally called the Aqueduct Bridge? It was originally constructed between 1837 and 1848 with sixteen stone arches and resembled a Roman Aqueduct." He picked up the toast in front of him and waved it around while he spoke. "It was part of the Croton Aqueduct that connected with the Croton River and was the first reliable and main water supply system in New York City. It was, in fact, the very first of its kind ever constructed in the United States. It leveraged a classic gravity feed, dropping a little over a dozen inches per mile and running forty-one miles."

He paused to take a bite of his toast and chewed it before continuing. As he was rambling, I shoveled a half dozen heaping forkfuls of the omelet into my mouth, still famished.

"The High Bridge Water Tower, on the Manhattan side of High Bridge, was added between 1866 and 1872. Water was pumped up one hundred feet to a seven-acre reservoir adjacent to the tower—which is now the site of a public swimming pool and a play center—and the forty-seven-thousand-gallon tank. This new improvement was fundamental to improve the water system's gravity pressure which became important with the advent of flush toilets and—"

"You're going to go on about the history of flush toilets in the city?" I interrupted him, tossing my fork down onto my now half-empty plate. "A lesson in the history of the city's water supply?

"What the heck is wrong with you? Didn't you hear anything I just said? The entire city is teeming with this madness. I can't even be with Gail because of this curse. And I think the hell-on-earth that's growing day by day is connected to this ancient curse. Ben told me something about an artifact that was hidden somewhere in this city. I need to find it. Destroy it. And instead of helping me, you're rattling off some random encyclopedic nonsense about how they got water to Manhattan?"

"You mentioned the High Bridge. That made me think about the history. Hey, just a few weeks ago, you were *very* interested in knowing more about the city's water supply, weren't you?"

"Yeah. But it wasn't even at High Bridge."

"No, the city stopped using that location around 1890 when they built the New Croton Aqueduct."

"I know. You told me about this. And about the water tunnel systems running under the city. I don't care about that now. I need your help finding the artifact I told you about."

"What makes you think I can help you find it? I know absolutely nothing about it. Or the curse you were talking about earlier."

"But that intuition you have. You *must* know something."

"I already tried to tell you—the things I know just come to me. I have no control over any of it. I either know something—like your lycanthropic nature, or where and when I need to be somewhere—or I'm compelled to spout off some random trivia. I can't summon those things up. They come when they come."

Buddy finished the piece of toast while I stared down at my plate. From the corner of my eye, I caught him glancing at his watch.

"You're about to leave, aren't you?"

"Yeah."

"I'm at a complete loss of what to do here, Buddy. I'm not sure where to turn or what actions I can take. If something comes to you, could you please reach out?"

"You know I always do."

"Thanks, Buddy. And thanks for your help. This morning, with my clothes. The other day when you helped Ben find me."

"Hairy wolf mother at your service!" He grinned, and his enormous belly hitched as he laughed at his own joke. His laugh always reminded me of John Candy in the role of the traveling salesman in the movie *Planes, Trains and Automobiles*. And, similar to that character's effect on Steve Martin's uptight businessman character, I couldn't stay angry at Buddy for long.

He wriggled his way out of the booth, stood up, and placed a hand on my shoulder.

"One thing I know," he said. "You'll figure this out. You and Gail. Together, you'll find a way to fight this. To beat this. It won't be easy, and it won't be quick; but that's never stopped you before. It's no different than writing a novel, Michael. You get writer's block? That's just a temporary setback in a much larger, much longer journey."

I turned to look up at him. "Is that a clue?" I asked. "One of those things that random muse voice told you say?"

"No," he grinned. "I told myself to say that."

He then walked out of the diner, and after a few moments of staring at my plate, I picked up my fork and dug back into the omelette.

Chapter Twenty-Five: The good news, the bad news, and the ugly news

Upstate New York

GAIL

My mother put the phone in the cradle and dropped her head to her fingers and massaged her temples. I resisted the urge to tease her about the landline—*Hey, Darina, the 80s called, they want their phone back!*—when I saw Iz watching Mom, her face pale and drawn.

"Mom?" I finally said.

She took a deep breath, and then looked up. Her eyes went over me quickly, and then lingered on Iz, who squared her shoulders.

"That was Mosegi," Mom said. "The good news is that your grandmother has confirmed that the Baloraye you and Ben found is not a fake. Every member of the coven who is not out searching for more is now working together to decommission it."

"Whoa," I said. "You can take magic away from things?"

"Magical items are," my mother began, but then she paused, seemed to reconsider. "The object will always carry hints of the curse in the eyes of those of us who know what to look for. But Roberta can neutralize the dark magic. It won't disappear, but it will become unusable."

"Cool. That's great news, right? So, we find the rest of these balor-thingeys, and then we ask Iz's grandmother to de-magic them, and the curse is over. Easy peas—" I stopped when I saw that no one else shared my glib optimism. "I mean, I know it's probably not *easy*." I glanced from Mom to Iz, trying to understand their gloom. "But it's always good to know the problem. Now, we fix it. Then we can all move on with our lives."

"It's not that simple."

"Should we go help? I mean, isn't that the whole point of the coven? Like, don't we do some sort of group ritual or something?"

My mother's eyes darkened, but I saw a tiny quirk at the corner of Iz's mouth before her expression settled back into a frown.

"Gail." Mom closed her eyes again, for a long moment, and breathed deeply. "Neutralizing magic this dark requires a blood sacrifice."

"So, like, we sacrifice a cat? I'd be happy to do that. Think of all the money I'd save on allergy meds."

"A great deal of blood is required from the High Priestess of the coven. Roberta is from a royal line, and she carries centuries of ancient wisdom inside of her, but she wears a human body. One that is, unfortunately, growing frail."

My chest hollowed. "Will it kill her?"

"She does not recover from this kind of ritual as quickly as she used to."

"Well why can't someone else do it? Iz is from her blood line." Isabeau's eyes flashed at me, and I corrected myself quickly. "Or me. I'll do it. Seems only fair. And I don't care about blood. I make more every day."

My mother didn't smile at me, but her face softened. "Even if you had the training, which you do not, you don't have the experience or the authority to call on such magic."

We'd been having such a nice day, given everything else that was going on. The entire contents of my mother's pantry had been removed to reveal a false panel in the back of the cabinet. There, she had hidden away a tiny secret pantry neatly packed with herbs, potions, minerals, and utensils. She and Iz had been telling me about all of them—their uses, their dangers, their histories. I'd been opening jars, smelling the herbs, taking notes, and breathing in their benign presence like they were the first snowfall of winter.

Now I chewed the inside of my cheek as I surveyed the mess we'd made, nervous about the sad atmosphere in the room. I picked up the jars and put them back on the shelves, though I knew they were out of order. Mom didn't alphabetize anything, but she had a specific and precise organizing system. Thanks to me, the once-tidy jars now tumbled into random spots, some rolling on their sides, some on top of others, packed in willy-nilly without any consideration for accessibility.

They watched me quietly as I tried to quell my anxiety with decisive motion. Finally, my mother put her hand on my arm and I stopped in my tracks.

"I know you want to fix this," she said quietly. "Because that's what you do. You act. It's your strength. But it can be a weakness, too, Gail. Barrelling in without understanding the consequences can be very dangerous." She took an amulet and a fragrant sachet out of my hands and set them back on the kitchen table. I sat back down next to Iz.

"What's the bad news?" Iz said. Her voice sounded small.

"What do you mean?" I asked.

Iz kept her gaze on my mother, who was now arranging the jars I'd shoved into the cabinet into an order only she understood.

"Darina said the good news was that Gran identified the Baloraye. What's the bad news?"

"I thought the bad news was the blood situation?"

My mother's hands froze over the shelves, and then, after an interminable silence, she turned and joined us at the table.

"Finn," my mother said quietly.

The knuckles on Iz's clenched hands whitened, her long nails digging into the skin of her palms. "I don't believe it."

My mother cleared her throat and spoke slowly. "Honey, no one blames you."

The air between them hung hot and tense like an overfilled balloon about to explode.

"But..."

"I know."

"He never..."

"He wouldn't have."

Iz's eyes darted wildly around the room, and her body trembled with whatever she had just learned. "We *trust* the Raichann Coven," she finally said.

"We do," my mother said. "We did. They are worthy people. That's probably why Artair singled him out—"

Whatever my mother had been about to explain was drowned out by the screech of Iz's chair against the hardwood floor. She jumped from her seat and ran out the front door.

I stood quickly. "I'm going after her."

"No. She needs some time alone." My mother's voice was calm, and she went back to organizing her spices as if this were a regular day in a magic household. Which, I supposed, it could be.

"Finn was someone you knew?" The name tickled at the back of my memory, but I couldn't place what he meant to us.

"Most of his people remain in Scotland, but several years ago he moved to New Orleans for work. The Boudreaux family has close ties with his family, and he became an honorary member of the Ulos. We all loved him. He and Isabeau became very close. He was a valuable Messenger, and he knew a great deal about the inner workings of the coven."

"What happened?"

"We've learned that he was working for Artair the entire time."

Now I remembered the name, and Iz collapsing into my mother's arms in the Boudreaux mansion. "So, he was some kind of spy?"

Satisfied that her cabinet was in working order again, my mother rejoined me at the table. "The problem with spies is that no one trusts them after they've done their job. Artair got what he needed: access to you. The second that portal opened, Finn was dead weight to him. That monster spilled magical blood as easily as if it was wol—" she had been speaking in a furious rush of words, but now she stopped herself and bit her lip.

"Say it."

"It's nothing," she said quietly. "Well, not nothing. It's an old phrase that we use. It doesn't mean anything."

"Wolf's blood," I said. She looked up at me, a strange look of almost-shame in her eyes. "You always used to say that to me and Ben. If the playroom was messy, you'd say we had no respect for our toys, and we were no better than wolves. If you didn't like the way something smelled, you'd say it stank like a dirty wolf." I barked out a laugh. "My god. When I was dating Robbie Garner in high school, you said he had the table manners of a wolf."

"It could have been worse. When I was a child, my mother would tell me to go clean the bathroom because the tub had a ring of wolf's dirt. If I caught a stomach flu, she'd pat my back and say, 'Good girl. Spit the wolf's blood out of ye.'" Her eyes were shiny now. "I'm sorry, Gail."

"It was in front of me the whole time, wasn't it? All those prejudices, just flying around the dinner table, and I had no clue."

"Prejudice is nothing but fear. We have a lot of that. Especially me."

"Well, I'm not afraid. And I'm not waiting around anymore." I jerked my chin at the purple velvet pouch on the sideboard. "Why don't you let me take that orb we made back to the city and look for more of those Baylor-things. Maybe that way, innocent people won't get hurt. If it's my curse, then it's my responsibility to fix it."

"You don't have the knowledge to wield such a tool."

"Then come with me," I said, stunning myself with the suggestion. Darina Sommers and I weren't exactly let's-take-a-girls-trip kind of people. "We can work together."

She looked weary, my mother. I had a sudden realization that she was getting older. Her beautiful dark hair had been graying since she turned thirty, but now I could see a fine web of lines on her face, a very slight sag to the sides of her mouth.

"Gail, on your own you would call attention to every Paranormal in the city. Together, we would attract them from all over the Eastern Seaboard. This is a Safe House. If we stay here, we are protected. For now. This orb was made for your brother. It is his job."

"But I've done this kind of thing before, Mom. Last year. I created an orb to help Michael find other members of the PFA hiding in New York. I just read how to do it in an old manuscript. It was easy. Like following a recipe."

"Most untrained witches would have caused real damage attempting that level of magic. The fact that you were successful, well," There was a gleam in her eye now, and her pride warmed me from the inside. "I've always suspected that your talent is a rare one, my daughter. But we cannot risk any more life, Paranormal or Mundane. Do you understand?"

"It's just that it seems kinda useless to have actual magical powers if I'm not allowed to use them."

"That's because you are still thinking like a Mundane. Obsessed with individuality. The power of the witch is always in the coven. If we don't work together, we are nothing."

I stood up and stretched. "Should I go find her?"

"No, you're on kitchen duty," she said.

"Don't tell me. The sink is as filthy as wolf's blood?"

She sighed. "I'll find Iz. We'll order in tonight, okay? Your choice."

I squirted some dish soap into the sink, turned on the tap, and stacked the various dished we'd been using into the basin. When my hands hit the hot water, I swished them and watched the ripples bounce off the walls of the sink.

"Water," I murmured. "Hey, Mom? Ben should go toward the water, right?"

She didn't answer, but I made a mental note to tell her when they returned. This had been happening to me frequently in the three days we'd been staying here. I kept having these sensations, somewhere between a daydream and déjà vu. Feelings would come over me, vague and transparent like mist burning off in a hot morning. The harder I tried to grab onto the tendrils of thought, the more they slipped out of my fingers.

Ripples, currents, streams, pools. Water.

But it was no use. The image was gone from my mind. I dried my hands, left the dishes to soak, and took the spell books back into the shelves in the living room. Once I put them back in their place—their proper place, my mother would say, no need to fling them around like I was raised in a wolf's den, for goddess' sake—I pulled my phone out of my back pocket to see that Jaya had left another string of frantic texts and phone calls.

How would I ever explain what was going on? My absence was simply too enormous to get my arms around, never mind trying to explain it to someone outside of this bizarre Paranormal circle I now lived in.

I scrolled back, reading through her various queries. Vendors, cash deposits, new hires. She had a dozen questions about the shop that I needed to answer. But I'd been so busy with my mom and Iz that I barely even looked at my phone anymore.

I'm sorry I missed all your texts. I've been super busy using frog's eyes in magic potions.

The text made me smirk, but I deleted it before I could accidentally hit send. Maybe someday I could tell people about my family.

But I doubted it.

Sorry I've been MIA. A lot of family stuff going down. Here's my mom's landline. Probably the easiest way to reach me. I'll be here for a while. I promise, when I get back you're all getting a raise.

I hit send and went back to straightening the books. Whether or not I actually could give anyone a raise wasn't important. I'd find the money. I'd sell fake love potions to drunk college girls if I needed to. Hell, I was a witch now! Time to make some money off the family business. Then I could make all of this up to Jaya and the New Girls.

My eye fell on a leatherbound book sitting on the table next to my mom's favorite chair. The book itself was nothing special—most horizontal surfaces in this room had a book on them, marked where she left off, ready to be picked up again when she sat down. But this one seemed to glow, and I recognized the misty feeling coming over me again. Instead of trying to reach out and seize the sensation with my hands, I decided to follow it.

I walked across the room and stared down at the book. It was a collection of Poe's short stories, one of my mom's favorites. I picked it up, and was startled that it felt warm in my hands. The pages fell open, and I found myself staring at a photo of a man walking across a long snowy bridge, his long black cloak drifting in the cold air behind him.

Gooseflesh rose on my arms, and when I exhaled, my breath fogged in front of me.

Friday August 4, 2017

Chapter Twenty-Six: The pages of one's life and the myth of fingerprints

New York

BEN

The day had started off foggy and overcast, but it soon burned off and the sun dominated the blue sky over the city. Ben stared out his window, looking from the bright yellow orb to the west and then back to the nearly formed moon, wan and lifeless over the western skyline. Every preschool on the planet told students that the sun and moon rotated in perfect symmetry around the earth; one showed up when the other disappeared. Now, of course, he understood orbits, and knew the simplistic 'one up, other down' animations he'd seen as a child were wildly inaccurate. Still, it always caused a disconnect in his brain when he saw them in the same sky, as if he'd stumbled upon two people having an argument.

He'd dedicated his life to studying mythologies of twins around the world, and been shocked to discover how many ancient civilizations considered the sun and the moon to be twin siblings, alternating their time in the sky. Most cultures believed that whether humans or gods, twins were different from other children, not only in the circumstance of their birth but in the makeup of their soul. Sometimes enemies, sometimes incestuous. Omens of good or evil. One soul tormented by the separation into two bodies or two souls shredded by hatred of each other. They either spoke their own language or they couldn't understand a word the other said.

As with the stars, the more people knew about twins the less they understood. Over the course of their lives, Ben and Gail had been questioned by curious singletons, some more intrusive than others. Do you share thoughts? Do you have the same fingerprints? Do you dress alike? Did you go to the same university? Did your mother treat you the same?

That one, at least, Ben could answer.

Gail finally knew the secret that had been kept from her for most of their lives. And now she was hiding away with their mother. Goddesses above only knew what would be happening in their little cottage near the Hudson. At this very moment, the two most important women in his life might be embracing or ripping each other to shreds. Neither scenario would surprise him. All he knew was, Darina had very little time to teach Gail centuries of information, and Gail would make every second of that education difficult.

Ben closed his eyes to the view and turned from the window. He hated the twinge of jealousy gnawing in his sternum. Gail had as much right to their mother as he did.

More, perhaps, considering that they shared…well, basically everything. In many ways, his mother and sister had the stronger connection, even though they couldn't be together for more than five minutes without arguing. Aside from their shared gender, which ought to act as a bond, they looked and behaved alike. They were both stubborn beyond all reason, wickedly funny, fiercely loyal, and enticing to nearly every man (and half the women) they met.

The magic, of all things, was what divided them. He blamed Darina for that. At the same time, he understood her reasoning. Gail was a troublesome child, at best. Ben had kept the secret even as an adult, knowing that when his sister found out, it would be catastrophic to their already-tenuous family ties.

Eventually, he hoped, they would survive this battle they were currently facing, emotions would settle down, and witchcraft would bring his mother and sister together.

And he would be banished to the other side of the circle they drew around themselves. Similar to them, but not one of them.

He had never doubted his mother's love for him, or his valued position in the coven. But now, not for the first time, he felt a longing for a father. Darina had forbidden Ben from searching for the man, but that had never dampened the yearning that burned in his heart. He had only asked his sister about it once or twice, thinking Gail would like to find a parent she didn't fight with all the time. But to his surprise, his sister never had much interest in finding their mysterious sperm donor.

His covert searching had yielded no useful information, and he was beginning to think it was time to give up. He didn't mention his desire to meet their father again, to Gail or to anyone else. Who did he have to talk to about it, anyway? There had never been a significant other in his life. There'd never been time for it. Not after he had learned, at an early age, the destiny his birthright had placed on him. Especially not recently, when searching for Baloraye took every spare moment of his time.

He turned over his hand to reveal the small blue-green orb that Gail and Isabeau had conjured under Darina's guidance. It would pulse whenever he came within a particular proximity to the hidden artifact. And it had to be him, because, as his mother informed him, were the witches to leave the coven stronghold in upstate New York, their magic would be easily detected, not just by Artair and his cronies, but also by other Paranormals and sensitive Mundanes. All types of creatures had been drawn to New York City since Gail and Michael unleashed the curse in full force.

Evidently, his sister was now having vague intimations of water. Ben wasn't sure how much they should trust Gail's Seeing, given how new she was to this life. But his mother seemed convinced that the visions meant something, so water was where Ben focused much of his search, walking the shoreline surrounding Manhattan. As he wandered, he reflected that water was considered, by most world religions, to be a purifier. Across faiths, it was blessed for cleansing rituals, and purified for sacramental consumption. It was the stuff of life and legends.

Ben drew upon those tales for company, the beautiful creativity of humanity, in all its splendid difference across cultures, locations, and times. Water, and mythology, never stayed the same. It was ever changing, inconsistent across time and age, necessary to survival but impossible to grasp.

The searching was the only part of his life that remained consistent.

Chapter Twenty-Seven: The searching woes of ceaseless pain while standing at wit's end

New York

MICHAEL
4:01 p.m.

I realized I was at my wit's end when I found myself picking up my phone to dial his number.

The past several days had been a combination of overcast days, heavy rain, and overall darkness.

Completely matching my mood.

Sure, I had finally shaken the Apatetic Spirit, but I was on my own—completely, without even Ben's companionship. I hated to admit it, but he was actually starting to grow on me. Despite the fact Ben was babysitting me, and our time spent together had been rather tense, I actually missed him. Gail had thought, all those years ago, that Ben and I would hit it off, that we had a lot in common. And I did admire two things about him: his pure and limitless love for his younger sister; and his steadfast determination and dedication to whatever mission he was tasked with.

Ben and Isabeau had sacrificed so much in favor of watching over Gail and me and questing to find the Baloraye. Watching out for us, in a protective way. What did they give up of their own personal desires and dreams so they could do that?

I had to keep checking myself against these thoughts whenever I migrated back to moping about the fact that Gail and I couldn't be together.

After Buddy had left me at the diner on Thursday morning, I went back to my apartment, trying to figure out what my next steps might be. I didn't even know where to start. The city was huge and, without any idea where the cursed artifact might be, I felt utterly hopeless.

Where the heck would I even begin?

I could track down a person like a bloodhound, but to do that I had to have some sort of a bead on their scent. Ben said the object emitted a distinctive high-frequency ringing sound. Given my Canis nature, and my ability to hear the sound of a dog whistle, I ought to be able to pick up on that sound if I could only get close enough to it.

Therein lay the challenge. Finding some hundreds-year-old, foot-high tchotchke tucked away in some corner of New York City? I'd have a better chance of cutting a diamond with a butter knife.

Nevertheless, I spent several days walking a grid pattern of the city, starting in the southern tip of Manhattan, and methodically moving back and forth along the streets, listening, and hoping beyond hope, to pick up on the pulsing ring tone of the cursed object.

All I got from the first several days of this tracking was soaked from the rain, exhaustion, and a really bad feeling about the state of the world.

During those days I used my special strength and abilities—close to the very heights of my powers given the proximity to the full moon—to prevent several dozen citizens infected by Apatetic Spirits from continuing to spread their mischievous and hateful mongering.

When I was out on my quest, I donned a hastily scrambled together simple disguise. I wore black jeans and a nondescript black t-shirt; and just before I leaped into action, I'd pull on a red running gaiter Gail had left at my apartment to cover my neck, mouth, and nose, and a black bandana I tied over the top of my head. It was simple, but far less goofy, than the swimming goggles and hoodie getup I'd donned before.

All I had to do was knock the spirit-infected people out and the black worm-like wisps controlling them instantly fled their bodies. Remembering how easily one had entered through the cut in my hand, I was careful to maintain my distance while these entities were leaving their human hosts. I couldn't be sure if the thin layer of cloth over my mouth would be enough to protect me from being reinfected by the evil plague.

I'd stopped several muggings, robberies, street-fights and vandals. But I might as well have been shoveling water. For every contaminated person I took down, there were another two in their place. I was like a man trying to clear a high rise infested with cockroaches with a hammer.

And I'd gotten no closer to figuring out where the artifact might be hiding.

I had just finished ridding another poor citizen of their Apatetic Spirit possession, but not before he had bludgeoned an old man to death with a pipe wrench inside a pizza shop on Fulton Street. I'd heard the ruckus from about a block away. And though I ran as quickly as I could, slipping my facial covering into place, I could tell the man being beaten was dead before I rushed in the front door. I tackled the assailant to the ground and put him into a sleeper hold. Not being a fan of punching innocent people who just happened to be infected with some sort of demonic entity, I researched how to render someone unconscious, and had plenty of practice using it on dozens of perpetrators.

I'd been too late to prevent the murder of that one man, but I had at least arrived and taken the bad guy out before he could hurt anyone else.

Because this had been the first actual murderer I'd stopped since the two gunmen near Madison Square Garden, I figured I should do something like tie this guy up and have the authorities process him.

My favorite fictional comic book hero would have webbed him up and left a cute note that read: *Courtesy of your friendly neighborhood Spider-Man*. But I didn't have web shooters. So I tore the guy's shirt into strips, tied him into a chair so he wouldn't be able to flee the scene, and confirmed that the woman working behind the cash desk had already called the police.

As I left, I wondered if that was the right thing to do.

Yes, the guy had murdered someone, and needed to be brought to justice.

But he had been possessed by an AP, and was not acting of sound mind. How would the courts deal with something like that? Particularly given that most wouldn't believe some unholy being had been at the wheel. The "insanity" defense, then, might be considered.

The way Ben had explained Apatetic Spirits to me was that they were drawn more easily to those who were already primed with strong emotions. That they not only fed on, but thrived on hatred, fear, and prejudice. It was like their presence enhanced the people who were hosting them to a point where their inhibitions were dropped. And they acted out.

It led to the age-old question: did the fault lie on the person, or the alcohol or drug they'd ingested?

"Sorry honey, I didn't cheat on you. It was the half dozen vodka martinis."

"Well then, I'm divorcing the half-dozen vodka martinis."

Here I was, hypocritically debating the idea all the while knowing I'd killed a man when I'd been under the influence of an Apatetic Spirit.

What did that say about me? About my inner self?

That's one of the reasons I found myself calling Detective Wagner.

He was part of a secret paranormal investigative unit of the NYPD that worked with a special task force of the FBI on supernatural threats. Gail, Lex, and I had collaborated with Wagner and his secret task force.

Neither of them knew of my lycanthropic ability and powers, but they had been aware of the power Lex possessed. The task force had even leveraged Lex's abilities to help in their fight with the PFA.

I found myself dialing Detective Wagner's number before even knowing how I would approach this. In Wagner's eyes, I was just another Mundane, like him, who had gotten mixed up with the paranormal neo-Nazi hate group because of my girlfriend's former ties to them.

"Michael Andrews," he said upon answering. "To what do I owe the pleasure of this call?"

"I'm sure that you've been busy with the elevated incidence of violence in the city."

"That's the understatement of the year. Do you know something? Have the PFA been back in touch with you?"

"No. But I suspect this violence might be related to the paranormal."

"What makes you say that?"

"I've seen some things." I had to, of course, play dumb. "Things I don't understand but that appear to be in line with the things your special task force focuses on."

Wagner was silent. I knew, through my experience in speaking with him, and my research into detective work, that it was an interrogation technique. People naturally sought to fill the silence, particularly when they were nervous. Leaving long pauses in a conversation usually resulted in the people investigators were speaking to saying more.

"I saw something in the whites of the eyes of someone who was acting in a very erratic manner."

"What'd you see?" I knew, immediately from the urgency in his voice, and the accompanying increased heart-beat I could hear over the phone, that Wagner knew exactly what I was talking about.

He was familiar with the Apatetic Spirits—or whatever he and his team called them; I doubt anyone else would pick such a convoluted name—but wasn't about to tip his hand. He knew that I was aware, via experience with the PFA, that paranormal threats existed in our world. But he was still part of a top-secret task force that kept this information from civilians. And I was, after all, a civilian.

"There were these black tendril-like fibers in the whites of his eyes."

Wagner's sharp intake of breath, though too quiet for most human ears, was not lost on me.

"These inky small tentacles swam across his eyes."

"How close to this man did you get?"

"Not close. Why?"

"Listen, Michael," he took a long breath. "I know that you're aware of several extraordinary things. And that you've kept it quiet. And I know you're familiar, as Agent Reynolds and I have explained to you and to Gail, of the panic that could set in should the average person become aware of them. But I have to share something in order to caution you: Don't get close to anyone you see who has those slimy worms in their eyes."

"Why?"

"We believe it's some sort of virus."

"A virus?"

"Yes. It can't be a coincidence that this started happening just a few weeks after the PFA tried to poison the city's water supply with that Berserker powder, trying to taint Manhattan with violent intentions. Your girlfriend Lex ended up stopping them, of course. But their leader, Marco, got away; and we believe he is the one responsible for this new type of transmission, which has similar side-effects to the ones he'd intended to release. Only this one is spread virally. We've seen evidence it can spread from one person to another through close contact, via contact with mucous membranes."

"But I thought Marco escaped and you haven't been able to trace him?"

"Do you remember that shooting incident outside Madison Square Garden last week?"

"Yes."

"I'm sure you saw reports of the guy in the swim goggles who killed one of the gunmen."

This time it was my turn to take in a sharp breath. "Yes."

"We believe that vigilante may have been Marco. We know he had super strength. And we suspect he injected it into the two gunmen, perhaps to test its effect, before spreading it to others. We can't figure out why he would have knocked out the one, and killed the other. Unless he was checking to see how lasting the infection might be. What might cause it to leave the contaminated body."

"You think Marco did that?"

"It makes sense. Poisoning this city with violence was part of his plan. He must have had some secondary infectious virus as a Plan B. He knew the authorities were on to him, because we had taken down his gang at One Bryant Park. So he had to take on a disguise. With Lex now out of the way, and unable to stop him, he must have begun his experiments with that backup contagion.

"But we know two things about it now."

"What's that?"

"The virus leaves the body when the infected person loses consciousness. That must have been what Marco was testing with the gunman. Why he knocked the one out. He must have underestimated his own strength when trying to render the second one unconscious."

"What's the other thing you know about the infection?"

"Lex's paranormal-reducing powers have no effect on it."

"Why do you say that?"

"Remember that solution from her emiction we'd used? The one you called Lex's Golden Charm?"

"Yes." Not only did Lex's proximity result in the blocking of paranormal abilities—including mine—but any of her secretions, including sweat and urine, had the same side effects.

"We tried it with an infected civilian we managed to subdue; but it had absolutely no effect."

I thought about that. Lex's magic-nullifying ability had come—like all the PFA's supernatural abilities— from a series of black magic-based ritual and scientific experimentation. The Proud Fighters for America had been trying to further their belief in white supremacy by generating a race of enhanced super-powered beings. Their ritual and experimentation led to unexpectedly different abilities in everyone who survived the indoctrination. Lex initially appeared unaffected in any way by the completion of the ritual. Marco had discovered her Black ancestry and expelled her from the group. Sometime later, Lex realized that she did possess a unique supernatural power. Only, her power was to block, or prevent, the paranormal.

Leveraging that ability was part of the PFA take-down plan.

But Lex's latent powers were useless against this current threat.

That made me wonder about the difference between the PFA's super-enhanced abilities brought on by a combination of science and magic rituals versus those who were born naturally into the paranormal world.

It was as if Lex's power only worked on PFA members, but not on those naturally Paranormal by birth, or the demons and evil beings conjured into this world, like the Wraiths and Apatetic Spirits.

I couldn't, of course, share that with Detective Wagner, and that filled me with a combined sense of guilt and uselessness. "So, what does this mean?"

"The challenge is that when a person contracts the virus, they often become manic, and are less prone to falling asleep on their own for some time. Which means they can engage in violence, and also spread the virus to others."

"Do police tasers work?"

"No. Frustratingly, because the taser disrupts the neuromuscular system, it has the opposite effect. The subjects get more violent. So, stopping infected civilians is that much more difficult. We have experimented with using a Halothane-infused tear gas that brings about unconsciousness, and are going to get that distributed among the force."

That was a good sign, because walking around the city and putting possessed civilians into a sleeper hold one by one was losing its charm rather quickly. And I had a cursed artifact to find.

"Listen," Wagner said. "I've got to go. It was good catching up with you. Please promise me that if you get any indication that Marco is near, you'll call me immediately."

"I will."

After hanging up the phone with him, I debated whether I should call him back and come clean with him, reveal my werewolf nature, and see how I could work collaboratively with his special task force.

I could tell him what I knew about Wraiths. About Apatetic Spirits. About the cursed object. And about the witch covens, and the other Paranormals outside the PFA who walked among us.

My worry had always been that if the authorities found out about me, they'd lock me in some sort of cage where they could study and experiment on me. I'd become nothing but an oversized lab rat for them. Only now, I wasn't the only one at risk for that. Gail, and Isabeau, and their families, would also be in jeopardy.

But I could trust Wagner and Reynolds.

I knew that from experience.

After all, upon learning about Lex's abilities to nullify PFA magic, they hadn't locked her up. They'd worked with her, with us. And Wagner had just shared a significant number of confidential details with me. He trusted me.

So why couldn't I trust him back in the same way?

There were too many unknowns.

This back-and-forth debate played repeatedly in my head, completely unresolved, for the rest of the day.

Monday August 7, 2017

Chapter Twenty-Eight: Once upon an August dreary, while I wandered, weak and weary

New York

MICHAEL
6:03 a.m.

I woke in one of the typical half-dozen spots in Central Park my wolf self seemed to prefer. This one was in a copse of thick foliage just a few meters north of the Bow Bridge. As disconcerting as it was to wake up not knowing where you'd be, it was at least comforting when the location had that sense of familiarity.

Don't get me wrong; it'd be much preferable to wake up in my own bed, cozy and surrounded by the comforts of home.

But considering the circumstances, this worked out just fine.

My stash of clothes from the night before was nearby, and so I was able to get dressed quickly and begin my journey home.

As I headed on the path that led across the Bow Bridge, past Bethesda Fountain and Terrace and on my way out of the park to home, I was reminded that I'd gotten no closer to finding the Baloraye artifact. Morphing into a wolf for almost twelve hours these past several nights didn't help. It merely reduced the time I was able to explore and search.

Turning up nothing so far in my search was getting to me.

Being alone was also getting to me.

Which was strange, because I'd spent so much of my time alone; and enjoyed it. As a writer, soaking in solitude was something I relished. And I spent several years being the only one aware of my werewolf curse.

Even after Gail had come back into my life three years ago, informing me she knew about my wolfish nature, and up until just a few months ago, I'd continued to spend most of my time alone.

That had changed with meeting Lex in Los Angeles back in June. And in those two months since, more people than ever knew about my affliction. Two of them, of course, were now dead. And though there were still a half dozen others who were privy to my secret, it's not like I could connect with most of them.

Stay away from my daughter!

Darina's words continued to echo in my head. I didn't even attempt to contact Gail, or Isabeau, or Ben. That was completely out of the question. I didn't know what might happen if I got close.

But I desperately wanted to talk to someone about what I'd kept debating back and forth in my mind.

All I knew was that there was an artifact hidden somewhere here in the city that I needed to find. But I was getting nowhere on my own after days of fruitless searching. I wondered if I would be better off revealing my true nature to Detective Wagner, explain the witch coven, the curse to him, and see if, working together, we could finally resolve this quest.

It was the whole *two heads are better than one* idea.

Ironically, I needed someone to talk to about my dilemma.

So, I did the only thing I could. When I got back to my apartment, I called Buddy on his cell.

He answered on the third ring with a low and groggy voice. "This is Buddy J. Samuels."

"Hey, Buddy. It's Michael. Did I wake you up?"

"Wolfman," he said, a little more life coming into his voice. "Yeah, you did." There was a pause. "What's wrong? It's not even five a.m."

What was he talking about?

"Buddy, it's almost seven."

"Not where I am."

"Where's that?"

"Denver."

"Denver? Are you there to mentor another unique individual like me there?"

"Nope," he said, and I could picture the infectious grin on his face as he spoke. "I'm doing a gig for the American Numismatic Association at the World's Fair of Money."

"What?"

"The random mentoring I occasionally do doesn't pay the bills."

"I see."

"So what's wrong, Michael? Why are you calling this early?"

"Buddy, I'm torn about whether or not I should reveal myself to someone."

"Who?"

"A local police detective."

"A detective?"

"Yeah, Detective Wagner. He's someone I've gotten to know and to trust, and he knows about the presence of some supernatural beings. He's part of a secret paranormal task force, and they are aware that supernatural beings exist. They've been tracking the Proud Fighters for America. Gail, Lex, and I collaborated with him and some others."

Buddy made an odd noise, as if he was in pain, and then he was quiet for a moment.

"I don't know much," he said, "but one thing I do know is that despite the countless compulsions I've had to help you and others like you over the years, the one thing that always felt right was keeping the existence of your kind a secret."

"But Detective Wagner already knows that people like me exist."

"Sure. And he's aware of the PFA. But does he know anything about the witches? How are you going to explain what you're looking for without giving away the existence of Gail's coven? It's not only your secret to keep. You've got to think about the impact this can have on other people."

I reflected for a moment on this. He was right; it wasn't my place to share anything about Gail's family, nor Isabeau's family.

"But, what about the bigger picture? Putting a stop to what's happening to the world right now. Who cares about keeping the witch coven from the authorities when there are demonic beings running around and possessing people?"

Buddy was silent again, and I heard him take a long and deep breath before he spoke.

"You know that strange feeling you get when you're about to do something and you know it's wrong?"

"Yeah."

"I get that, but for me, it's extreme. I told you the other day that I get these compulsions to be somewhere; an overwhelming sensation to say or do something. I'm not sure where it comes from, but it's an all-consuming instinct. And if I attempt to act in any way other than whatever that inspiration tells me to do, it's like someone is playing a game of whack-a-mole on my stomach. And when I feel *that*, I know it's wrong."

"Okay."

"Just a moment ago, when you asked my thoughts about revealing yourself to the authorities, it felt like Rocky Balboa just sucker-punched me. So maybe you might be able to trust that one cop you mentioned. But something inside of me is screaming that telling him is a bad idea. I don't know what that means, except that I strongly recommend you keep this to yourself."

"Okay, Buddy. Thanks."

There was so much I didn't know about this world I was trying to navigate. Trying to make my way in society as a man with heightened powers and who turned into a wolf was something I'd somehow gotten used to. But interacting in a world where there were so many other paranormal beings at play was still so new and fresh. Buddy, being the only friend I'd known since moving to Manhattan, was a person I had always been able trust. So there was no way I wasn't going to heed his advice.

"Listen, Buddy, did you get any insights or whatever it is you get regarding where the artifact might be hidden here in the city?"

"None that I can tell. I would have reached out to you if that were the case. But, like I said, these things come to me automatically. I can't force them; and I've given up a long time ago trying to even understand what I'm being compelled to do."

"Okay, thanks."

"You'll figure something out. You always do. And, like I said, if something comes to me, you know I'll call. I pretty much have no other choice but to obey that voice in my head."

"Thanks, Buddy."

Disconnecting the call, I felt more alone than ever.

I went into the kitchen and put on a pot of coffee before heading to the washroom and getting into the shower. The plan, like it had been the past several days, was to write for an hour or so, then head out to do my searching.

1:16 p.m.

I was heading west below the shadow of the Williamsburg Bridge as it ramped up through the Lower East Side, and about an hour and a half into my combination of the daily sweep of Manhattan and neighborhood patrol, when I heard something that had me instinctively pull my neck gaiter up over the lower half of my face and reach for the bandana in my front pocket.

Across the street and inside a twenty-four-hour parking garage, someone—a lone man by the smell of it—was going all Carrie Underwood on the cars parked there. My best guess, based on the sound of metal hitting metal and smashing glass, was he was using a solid metal object like a crowbar to do his work.

As I slipped the bandana over my head and prepared to rush across the street, my phone rang.

I ignored it and rushed into the garage.

The young man in his mid-twenties was attacking the hood of a late 70s Chrysler LeBaron station wagon with light and dark brown wood paneling along its side; it reminded me a little of the vehicle Chevy Chase had taken his family across the country in in *National Lampoon's Vacation*. The other car, to his right, and closer to me, had already had its turn beneath the fury of his crowbar.

"Hey, pal," I called out as I moved closer toward him. "I know it's a mercy killing, but don't you think that's for the owner to decide?"

Startled, he stopped swinging his weapon down on the car and turned his head to look at me. He didn't react to the fact my face was mostly covered in my makeshift mask. This was a man extremely focused on his mission.

"The owner doesn't care," he said. "Nobody cares. These things are responsible for greenhouse gas emissions. We have to do something about it." He then pointed to a stack of garbage against the wall that had a two-foot piece of wooden board with nails poking out of it laying across the top. "Grab that two-by-four and help me."

As I got closer, I saw the tell-tale flicker of the black worm-like tendril cross the white of his left eye.

"C'mon," he said, turning back to the car and lifting the crowbar up high for another top-of-the-hood strike. "We got a lot to do."

I stood looking at him for a minute, knowing I had to knock him out to get the infecting spirit to release its hold on him, but not feeling good about it. I didn't disagree with him. Fundamentally, we did have a lot to do about greenhouse gas emissions. A hell of a lot. But randomly smashing cars wasn't the solution.

I moved around behind him and slipped my right arm around his neck to put him in a sleeper hold. He was unconscious in a matter of seconds, and I quickly laid the top of his ragdoll body across the dented hood of the car, keeping clear of the escaping black wisp of the Apatetic Spirit as it floated up, out of his nostrils.

"One more down. God knows how many more to go!" I triumphantly said to nobody.

I was about a half block away, my face again uncovered, and moving south on Columbia Street, when I checked my "missed calls" notification to see that it was Buddy who had been trying to reach me.

He answered right away.

"You have something for me?" I asked.

"Yeah. This morning I was in a meeting to discuss the evaluation of a white metal medal from 1842. Immediately after I learned about the medal's history, I had an insatiable urge to call and share these details with you."

"Hit me."

"The medal, designed by Robert Lovett, was created to commemorate the opening of the Croton Aqueduct. This 51-millimetre coin that was manufactured outside the Mint was considered oversized. But it's such a unique item because the coin itself has so much information and legends printed on it that it reads almost like the back of a baseball card. One side of the coin depicts a cross-section of great aqueduct on one side and on the other, the terminal Manhattan reservoir that was located at 42nd and Fifth Avenue, where the New York Public Library now stands. There are statistics about the amount of water that flowed through the aqueduct—sixty-thousand gallons a day—as well as its slow, steady descent, the width and depth of the pipe, and more. This medal also includes a date: July 4th, 1842."

"That's it?"

"Yeah," he took a long breath. "That's what I needed you to know."

"Anything else?"

"Nothing else. But let me tell you, this coin we were looking at is in such great condition. It's a real beaut."

"Do you think the coin is some sort of clue?"

"No idea. Like I said, these things come to me, and I'm compelled to share them."

"What images did you say were imprinted on the metal?"

"The one side had a cross-section of the Croton Aqueduct. The other is the large terminal Manhattan reservoir which looks like a big brick fortress."

"And you said that was located at 42nd and Fifth?"

"Yeah."

"The main branch of the New York Public Library."

"Indeed. The location that was once a reservoir that supplied the city with much of its drinking water through most of the nineteenth century evolving into a different kind of reservoir. A reservoir of knowledge. The New York Public Library is the second largest public library system in the country, behind the Library of Congress, and the fourth largest library in the world. The main branch, as it is commonly known, is technically called The Steven A. Schwartzman building. It was officially renamed that after a hundred-million-dollar renovation, resulting from a gift from the philanthropist it was named after. The building itself was built between 1902 and 1911, when it was officially opened in May of that year. Fifteen thousand people attended the ceremony that was presided over by President Taft. A remnant of the old distribution reservoir is still visible in the foundation of the South Court. There are more than eighty-four miles of stacks not open to the public that are located under Bryant Park and contain roughly one point two million books."

"Is that another clue?"

"I'm not sure. I just thought it was interesting and wanted to share it with you."

2:44 p.m.

It took less than twenty minutes to catch a cab to the main branch of the New York Public Library, and half that time to convince one of the staff members to let me into the subterranean passage, not accessible to the public, that lead to the stacks under Bryant Park.

While it wasn't at all helpful when trying to fight crime in my vigilante manner, being a recognizable bestselling author often came in handy. It was easier because I was well-known to the staff of this library, regularly spending time here either researching or just enjoying the magnificence of working in the Rose Reading Room. Not to mention the multiple generous donations I had made to the library over the years.

Denise, the librarian who oversaw this area, was more than happy to take me on a bit of a tour, which worked well for me. I had explained to her I was going to be basing a character in a forthcoming book on an employee who worked down here and wanted to get a feel for what it was like.

About five minutes into the tour, she received a call for something she had to attend to upstairs.

"I've got to head back up," she said. "Have you seen enough?"

"I was actually hoping to be able to see more. It can take a bit longer to get a good feel for a place. Really absorb it."

She paused, biting her lower lip, before making a decision. "Normally, people are never left unattended down here. But I'm sure you'll be fine if you're just walking about. Do you promise not to touch or move anything?"

I would most definitely be touching, and also taking, the artifact. If I found it.

I nodded. "I will not lay a finger on nor move a single book or periodical. But I must admit, it'll be hard for a book nerd like me."

She grinned. "I shouldn't be more than ten or fifteen minutes."

After she left, I hastily made my way through the long rows of stacks, listening intently for that high pitched ringing sound. By the time Denise returned, about fifteen minutes later like she'd said, I'd finished my patrol without picking up anything useful.

"So?" she said, a big smile on her face. "Has inspiration struck?"

"Not yet," I said. But at least I'd eliminated yet another location. "But I find that inspiration usually comes to me well after I've taken in and absorbed a place."

She led me back out to the main area of the library, and I was heading out the front entrance doors when I picked up a familiar scent.

It was Ben.

I traced his scent up to the third floor where I found him in the Brooke Russell Astor Reading Room.

I spotted him across the room, pouring over a small pile of books laid out on the table before him. He didn't notice me as he slowly flipped through one of the books, intently searching for something. I was struck with just how handsome he was. Like his sister. They shared the thick dark hair and deep-set eyes of their mother, but Ben had a squarer jaw and a persistent stubble that gave him a rougher-around-the-edges look than his twin. He actually reminded me a bit of the actor Tom Hardy, and as I looked at him consumed by the pages in front of him, the opening of one of my favorite poems came to mind.

Had he and I but met
By some old ancient inn,
We should have sat us down to wet
Right many a nipperkin!

It was "The Man He Killed" by Thomas Hardy. We had studied it in my senior year of high school English and, just like certain other passages and phrases that grabbed me immediately by the throat, this one stayed with me.

The poem was one of several Hardy had written about war, inspired by the Boer War and the First World War. It explores, in such common sentiment, the internal struggle of the narrator as he is forced to kill a complete stranger who could have, would the situation have been different, been considered a friend.

That described Ben and I effectively. We weren't enemies, but my very existence was a threat not only to his beloved twin sister, but to the world at large. I suspected that, in almost any other circumstance, the two of us might be good friends.

He glanced up from the book he was scanning through when I approached the table. Unlike some of the previous times he'd looked at me, this look—and the accompanying emotion coming off him—wasn't that of anger or frustration. It was of curiosity.

He gestured for me to sit down in the chair across the table from him.

"You've been searching for it, haven't you?" he asked with a wry grin.

I nodded, slipping into the seat.

"Welcome to my life."

We stared at one another across the table for a few seconds of silence.

"I can't imagine how you've been persisting at this for all this time," I said. "I'm already exhausted. I remembered that low level vibration you explained the

Baloraye gave off, so I walked the streets, hoping I might be able to detect it. I'm at the height of my..." I paused, leaned forward, and spoke in an even lower tone... "power, my enhanced senses. It being a full moon and all."

"Do you really think you'd be able to detect it nearby, through the noise of the thousands of sounds bombarding you from all around?"

I nodded vigorously. "At first that was overwhelming to me. But over time I've learned to ignore or block out most of it. Otherwise, yes, it would be nothing but a barrage of noise, no more meaningful than static. Not just static, but static on acid. I tune out a lot of it, automatically. I can also focus in on something specific when I need to. Sounds, smells, tastes."

"I've never known..." it was Ben's turn to lower his voice and lean in. "...a wolf before. I've read so much about them, and heard stories about our coven's past with them. But you're the first I've met. We were raised to fear and hate your kind. But I've always been fascinated with how a people could hate another group for something that happened between two individuals so long ago. When I was younger, I would have given my left arm for a chance to study and learn about your kind."

I was reminded of my previous thoughts about the authorities finding out about me, or even Ben's family, and locking us away to study us in a lab. The anxiety on my face must have shown, because he immediately added more.

"I wish, when Gail had introduced us all those years back, I had been open to getting to know you. But I was afraid. From my upbringing, what I knew about your kind and my kind. From the prophetic curse. And that champagne you'd brought to the Fourth of July picnic the day we met? It's one of my favorites. Wish we could have—"

"Wet right many a nipperkin?" I interrupted, smiling.

"Yeah." He laughed. "Something like that."

"It's water under the bridge," I said.

"So what brought you here?" he asked. "If you only started the grid-walk patrol of the city in Lower Manhattan a few days ago, it'd be weeks before you arrived here."

"Well, speaking of water, that's kind of why I'm here. I've also been researching." I didn't want to explain Buddy's inexplicable intuition. "One of Buddy's tangential monologues lead to an old coin showing the reservoir that used to be located here. I thought I should check out the labyrinth of archives below here and Bryant Park."

"Obviously you didn't find anything useful here."

"No," I said, thinking about how Buddy's clues were sometimes indirect in fashion. But his instinct led me here; that had to be worth something. "Not underground. But perhaps this is still a good thing. We can work together and cover more ground. Two heads are, after all, better than one, aren't they?"

Ben nodded, and grinned.

"What are you working on?"

"Poe," he said, gesturing at the half dozen books splayed out in front of him. "Gail had a vision that involved Poe. She was convinced the answer would be here in one of these books."

"Do we know what we're looking for?"

"No," he said. "But the way this works is much like my experience in anthropology. It's one of those, *once you see it, you'll know* type of things. You know?"

I laughed. "Yeah, I know."

He slid one of the books across the table at me and then returned to scanning through the book he'd been looking at.

For the first time since we'd met, I smelled a genuine warmth for me radiating off him.

Chapter Twenty-Nine: Water, earth, air, fire, and the other parts of this structure of mine are no more instruments of your life than instruments of your death.

Upstate New York

GAIL

A palm covered my mouth, and I heard a low voice in my ear.

"Don't move," she whispered.

I opened my eyes and saw Iz crouching next to me on the bed. My heart sped up, and I remained frozen there, straining to hear what she was listening to. I wanted to shove her off me and drift back into the blissful, dreamless nap that had become part of my afternoon routine. I'd continued sleeping with Iz since that fight with my mother, because I felt safer near her. I took care of her as she healed, and she kept trying to teach me. The one thing I'd learned over the last few days was that I didn't understand a fraction of what was actually happening and should probably just keep quiet.

We moved off the bed and slipped into our shoes. Iz had a look of concentration on her face and I had what I imagined was a sort of stupid confusion on mine.

A heavy thump from the front of the house sent Iz flying out the door, and I jumped up and followed her. We reached the living room and saw my mother collapsed on the ground. Artair stood over her. He looked up and saw Iz coming down the hall, but before she could raise her arms, he fled through the front door. Iz crouched over my mom.

"Go after him," mom whispered. "I'll be okay in a minute. Just stunned. He caught me by surprise."

Iz jumped up and ran after him without looking back at me. I glanced back at my mother, splayed backward with her eyes closed. Without speaking, I closed my eyes and opened them again, allowing my vision to drift into Seeing.

There were several beings, clones of Artair, out in the field. Iz was running into a trap.

I turned my gaze to my mother. A pulsing wound radiated from her right arm, but even as I watched, I could see the cells knitting themselves back together. She was in pain, but it was slowly ebbing.

"Mom. What do you want me to do?"

The question hung in the air between us, and I could have screamed with the time she took to answer. But I bit my lip, hard, and waited.

Finally, she opened her eyes and looked at me. There was a tiny shine of triumph in her face; the very question seemed to have satisfied her.

"Go help Isabeau," she whispered. "Do what she says, and nothing else."

I stood up and ran to the kitchen to take the carving knife from wooden block on the counter, and as I tore through the house, I grabbed the heavy iron fire poker from the fireplace set. I bolted out the open door. Iz and Artair stood in the center of the field, with their arms in front of them, sparks flying from their hands. I reached them quickly and threw the knife so it landed firmly blade down in the grass at her feet.

"On your left!" I screamed.

She shot a jet of yellow light at Artair and, before it even hit him, she turned in a fluid circle, grabbed the knife with her right hand, and flung it into the gut of the approaching attacker on her left. These were the same Artair clones who had come after us on the bridge. Iz kept fighting, and I closed my eyes in order to See again. Time slowed, and I saw inside the skin of the approaching men. Translucent black snakes wriggled over their bones, to their fingertips and back over their legs and feet, crawling up along their spines. Hundreds of snakes coiled and stretched, sometimes rising up to the skin and appearing like tattoos.

I opened my eyes again and time caught up with me. Iz had finished her perfect swirl/knife throw, and was facing Artair with her palms up again. But rather than shooting spells at him, she cartwheeled a kick to his head and knocked him out cold. She shrugged at my shock. "Lucky for us, physical violence also hurts them. Just not for long. We have to move fast."

"There is something else coming…" I stopped. I didn't have words to describe what I saw.

"Need you to talk," she panted, pulling metal stars out of her boots. I stilled myself and focused again, and she ran to retrieve her knife.

"I don't know what it is," I finally said. "Something is coming from the road. All I can see is that it's big."

"Anything else?"

"Snake men. Two more on your left, three on your right."

Iz took a deep breath and turned a circle, eyes scanning the trees ringing our property. "They have found us," she murmured. "So, the Sommers home is no longer a Safe House for us." She put her hands up in front of her as a man leaped easily over the old fence that bordered our property. Her eyes narrowed, but her lips moved into a smirk that looked almost gleeful. Was she actually having fun?

"Do you think you can do the Ritual Power again?"

"What is that?"

"The thing you did on the bridge?"

"The one that pissed everyone off? I thought I wasn't supposed to."

"It would sure help in this situation."

I gripped the poker tighter in my hands, which were shaking in fear. "When I tried to repeat it, I couldn't do it."

"No matter. Lob energy balls, like I taught you. Concentrate on fire," she nodded to the neighbor's house, where a thin plume of smoke rose up from the Green Egg smoker they used to cure bacon. "If anyone gets close to you, use this." She handed me the knife and fired off her first spell toward the approaching man.

I turned to the other side of the yard, and slipped fully into my Seeing vision. The Artair clones approached on foot.

"Wait until they get close before you try anything," she said, her voice already breathless. "You're not strong enough to hit them this far away." *Zip!* Another pulse of energy left her palms. "And they're too dumb to hit you from their distance."

I cocked the knife behind my back, and as soon as I saw their hands on the fence, I lobbed it forward, trying to imitate Iz's graceful impaling.

Of course my attempt failed miserably, and the blade landed with a dull thud on the grass near their feet. The men chuckled at my lame throw and the one in front, a particularly ugly copy of Artair, picked it up. He held it by the blade and wiped the handle on his shirt, leaving a smear of blood on his shabby clothes and a bloody slice across the flesh on his palm. I watched in fascination as he tossed the blade from hand to hand, coating it in his own blood.

"Gail!" Isabeau yelled. I snapped out of my hypnotic state. I was even less trained in physical combat than I was in witchcraft, but Iz was holding off three men on her side of the yard; I had to contribute something. I dropped the useless poker to the ground and put my hands in front of me. I closed my eyes and sensed the energy of the smoker next door. The ball formed in my hands and the heat of it warmed my palms. I flung it toward the warped clone, and to my shock, he fell backward, his clothes in flames.

I turned to the other man and did the same, but my aim was off, and he dodged it. The ball hit the back fence and exploded against the old wood, embers sparking onto the dry grass.

The second man lowered his head and charged me.

I picked up the poker at my feet and swung wildly. He dodged the first three swings, but eventually I got a good blow to his skull. It didn't knock him out, but it stunned him for a second, buying me a bit of time.

I used that opportunity to try the triangle-hand thing I'd used on the bridge, but once again, it was unsuccessful. Worse, it had cost me precious seconds.

The man was up again and coming at me. I called up another fire sphere and flung it at his head, and then screamed in fear when his hair went up in flames and the acrid scent hit my nose. I looked down at my palms and saw that they were unharmed from the flame I had just held.

I turned and saw that Iz had one snake man left. She was still fighting valiantly, but I could See how tired she was. I conjured the biggest fire sphere I could manage in my hands, the feel of heat now comforting to my senses, and flung it with all of my might into his midsection. The sickening smell of burning flesh and hair stung my nostrils, and I gagged and staggered back.

"Gail!" Iz shouted.

Artair was up again—these bastards just never seemed to die—and even worse, the fence along the side of our yard was up in flames. I turned to run away from the fire, but she stopped me.

"Put it out!" she yelled.

Great. Now she thinks I'm a firefighter.

I considered the hose on our back patio, but then remembered the Johnson's pool next door. I turned back to the fire and closed my eyes to conjure another sphere, and flung it at the fence. This one exploded in a shower of pool water, and the stinging scent of chlorine drowned out the stink of burning flesh.

Artair was on his feet, staggering toward Iz, and she was on her knees from exhaustion.

"Has to be right here," she pounded her chest with her fist. "Think of vampire stories. Stake him through the heart with solar energy."

"I don't have that," I said. I held the poker over my head again, hoping I could at least knock him out.

"You have air, you have fire, you have water," she wheezed. "Having that many Talents never happens. Let's see if you have solar. Concentrate it into a beam this time, not a sphere. Get him right in the heart, or he is gonna be one pissed off snake creep."

The hairs on my arms stood up, and I spun around. The amorphous being now hovered in front of my house. It was even bigger than I first thought, towering over the roof, morphing in and out of existence like a smoke cloud.

"Something else is here," I whispered.

"It has to get through Darina first," she said. "Focus on Artair. I know you can do it." She pushed herself to her feet and took the poker from me.

I watched Artair stumble toward us, and fear coursed through my body. How I was in this situation was beyond me. I was a woman who liked red wine and getting manicures, for goddess' sake. Setting snake men on fire in my backyard was not something I'd ever imagined doing.

I closed my eyes and focused on harnessing the sun's powers. The flames didn't burn my hands in the same way the fire sphere had, and I couldn't grip it tightly. But I didn't pause to consider this before I let it loose on Artair. Instead of being a dagger through his heart, the energy dissipated, barely knocking him back a few steps.

Iz raised the poker over her head, but Artair shoved her to the ground as if he was flicking a mosquito away.

He laughed, a rasping, manic sound, and then leaped so fast I almost didn't see him. He was on me in an instant, pinning me to the ground, and fear paralyzed my limbs.

"'Man is stark mad,'" he said. "'He cannot make a worm, but he will make gods by the dozens.'"

I could smell his breath, foul and bitter. I struggled underneath him, trying to get purchase with my legs so I could knee him in the no-goods, but he was heavy and solid as a cement block against me.

"What is with the Montaigne quotes, weirdo?" I grunted as I struggled underneath him.

"You believe in a god, dontcha girlie?" he snarled. "At least, you believe in your wolfman."

Iz appeared in my vision, the poker raised over her head, and she slammed it into his back. For all the damage it did, she may as well have hit a brick wall; Artair barely flinched. He raised one hand behind him and Iz fell backward into the arms of a pair of snake clones with the force of his spell.

I used the moment to slap his face, but he only smiled as he pinned my arm down again. It was a wild, animal smile, and my blood ran cold.

He pressed his lips against my ear and his wet lips darted against my flesh when he spoke. "I'm going to eat you for lunch, girlie, and then I'm going to find your boyfriend in the sewers and I'm going to eat him. Then I'll use his pointy rib bones to pick your flesh out of my teeth."

A crashing sound came from inside the house, and all at once every window shattered out. Shards of glass landed all around us, and the yard sparkled like a sequined ball gown.

I heard Iz moan. "Focus, Gail."

Her voice was so low that I almost didn't hear her words. But somehow, I Saw them, hovering in the sky over us, drawing my gaze upward.

Once again, I closed my eyes and time slowed.

Something was attacking my mother. Iz was fighting off a pair of demon creatures.

And this freak show pinning me down was going to eat Michael. I could see the snakes writhing all over Artair's skin, teeming with voracious hunger to get to me.

It was time to listen and do what Iz had taught me.

I drew in a breath and absorbed the sunlight, heavy on my skin in the pounding summer heat. With my hands pinned over my head, I couldn't make a shape, but I saw it in my mind: a dagger of pure sunlight stretched between my fingers, searing my hands with a heat thousands of times more powerful than the fire energy I'd previously held.

Curiously, it didn't burn me, even as I gripped it so hard the muscles in my arms bulged with the effort. I controlled it.

I opened my eyes again and looked Artair dead in the eye. A snake writhed across his cheeks and then trailed over his ear. Instead of nauseating me, the sight filled me with pity. He had no idea what was about to happen to him.

But I did.

The bolt of sunlight shot out of my hands and plunged into his heart. The force blew him off of me, and he crashed against a terra cotta planter on the patio.

There was a limpness to his body that I had not seen before, and I knew that this time, he was dead. The other attackers began to fade in the sunlight.

"Iz," I ran to her side and helped her up. "We have to go help my mom."

We took a few steps toward the house, and the back slider opened slowly. A tall figure, decidedly not my mother, stepped out and gazed up at the sun as if gauging what to wear today. I stared, dumbfounded, trying to place her. Brown skin, glossy, shoulder-length hair, a patterned tunic, and a pair of dhoti pants in a shade of plum I had always been obsessed with.

"Jaya?"

What the hell?

Her eyes met mine, and they were cold and flint-hard. Her gaze slid to Artair, and she bent over him, stroking his hair with her bejeweled hand.

"My love," she murmured. "*Mera pyaar amar ho gaya hai.*"

She stood and faced us. "My love has become immortal."

My jaw dropped to my chest. "How did you know where to find me?"

She made her way down the concrete steps to the lawn. "Darling, witches today don't need crystal balls. We have the internet. As soon as you revealed your mother's phone number, I found her home. What a delight when I saw that it was protected by charms. I knew right away it was the Coven's Safe House. Once you gave me access to that, I had access to everything." She smiled in a way I'd never seen before.

"I don't understand. What the hell is going on?"

"I thought it was very clear. We need *you* dead." She nudged Artair's limp foot with her stilettoed heel. "I hoped I would not lose him in the process, but this is life, is it not?"

My shock was a physical presence inside my body, sucking away all reason, logic, and strength. My knees buckled underneath me. *I don't know what this is, but I know I'm not strong enough.*

Movement by the smashed-out sliding glass door caught my eye, and I saw my mother step onto the patio. Her wrist hung at her side at a horrifying angle. Nonetheless, her face had the same steely anger I'd seen on the bridge.

"Not today, Laxmi Mohan, clan Dakini."

Jaya turned to regard my mother. "How nice it is to hear my real name once again."

A loud explosion shook the air. The shards of glass speckling the grass danced with the sound and formed into a cage around Jaya.

Her scream echoed through the air as it sealed shut.

My mother's eyes ran over the destruction of the now-empty back yard, and she looked back at me with a gleam of pride in her eyes when she spotted Artair, finally dead. "It's no longer safe here. We must move quickly."

Our neighbor, kindly old Mr. Johnson, owner of the fire-quenching pool and the bacon smoker, peeked over the fence. "Darina? You all okay over there? Sounds like quite a party."

"Get back inside your house, Omar," my mother said, her voice strong. "It's not safe out here."

She smiled sweetly, waving her good hand in the air like it was a typical Sunday morning and her back yard wasn't smoldering with the final whisps of dying demon clones. Mr. Johnson stared for another moment, and then backed away, locking his glass slider behind him.

My mother opened a portal, and we stepped through.

Chapter Thirty: Two heads are better than one toss of the coin, to mix metaphors

New York

MICHAEL
7:40 p.m.

The artifact—the Baloraye—was here.

It had to be.

It was hard to believe after days of searching the city, in less than two hours together at the library, we figured out the Baloraye was hidden here in the High Bridge Water Tower. And we had been so darned close to it, too.

I turned to look at Ben and shook my head as a wry grin spread across my face. Who would have thought we'd make such a good team? Besides Gail, all those years ago.

The clues had come together like the final pieces of a jigsaw puzzle right after I'd found a black and white sketch in a 1952 Great Illustrated Classics edition of tales by the author.

It was a melancholy sketch of Poe, bundled in a long, billowing cloak in winter, walking across a bridge that disappeared off into the bleary winter scene behind him. To his left is a white landscape of barren trees that drops off in the distance alongside the bridge. After finding it, I slid the book across the desk at Ben. He snapped a quick photo of it on his phone and texted it over to Isabeau, who confirmed that was the specific image of Poe Gail had seen. We solicited some help from one of the librarians and learned it was a picture of Poe walking on the High Bridge. Near the time of the bridge's completion, Poe was a resident of a tiny cottage in the Bronx and apparently making the long trek to and across the bridge, to gaze at the picturesque view of Manhattan to the south was one of his favorite recreational activities.

The High Bridge and the Old Croton Aqueduct were connected to the New York Public Library. It now all made sense. Ben had been searching near water. Buddy had shared details of the Croton Aqueduct Medal; only I had focused on the flip side of the coin, of where the water ended, at the location that was now the New York Public Library. Combining that with the vision of Edgar Allan Poe walking the High Bridge made it all click into place.

I turned from Ben and looked off to my right. Though I couldn't see the High Bridge from where we stood in front of the two-hundred-foot stone tower, I knew it was there, just a few meters beyond the thick foliage. I pictured the bridge in my mind, felt its presence to the core of my being. The proximity of the last place I'd been with Gail didn't just linger in my mind, it took up a dominant residency there, the way a selfish jackass might manspread on public transit.

The High Bridge was where Gail and I had our last kiss.

Before the deer, the rodents, and the demon army appeared, all hell broke loose, and Darina saved the day and transported my sorry ass far away from her daughter.

Stay away from my daughter.

I turned back to look at Ben, who was staring at me, a sympathetic look on his face.

"Maybe one day soon," he said. "If we can find and destroy the artifacts."

I nodded.

Ben looked down at the small detection orb in his hand. "I'm getting nothing. Can you hear it?" he asked.

"No. Not from here, anyway. Let's go inside and check."

The tower wasn't open to the public today, and I could sense there wasn't anyone inside. The pool to our left, which had recently closed for the day, was empty; and only a few scattered folks were still wandering about near the pool and the adjacent recreation center.

We walked around the side of the tower. The locked door didn't delay someone with my enhanced strength for more than a minute. Entering the building, we ascended the metal staircase. I felt an odd sense of déjà vu from the encounter I'd had with the demon horde in the dark. But I didn't mention that to Ben as we silently climbed, him focused on the orb in his hand, me listening intently.

"I feel something," Ben said, before we got more than ten feet up. "A light pulse." He paused, closing his eyes. "Yes. There it is again. Another pulse. It's near. Do you hear it now?"

I closed my eyes, and picked up a faint auditory vibration.

I ascended a few more steps. The almost imperceptible ringing was a tiny bit louder.

"Yeah," I said. "I think so."

Ben and I grinned at one another, and he laughed. "Having your hearing and this orb Gail fashioned sure beats the years Iz and I had to search before we found that other one."

I shook my head. "Not sure how I expected to pick up this sound in the middle of a bustling Metropolis. You noticed it first."

"Gail was right," Ben said.

"What do you mean?"

"All those years ago, when she insisted we meet. Saying we'd get along if we just gave it a chance. She was right."

For the first time in many days, I felt a sense of hope and warmth come over me. We were one step closer to finding this artifact and potentially returning to a normal life.

And yet something kept bothering me.

I pushed those negative feelings aside as Ben and I continued our walk up the stairs. The further we went, the louder the humming became. I was also aware of the stale sweat of thousands of tourists who'd come through here, combined with the scents of metal, wood, and new and old brick of the building.

When we reached the main lookout platform near the top, where the pairs of tall arched windows offered a panoramic three-hundred-and-sixty-degree viewpoint, I spotted an odd dark cloud from the direction of the High Bridge out of the corner of my eye.

I turned to look out across the bridge, but there was nothing there. However, I caught a sulfurous odor drifting in on the wind.

There was something evil approaching. But I couldn't see it.

"Ben," I whispered. "There's something wrong."

"What?"

"I'm not sure, I…"

I stopped, suddenly aware of a distinct drop in the temperature.

Scanning left and right, I couldn't see anything to explain what I'd been smelling, or the instantaneous chill in the air.

When I looked back out of the tower window, I noticed the dramatic length of the shadow of the tower to the east. I turned and looked at the sun lowering itself behind the buildings in the western sky.

I'd been so involved in this search that I'd neglected to notice the time.

"The sun!" I yelled to Ben. "It's going down."

Before Ben could even respond, a bright flash of light appeared in the air between us, making us both step back as far as the opposing walls of the tower platform would allow.

I smelled all three of them before they stepped out of the portal and onto the wooden platform of the observatory deck just a few feet away from me.

Isabeau and Darina.

And Gail.

Chapter Thirty-One: Are you ready? Say that you're ready for this!

New York

GAIL

We landed hard on a wooden platform. I stumbled under the weight of Iz and hit the ground.

These fucking portals, man. They may be an efficient way to travel, but I couldn't imagine ever getting used to them. If I ever became a real witch, I planned to look into the broomstick market. Anything would be better than this.

"Stand up. Laxmi will be right behind us."

I put my arms under Iz's shoulders to help her to her feet, but before I could move I heard my mother swear under her breath.

"What are you doing here?" Her voice was as icy and cruel as the Hudson in winter.

A familiar voice answered her. "Searching for the Baloraye."

Michael.

I tried to twist my body to get a good look at him, but my mother's good hand came down hard on my shoulder and didn't move.

"How do you know about that?"

"Ben told me. I thought you were keeping Gail hidden."

"We've been compromised."

Iz struggled beneath me, and I shook my mother's hand off and helped her stand up. She immediately took Mom's broken wrist in her own hands, her eyes closed as she Healed her.

"Ben, it was Jaya. From the store. Her real name is Laxmi, and Mom knows her. She's a witch," I said. "She came to the house."

My brother stood next to Michael on the platform. His hair stood up at all angles and he looked like a teenager again.

"Get the w- Get Michael out of here," my mother said.

"I'm not leaving Gail," Michael said.

"You can't protect her," Iz wheezed.

"Neither can you. Isn't that why you're here?"

There was a long silence. The mounting tension nearly choked me.

"Mom. Maybe he could help us fight?" Ben said quietly.

Mom studied them for a long moment before replying. "Keep him far away from Gail, and promise me you will protect yourself, my son, no matter what happens to him."

"Michael," Ben said. "Come with me."

Michael didn't move, only stared at me, waiting to see what I might do next. I knew he was expecting me to argue.

I took a deep breath. "She's right, Andrews. Stay with my brother."

He looked stunned by my words, his face hollowed out by hurt.

"Wraiths," Iz yelled. "Coming from the far end of the bridge."

"Move him away from her," Mom said to Ben. "The two of them together are going to attract every Paranormal in the state." She watched Ben lead Michael down the stairs, then paused and closed her eyes. "Demons, too. Laxmi's calling them to her." Her eyes snapped open and she looked at Iz. "How long until you are at full strength again?"

"Already there."

Iz had a half-dollar sized lump on her head, but her face was fierce, and she rolled her shoulders and shook out her legs.

My mother turned to me. "You've learned a lot in the last few days. You can help us, if you only use what you already know."

"I will," I said in a quiet voice.

She offered a tight-lipped smile in return. "Okay, we need to get down out of this enclosed space to face her."

"But the wolf," Iz said. "We need to keep Gail and him apart."

"He's far enough away, and Ben will keep increasing the distance. Staying here is a death-trap."

My mother descended the stairs, and Iz and I followed.

When we were back at ground level, the air in front of us shimmered. I glanced at my mother and realized that she Saw, too.

"That's a portal. It will be Laxmi."

"You can tell?"

She nodded. "You'll be able to soon. You can already see the portal before it appears. That's incredibly advanced Seeing."

The portal opened, and the stench of rot seeped into the air around us. Laxmi stepped out as if she was walking a runway.

She and my mother stood face to face, and then Laxmi took a step to her right. My mother moved to her left.

"Oh, Darina. Can't you learn any new tricks?"

They stepped again, in tandem.

"We learned all the same tricks together, Laxmi. From my mother. And then we ate buttered bread with sugar. Those were the good old days."

They continued to move slowly, their eyes never leaving each other's faces, the circle growing ever tighter.

"They weren't so good. Your mother was a terrible cook."

"At least my mother didn't consort with Demons."

Laxmi's eyes narrowed and her hands went above her head. But my mother moved faster, pushing her hands in front of her so that Laxmi slid into the bushes behind her. Iz conjured a wind sphere and flung it at her. This was far heavier than the pebble ones she trained me with—it looked more like Iz flung a bowling ball at her head.

Laxmi reeled back with the force of the blow, momentarily stunned. But she righted herself quickly and pointed her index fingers toward my mother and Iz. Coiling ropes emerged out of her fingers with a loud cracking sound, and they snaked around Iz's and my mother's ankles. She did it again and more ropes came out, wrapping their wrists over their heads.

"Ladies, please don't waste my time," she said. "I'm not here to reminisce. I'm here for her." She advanced toward me. I put my hands in the triangle position and her face lit up.

"Oh, this will be fun! It's like trying on Mummy's lipstick, isn't it Gail? Except instead of looking like a clown, you'll look dead."

Before she finished her sentence, I'd shifted my hands and conjured a wind sphere of my own and flung it with all the strength I had. She crossed her arms in front of her and the sphere parted around her.

"Gail, I tried to talk to you so many times," she began.

But I was bored of the talking. Bored of this fighting, bored of these ancient grudges. Laxmi wanted me dead? She'd have to fight me. I wasn't going to sit around and listen to her villain monologue in the meantime.

I had a family to protect.

I moved my hands back to face each other again, closed my eyes, and Saw all of the energy around me. A small house fire less than a mile away. The river under the bridge. The light breeze. The animals hiding in the vegetation. Every microscopic organism in the soil. The Atlantic Ocean. The sun. The stars. The Universe. All of it vibrated with energy.

Mine for the taking.

I shot sphere after sphere into her gut, and each knocked her back a bit farther. Wind, fire, water, earth, life, breath—one after the other. She hardly had time to recover before the next one hit her, because the one thing I had on her was speed. All those years of outrunning my brother, and anyone else who got in my way, had made me fast enough to outspell her. Maybe I would be a good witch after all, just by sheer force of stamina.

I hit Laxmi with a particularly nasty mud sphere, which ruined the pretty tunic she was wearing, and she fell backward into the hedge. I took the moment to assess the situation. Off to my left my brother and Michael, who hadn't gotten very far, were tussling with several Wraiths. Pebble-skinned demons approached my mother and Iz, who were still bound in Laxmi's coils.

"Use a sun bolt on the ropes," Iz yelled. "A small one this time. Please don't kill us."

My mother's hands, bound palm to palm, were bright red from the exertion of trying to break free. I conjured a fire bolt in my hand, a tantalizingly familiar pain, and chopped my hands through the air, slicing the bonds cleanly off their limbs without touching either of them.

"Nice," Iz said.

My mother had already turned to the approaching demons, but I grinned at Iz as we turned back to Laxmi, already back up and running at us.

Iz stood in front of me, palms up, and fired a tsunami of wind energy. The force was so strong it ripped the wrought iron bench out of the concrete and knocked Laxmi off her feet. She landed on her back about twenty feet away.

Iz watched her for a second with no small amount of pride on her face, but then swayed on her feet. "I'll need a minute." She was panting with effort.

"I got this," I said.

I remembered the trick my mother had used on the bridge. A twirl, almost like a ballerina, and the ancient understanding of the spell landed in my brain as gently as if it had always been there. Which, maybe it had. Perhaps that was how ancient wisdom worked, and what mom meant when she instructed me to use what I know. All I knew was that the energy was already in my hands, and I could distribute it at will for as long as I wanted. The power was infinite.

The only thing I didn't have was my mother's grace. As if that had ever stopped me before.

Flinging my hands to the side, I turned in a circle, my arms whipping against my body. The chaos of energy shot out of my hands—fire, water, wind, and earth. Despite my flailing limbs, I held the picture in my head of the creatures I wanted to repel. The Wraiths and demons were forced off my brother, my lover, and my mother. They flew back, stunned, while my family remained still in my Sight, each protected from my onslaught by a solid wall of shimmering sunlight.

When I stopped turning, a wail of fury erupted from Laxmi. "You stupid little cow!"

She pulled a two-foot broadsword from the billowing fabric of her pants and advanced upon me faster than I'd ever seen a human move. I ducked to dodge the blow, and the flat side glanced off the side of my head. I landed on my knees and the impact rattled my teeth, but I didn't stop to consider the pain. I'd already been stabbed one too many times in my life, and wasn't about to let it happen again. I stood again, wrists crossed, and warded off the next blow.

Before she could reset, my brother reached us, and tackled her from the side.

My mother, free of the demons, came to Ben's side and stood over Laxmi. "Give up. We outnumber you. And we can call upon witches from every coven on earth."

Laxmi seemed to consider this, and I saw my mother's shoulders relax slightly. But without warning Laxmi's arm extended and swept my mother's feet from under her. My mother hit the ground with a sickening thud. I ran to her and pulled her off the pavement.

Ben moved in front of us, fists up, and Laxmi laughed.

"Oh, this *is* going to be fun!" she crowed.

Ben swung—a good punch that landed hard on her cheek, and Laxmi stumbled back a few steps. But it didn't stop her. She sliced her arm diagonally in front of her, and a cracking sound shot through the air. A slash of blood appeared on my brother's chest, and his face went pale.

Laxmi lunged forward to impale Ben with the sword, but out of nowhere, Michael intercepted the blow by stepping in front of Ben. He knocked Ben backward, out of harm's way, and the sword dug deep into the top of Michael's left chest, near his shoulder. He let out a howl of pain.

I jumped closer to them and started my barrage of spheres at Laxmi again.

Iz rushed to Ben's side and put her palms on his chest. The blood stopped seeping, but he looked as pale as a ghost, and couldn't seem to rise.

Laxmi had gotten her hands in front of her and was deflecting my spheres as she advanced toward me. Iz left my brother's side and took up a spot beside me.

I took the opportunity to survey the scene. Michael had fallen to the ground, confused and delirious. My mother sat up, her hand on her forehead, blinking at us.

Iz was tiring, so I stood next to her, wrists up, trying to hold a defense in front of both of us. Finally, Laxmi stopped her attack. Iz staggered back into my arms.

"Your death will mean the end of the reign of the covens," Laxmi said, stopping to pick up her sword. And the death of your," she paused, spitting the next word out, "*lover* will end the tyranny of the wolves. And every one of the rest of us will rejoice to be free of your kind."

"She is not strong enough," I heard my mother say from behind me.

Laxmi laughed again, and swung her arm in a slow, graceful arc. The tip of the sword left the dirt and sailed high into the air, circling over itself until it peaked and plummeted back toward the ground. I Saw this in slow motion, but Iz was sinking in my arms, and a Demon had reached my side, ready to snatch her away.

The blade was aimed at Michael, who was on his hands and knees, unable even to lift his head, his shoulder bloodied from the sword; but there was something else. His face was elongating, and this time I was seeing it with my Mundane eyes, not my special Vision. The sun was setting. He was turning.

I'd witnessed this moment several times. The transformation never stopped terrifying me.

At the very moment I realized the sword's trajectory, and Michael's total vulnerability, a blur flew through my Vision. A swish of a long skirt, a haunting wisp of neroli, and then my mother skidded to a halt in front of Michael. She flung herself across his body, arms up in a defensive position to ward off the sword coming toward his heart.

But Laxmi had an armory in her billowing pants. She pulled out two knives, shorter handled with thick, leaf-shaped blades tapered to a deadly point, and vaulted close to my mother. At the exact moment the broadsword deflected off my mother's shield, Laxmi extended her arms and plunged the blades into my mother's neck.

Chapter Thirty-Two: Wolf Interlude

*T*he wolf woke to the pressure of a human lying on top of him, the sound of a human wailing a single syllable over and over, though he had no idea what that word meant.

Mom! Mom! Mom!

The smell of human blood was thick in the air. There were other humans nearby, as well as other creatures, the likes of which the wolf was not at all familiar with. Not human, but not quite animal. Instinct kicked in, and the wolf slipped out from under the body on him and bounded across the hard-surfaced platform where the humans and other creatures struggled. He leaped over a small barrier and into the nearest wooded area.

As he ran, burning pain tore through the part of his left leg closest to the torso, and the wolf realized he had been injured, pierced by something sharp. He stopped when he reached the cover of bushes and turned to see if any of the humans or other creatures had followed. None of them had, which was good.

Fresh blood matted his fur. The wolf licked at it, attempting to soothe the pain, and took more detailed stock of the scene. Humans and several bipedal non-humans were standing in separate groups. Four of them smelled familiar to the wolf. One was far more familiar; intimate, even. He homed in on her scent and breathed it in. She stood with two others the wolf felt smelled vaguely familiar.

Yes, he knew that woman. And trusted her.

He sensed that this human female he knew, and could trust, was overcome with some sort of intense emotion. Negative emotion. She was in pain. Maybe she, too, had been impaled by a sharp object. The wolf sniffed for fresh blood but could detect none of hers.

He considered going to her.

But the wolf was unsure of the others. Could they also be trusted?

He remained hidden.

As the voices and conflict between the humans and the other creatures in the open field grew, the wolf slunk further into the safe foliage of the trees and continued to lick his wound.

Chapter Thirty-Three: The stars are not wanted now; put every one out. Pack up the moon and dismantle the sun

New York

GAIL

Laxmi stood up tall over her and held the knives over her head. My mother's blood dripped off the knife blades and slid down her arm.

She grinned at me. "Baby girl, you're next."

"Bitch, you're fired," I snarled.

I stood up, stunned that my legs held me, and glared at her with my fists raised. I had the energy of the earth at my fingertips. But all I wanted to do was punch her hateful face.

But, before I could, Laxmi turned and gave chase after Michael.

I started to run after her, but my brother caught me around the waist and held firm.

I pounded my fists against Ben's arms, locked around my abdomen. "Let me at her!" I screamed.

Iz shot ropes to try to catch her, but Laxmi ran swiftly, and was gone in an instant.

She's not strong enough.

Her very last words a condemnation of me.

Ben and I dropped to our mother's side. I was afraid to touch her, as if death might be contagious, but Ben gathered her in his arms, resting her head on his lap. He brushed her thick hair out of her face, gently lifted a twig and several leaves out of the strands, and stroked her cheek. Her face still looked so alive. The fine lines I'd noticed earlier were smoothed as she lay in repose. She looked like a younger, more serene version of herself. Happy and peaceful. The woman she might have been before the curses, the fighting, the danger.

Before me.

"Mom?" Ben whispered, his voice a question, as if she might wake up and answer him. "Mom?"

I put my hand on top of his, leaned against him, and let him cry into my shoulder.

The holy moment could have gone on forever. I held my mother's limp hands in mine, and grief settled over me like a storm cloud.

I gasped and looked up. I was a Seer, wasn't I? My eyes scanned the area around us. The trees, the bridge, the river. Mom hadn't left us that long ago. Could I See her again? She must be right here. Wherever she was going next, she couldn't have gotten that far.

"Mom?" I screamed. "Darina!"

The Vision had disappeared. Maybe whatever witch powers I'd briefly had vanished when my mother died. Only minutes gone, and I already missed my Seeing. Now I only saw what everyone else saw. The lingering heat of the late summer evening still pulsing off the concrete, the remnants of a fiery sunset, and three broken people bent over an oddly beautiful body.

"It won't work, Gail," Iz whispered. "You can't See people after they die. She's gone."

She knelt by my side, one arm around my shoulder. My back ached where her hand touched the Druid blade wound, but I didn't ask her to move it. The steadiness of her touch was the only thing that felt real. Everything else around me blurred and fuzzed.

Ben hadn't taken his eyes off of Mom. He rocked slightly, back and forth on his knees, her head swaying with his movements, and he keened into the sky.

Chapter Thirty-Four: Wolf Interlude Two

*T*he female bipedal human running at him clenched objects in both of her forepaws—the human word "hands" flashed quickly in his mind—coated in the blood of one of others whose scent seemed familiar.

Despite the pain in his left leg, the wolf bolted through the underbrush, knowing the female human rushing toward him was intending to kill.

He couldn't gallop as quickly as normal because of the injury, and this area was completely unfamiliar. He moved slower than normal, barely increasing the distance between him and his attacker.

The familiar sound of traffic came from far off to the right, near the bottom of the sloping and wooded hill. To the left, across a broad open field, a group of humans were engaged in an activity he had witnessed before in part of the large green space he normally found himself in. The distinctive metal twang of a small spherical object being struck by a thick stick, combined with the heightened excited calls of other humans standing nearby was familiar enough. It was one of the ambient noises telling the wolf this was a direction he did not want to head off in. Most humans were dangerous, and the female human pursuing him now was an even greater danger.

He darted through a set of trees and the burning in his leg became too much.

He stopped and crouched behind a low outcropping of rock. The female human was still coming, not all that far behind. She couldn't maneuver as quickly through the wooded area as the wolf. In a normal situation, he would have already left her far behind.

He realized that outrunning her was not likely, so he braced himself to strike the minute she cleared the rock.

As she neared, she called out words he couldn't decipher. He knew they were taunting in nature, from the slight shift in her scent. She believed she was in control, that she was the predator, and he was the prey.

That infuriated him. He recognized fury as a human emotion. One of many human emotions he occasionally and unexpectedly experienced.

He pushed that human emotion away and let instinct return.

This wasn't yet his territory, but it was also not hers.

That would change now.

He would establish his dominance. He would kill her, and show that the wolf was in charge.

This was his territory now.

And these humans were part of his pack, and under his protection.

He lunged from his hidden spot with a blood-thirsty growl as she passed the rock, his teeth bared, aiming for the pulsing vein at the side of her throat.

Just as he reached her, intent on sinking his teeth into her exposed neck, he struck something hard—some invisible barrier.

He whined and fell to the ground in front of her.

She laughed and swung one of her forepaws at him, attacking faster than he'd ever seen a human move before.

He easily dodged her blow and lunged at her again, this time aiming toward her mid-section.

For a second time, his snout slammed into a hard invisible surface.

He sniffed, unable to detect what it was that appeared between them.

She swiped her other forepaw at him, and again he was able to leap out of the way.

This time he twisted and struck. No invisible barrier stopped him. He sunk his teeth into the top part of her leg, feeling the satisfying taste of her blood filling his mouth.

She let out a scream and fell to the ground, and he howled in triumph.

Setting his forepaws on her chest he peeled the lips from his teeth and raised up, preparing to strike at her throat.

But he paused as a sudden shift in the wind brought the scent of the familiar humans to him. Something was different. The scent now was of only two of the four humans.

And with the smell of the one he was most familiar with, a human word, a name, "Gail" came to his thoughts. She was giving off an emotion that he understood as an extreme sense of longing and loss.

And of fear.

She needed his help.

The wolf was suddenly confused at the conflicting emotions raging inside of him.

He shook his head, leapt off the prone woman—he would return to finish her after he dealt with protecting the woman he knew.

He turned and ran back in the direction he'd first come from, toward the scent of the familiar humans.

Chapter Thirty-Five: When the night has come, and the odds are long, and the moon is the only light we see

New York

GAIL / WOLF

"Laxmi will come back," Iz said. Her voice was no longer gentle. She had turned commanding in the minutes—seconds? hours?—since we'd been alone here. She stood up, brushed off her hands, and looked down at us. "We have to get Darina out of here."

We looked up at her, and she froze, blinking at us for a moment. "Wild," she murmured. "Sometimes I actually forget y'all are twins."

Ben and I turned toward each other, each of us looking at a slightly warped mirror. I saw my whole life in his eyes. Our childhood adventures, our teenage brawls, or adult friendship, our eternal loyalty, and now, the greatest loss we'd known. His face was soaked with tears and mine was still dry, but I knew my eyes reflected his. Red rimmed, wide open, and terrified.

Iz shook her head. "We need to move. As soon as she finds Michael, Laxmi will return."

"She won't find him," I said. "He knows how to hide."

But Iz's hands were already up, and a portal shimmered in the air in front of us.

"She'll find him, Gail. Any minute now. She will kill him. And then she'll come back for you."

All at once, the enormity of the day hit me, and the shock waves coursed through my body. I took a deep, rattling breath, tilted my head to the sky, and tried to choke back the sobs.

"Stop!" Isabeau's hands were on my shoulders, and she forced me to look in her face. Once again, her hands brought me back to solid ground, back into my body. "Do. Not. Freak. Out. We have to act right now. Do you hear me?"

I nodded, and she squeezed my shoulders and turned to Ben.

"I'm sending you to the mansion. Tell Gran to send help."

"What about Mom?" Ben asked, his arms tightening around her.

"You'll take her," she said. Ben's face crumpled, and Iz squatted next to him. "Ben. You know they'll take care of her. Better than we can right now."

She stood again and looked at me. "After I conjure the portal, I'll be weakened for a few minutes. As long as we stay right here, it won't be a problem."

"I'm not staying here," I said. "I'm going to help Michael."

"The fuck you are," Gail replied. "You're staying with me until I'm at strength again. All we can do is hope that Laxmi doesn't return before Gran can send help."

I wanted desperately to argue. I think she expected me to argue. But I had nothing left in me. I stood facing my brother and his tear- and dirt-stained face, holding my mother in his arms, and Iz, so scared and yet so strong, and had never felt more out of my depth in my life.

My brother took one last look at me. "Stay alive," he said.

He stepped into the portal and disappeared.

Iz's hands remained up until the air stopped shimmering, and then she collapsed in my arms. Holding her close, I slid down to the ground with her.

Reaching the final clearing of the wooded area to the hard surfaced space, he stopped, spying the two familiar humans huddled together. The smell of anxiety coming off them was stronger, but they were under no apparent threat. The other two that had been with them were nowhere to be seen; and their scents had completely vanished.

He paused just shy of the clearing and gazed at the two female humans, Gail and her familiar-smelling friend. He debated moving toward them or going back to finish off the female he had left behind in the woods.

Iz and I remained in silence for several minutes. At first, every noise made me jump out of my skin. Every twig cracking, every bird, every conversation echoing off the bridge above us. I kept expecting to see Laxmi, returning with her own army and Michael's dead body cradled in her arms, the way Ben had cradled my mother.

His death, I knew, would not be fast, nor would it be painless. She would enjoy prolonging it. She would make sure to cause pain. She would make sure I saw his agony.

"Iz?" I whispered.

"What?"

"Did you hear what she said?"

"Who?"

I swallowed past a large lump in my throat. "Mom. Did you hear what she said? She said I'm not strong enough."

Iz took in a long breath. "Gail. She didn't—"

But her voice froze in her throat.

I looked up. The sky was darkening, but light from the bridge above us bounced off the rippling water, giving a luminous glow to the clearing where we rested.

I felt the prickly sensation of eyes on us.

As he continued to watch over Gail and her friend from cover of the bushes, he spotted some of the other non-human creatures approaching them from the other side.

The smell emanating off those creatures, like that of the female human he'd attacked back in the woods, was pure evil.

He bared his teeth, growled, and then let out a stiff bark to warn Gail and the other.

Crouching in front of Iz, I scanned the foliage, holding my breath. Glittering out from a large bush were two eyes, bright white, glowing. I smelled the animal musk of an apex predator, the coppery tang of blood.

"Iz," I whispered.

"I see," she breathed in my ear.

A low growl filled the air, and the hairs on my arm stood on end.

The growl rumbled louder, a chopper being revved again and again, each rumble ending with a deep animal bark that rattled my teeth.

We rose, slowly, hands in front of us, ready to spring, and the wolf slowly emerged from the foliage, lips peeled back, and dagger-like fangs exposed.

Chapter Thirty-Six: One love, one fight. Let's stand together and kick some ass

New York

GAIL / WOLF

His ears lay flat against his head. His grey fur folded slick on his skin, taut over the rippling muscles of his lean canine body. His lips were open, curled back past his teeth, which gleamed in the dark of the evening.

Neither Gail nor the other human seemed to understand his very clear warning.
There was no time for communication. It was time to act.

The wolf ran at us with a sleek, vulpine grace, his forepaws extending out in front of him again and again, grabbing the earth and then pushing it away from him. With an almighty leap of his muscular legs, he vaulted off the earth, only inches before he reached me and Iz, and sailed over us. If I reached up a hand, I could have stroked his belly, furred and soft over the straining muscles of his abdomen.

We followed his trajectory over our heads until he landed, claws extended, on a red-skinned demon approaching behind us.

Before the demon even hit the ground, the wolf had his jaws locked onto its throat. The creature tried to fight, flailing its arms against the attacking wolf, before falling still under his assault.

The wolf stepped off of the inert body, which was already dissolving into a sticky tar. He licked his lips and surveyed the scene around him. His gaze landed on me, and he studied me without blinking.

I didn't lower my eyes, or change my stance. If this was how I was to die, it would be on my feet.

His eyes were a hot, ember orange, fathomless, ringed by thick, black-lined lids and a heavy brow that dominated his narrow face.

The taste of the creature he'd just killed was even more foul than its scent.

He circled his tongue around his maw, removing the blood, but not the repugnant after taste and mild burning.

Why didn't Gail understand his warning to her?

Why had she and the other female human with her seemed afraid of him?

I braced myself for the attack, but suddenly his stance changed. A blink, a pause. The almond shaped eyes widened, and his head cocked a fraction to the side.

"Michael?" I whispered.

He could not form the human words as he looked at her, wanting to speak her name.

"Gail."

He blinked once. Twice. He remained facing me, his gaze never leaving mine, his stance never weakening. But slowly, I saw his chin lower. Just a fraction. An acknowledgement. I did the same, nodding to him without lowering my eyelids. An understanding passed between us.

Suddenly, every hair on his body stood on end; his body tensed, his claws extended, and the low growl rumbled from deep inside him. I watched his lips curl back up over his long front fangs, and when he let out a deafening bark, I saw the expanse of teeth, bright white in his mouth, still spotted with the sticky blood of the demon's neck.

In an instant we were surrounded by Wraiths and demons. They approached in groups of twos and threes, some armed, some with fists up, most of them sporting bloodthirsty smiles.

"Move away from him," Iz said, her voice trembling. "You are attracting the enemy."

My eyes hadn't left Michael's.

"Good," I said. "We want to attract them."

She was part of his pack.
He would protect her to the death.

We held our gaze for one long moment. I saw Michael's lids narrow in an acknowledgement. A surge of energy coursed through my body, stronger than the understanding of the earth's energy I'd experienced before. This was the energy of combined forces, drawn together at last, caustic and explosive.

Powerful.

A grin tugged at the corner of my mouth, and then we moved at the same time.

Michael leapt again, soaring over my head.

As he landed on the demon approaching behind me, I shot two bolts of sun energy into the chest of the Wraith on his heels. Iz, to my side, hit the approaching demons on the left and right with water spheres.

We repeated the movement, Michael leaping over me while I turned to hit the demons behind him. We landed, back to tail, ready to face the next onslaught.

The human fighting beside them was strong and confident.
That made her a packmate; a fellow warrior.

He let out an anticipatory growl as more creatures closed in.

Among them were creatures that seemed oddly familiar. He understood, from somewhere in the back of his consciousness, how best to kill them.

He needed to show his packmates.

Wraiths and demons reached us as we rotated in our tight circle, me shooting sun bolts at demons and him swiping ferociously at Wraiths.

I heard a yip, a high-pitched sound that took my attention, and I saw him standing on top of the prone body of a Wraith. He leapt back onto his hind legs and came down hard with his forepaws onto the chest of the waking Wraith. He rose up again, and this time landed his paws onto the Wraith's head.

To my astonishment, the Wraith disappeared into an explosion of dust, and Michael was left on the ground where he'd been. Quickly, he turned his eyes to me, and I could see a question in them.

Do you understand?

I nodded.

"Iz!" I shouted. "The head! Hit them in the head with all you've got."

"Got it," she called back.

She turned her wind spheres to demons and when the next Wraith approached her, she cupped her hands into fists and exploded them onto his face. She didn't stop to enjoy the shower of Wraith dust, but immediately moved on to the next.

The wolf lunged at the closest creature, sinking his fangs deep into its neck, then whipping his head left and right, tearing flesh out and spitting it to the side. It collapsed and then disintegrated to nothing.

He grinned and licked his lips, turning to watch Gail and the other strike in their own vicious ways.

Humans were not at all good at understanding clear and concise communication. But these two members of his pack had picked up on it and were in complete sync with him.

Momentarily distracted, he failed to attend to a creature that closed in from his left.

It grabbed hold of his front leg and a white-hot bolt of agony shot through his body.

Hearing a squeal of pain, I looked to see that a demon had reached Michael and held him in the air by his muzzle and his injured leg, twisting in opposite hands.

I dropped the demon coming toward me with a well-aimed fire bolt that burned the skin of my palms, and then I spun.

This time, my arms didn't flail away from my body; I kept them aloft, reaching outward, repelling all demons and Wraiths away from us while we three remained in our protected walls of light.

I collapsed onto all fours, panting.

My eyes met Michael's again, and his gaze lit up when he recognized me. Energy surged through me again, electric and glittering, and I knew Michael sensed it, too.

It coursed between us, gathering speed and strength, force, and velocity. I suspected that it seeped out of our pores, twin filaments blazing together to create a searing beam of light.

We stood again, ready to face the new onslaught.

He had always hunted and defended his territory on his own.

But she was more than just a worthy warrior.

A triumphant howl escaped from his mouth.

Then the scent of the evil female human he had fought in the woods drifted in.

This time, they surged forward as a group, led by Laxmi. She walked with a slight limp, and blood coated her outer right thigh. She had lustrous snakewhips coiled in her hands, and she let the length of them drop to the ground, clasping the handles in her palms. The taunting grin she'd been wearing had vanished, as had the gentle roundness of her body that I thought I had known and loved these last five years. Now she was solid, bulky, menacing in her attack.

The snakewhips, writhing in an s-pattern on the ground at her feet, hissed a piercing screech in the air. She raised them above her head, ready to snap over our flesh.

Without looking at each other, Michael and I raced forward.

Just before reaching Laxmi, I slid low, my legs skidding on the ground and my palm on the dirt to steer me, aiming for her feet. Michael went high, using his massive thighs once again to vault him into the air toward her face.

We landed at the same time, dropping her to the ground.

I stood quickly and turned on my heels again, pushing the demons off Iz, who was fighting valiantly but catastrophically outnumbered. The push spell didn't have any effect on Laxmi, but it bought Iz some time and space.

Laxmi whipped one of the coils toward Michael.

He saw it coming and dodged the full force, but it lashed across his face and a sharp squeal echoed across the field.

She wound her other hand over her head, ready to dole the same punishment on me, but I was standing near Michael. The surge of our combined power coursed through me, and I took a running leap, feet forward, and flattened her back on the ground.

I was pleased to see the footprint of my boot across her buttery soft cheeks.

I stood up, towering over her, fists raised, but her arms came up again.

Both whips shot out from her hands. One swiped around Michael's four paws, upending him on the grass. The other snapped around me.

I collapsed from the shock of it, the sheen of the snakeskin tearing at the flesh of my neck.

He struggled and flailed on his side against the coil that bound his legs together.

Straining against them, he tried to break their hold, but part of the rope that held his legs bound together dug deep into the open wound of his left front leg. The burning was too much, and he had to stop resisting for fear of blacking out from the pain.

Laxmi let go of the handles of the whips. They didn't need her to do their work; they continued to tighten on my larynx, choking the breath out of my body.

Broadsword once again in hand, she sauntered to me, once again enjoying her dominance.

"Gail," I heard from my right side. I couldn't turn my head against the knot of the whip. Iz's voice was weakened, gasping as she continued to fight, but she spoke firmly to me.

"Your mother wasn't saying you were too weak."

I grasped at the coils at my neck, desperate for air. Her words didn't register.

Iz repeated them.

"She didn't say *you* were weak, Gail. She said that Laxmi was weak against you."

What filled me then was different than the electric surge that happened when I fought with Michael. This time a pulsing warmth radiated from the ground and into my blood, expanding my skin like a latex balloon.

My mother thought Laxmi Mohan, High Priestess of Clan Dakini, could not withstand me.

I closed my eyes, opened my mouth, and inhaled a smooth, cool drink of air.

The whipsnake slithered from my neck and into my own hands.

I stood tall, holding the whip handle in my right hand, and shot an energy ball toward Iz. She reached her hands above her, absorbed it, and in one fluid motion turned it upon the Wraiths attacking her.

As one, they dropped to the ground.

I turned to Michael and swung the whip, lasso-like, around my head. The fang end snapped the coils that clenched his paws, and he leapt free.

Michael and I stood, shoulder to haunch, and faced Laxmi.

"Cute trick," she drawled.

My patience for witty repartee was gone. It was time to end this evil witch bitch.

Arms outspread, Laxmi threw her head back and screamed at the sky.

Fire erupted from the tips of her fingers and caught the grass, trees, and bushes surrounding us. The dry day turned them into tinder, and they exploded with her ignited fury.

Iz and I fired water spheres into the encroaching flames. Every time Laxmi laughed, the flames blazed hotter, higher, creeping ever closer to us at terrifying speed.

The wolf had never experienced anything like the bright flames that had suddenly sprouted on the trees, bushes, and grassy areas.

It burned and scorched when he swiped at it.

Instinct screamed at him to get away from the fire. But how? It was all around them.

Michael charged and retreated, unable to do anything except paw at the flames. The acrid scent of his singed fur stung my nose.

Sweat poured down my face; smoke filled my lungs. I swayed on my feet.

A shimmering caught the corner of my eye, and I turned to it in surprise. Hope stirred in the depths of my heart.

"Mom?" I shouted.

But this was no ghostly visitor. This was a portal.

My Vision was still there.

The portal opened, and my mother's younger sister, Aunt Bridget, stepped out.

"Momma Boudreaux called. It seems we have some family vengeance to enact?" Her voice was light, and she attempted a wry smile, but the pale, pinched look of her face told me that she knew what had happened to her sister.

Bridget's daughters, my cousins Aileen and Maeve, followed her. The three of them wore long peasant skirts, similar to how my mother always dressed, and they each held daggers in their hands.

Another portal appeared on the left, and Aunt Sheila arrived with cousins Lonnie, Grace, and Rosie. All three shared the dark Sommers brows but had shockingly blonde hair, giving them the look of enraged spirits. Their arms were already up, hands out, water spheres forming in their palms, and they immediately took aim at the encroaching flames. The force, and sheer magnitude, of the water they summoned nearly drowned our surroundings. I had just enough presence of mind to remember that Sheila and her girls had always lived on a tiny island off the coast of Southern California, as close to water as humans could live.

A new opening, behind Laxmi, and here was Aunt Cait, with her twin daughters Nessa and Norah, my favorite childhood playmates. They looked at me with cool appraisal, and I saw Norah nod, before her eyes settled on Laxmi.

Finally, to my right, the prettiest of the stunning bunch of them, my Aunt Neve arrived. Husbandless, like all of them, but also childless, she arrived on her own, wearing leggings and a spandex workout bra like she'd just come from teaching a Spin class. Which, if I knew Aunt Neve, she probably had.

The other humans that appeared were not known to the wolf; but they had a scent that was familial to Gail's. They were her kin. And thus, an extended part of his pack.

He became aware of how their presence, like his own, strengthened Gail's aura of confidence.

The fire now dealt with, the Sommers women raised their arms, and in a symphony of coordinated movement, attacked our attackers.

Iz joined the battle, and in the crashing din of screams and curses, bolts shot between us, always missing the witches, always hitting the enemies square in the chest. I heard grunts of exertion, crashing thuds of bodies hitting the ground, hollering cheers of encouragement, and howls of despair from the Wraiths and Demons.

Through it all, Michael and I stood back to haunch, easily warding off everything that broke through them to reach us.

I backflipped over him and landed on a Wraith; then ducked as he sailed over my head to claw a demon.

Again and again, we stood, attacked outward, leaned back to each other, switched places, turned and twisted, swept ankles, extended our arms. It was an elaborate, unrehearsed, perfectly choreographed dance.

There was a special rhythm to the world the wolf had always appreciated.

The soothing, rhythmic sound of water flowing along a stream.

The assuring rustle of the wind as it tickled the leaves of the trees, bringing in tantalizing scents from across the forest.

Even the odd, foreign, yet comforting sound of the rhythm of noises that came from the sounds from the humans, of the strange objects that transported them quickly across the land, the pulsing beat and whine of engines.

But this rhythm, this gracefully coordinated attack, perfectly in sync with Gail, was a cadence he did not know was possible.

He'd always been a lone wolf, but the confident uniformity of the way they struck and defeated their attackers, as if working as one mind, was an unexpected revelation.

Their collaborative movements struck a cadence deep within his very being.

The pace slowed. The Wraiths and demons halted, though I could see that their numbers had not diminished. They generated endlessly, a constantly replenishing onslaught. I turned to see what was stopping them, and froze in my spot.

Laxmi had my Aunt Bridget clasped to her body, one arm tightly around her neck and the other hoisting the H-shaped handle of the short katar knife she'd used on my mother, ready to plunge into Bridget's neck.

Bridget's sisters and nieces, all sensing the pause in the action, turned to see what was happening. Their eyes widened when they saw the threat.

"I killed your last High Priestess," Laxmi snarled. "Now I will kill this one. Then her," she jerked her chin at Sheila, then Cait, then my beloved Aunt Neve. "Then her, and her, and her. Until I get to you. And once I kill you," she showed me her teeth in a poisonous smile, "Fraus will smile down on my victory."

Her anger scorched through all of us, landing, finally, on me. Her words had the acid sear of the Druid blade that still burned my skin.

A low growl emanated from Michael's throat. Too low for anyone else to hear, it seemed directed at me, though his eyes remained locked on Laxmi.

Wolf and human instinct merged.

A word formed in his mind with the same desire to pass through his lips as he'd had when first wanting to speak his mate's name.

"Kill!"

"Yes," I breathed. I wasn't sure I had even made a sound, but I could tell by the way the fur on Michael's back lowered onto his skin that he heard me.

Michael and I sprang toward her at the same time, leaping into the air together. I saw her blade lower in slow motion, a wretched arc toward my aunt's neck, but I was moving at a speed I did not know I possessed.

Before we hit the ground, his eyes turned to mine.

In Mundane time, it was a fraction of a second, an unseeable movement. But in my Vision, I saw him look at me, take me in. I saw the liquid warmth of love in his eyes. I saw the gleam of anticipation in his gaze. And then his eyes turned black, and hardened, and his fangs landed in Laxmi's neck.

My heavy boots landed hard on her wrist, knocking the knife out of her grasp.

Her head hit the pavement with a dull thud.

She tore at Michael, ripping out chunks of fur from his back, but he didn't release his vice-like grip on her throat.

I spun on my heel, easy in the movement now.

All demons and Wraiths were pushed away from my family, and I raised my hands into a triangle formation. My Aunt Bridget's eyes widened in horror, but I knew my face remained placid.

Sexual ritual. Community Ritual. Service Ritual.

I understood their power. I possessed them now.

I struck my hands toward the ground and a bright bolt, neither sun nor water, air nor earth, but somehow all of them together, combined, into one massive, deadly cannon of energy into Laxmi's heart.

She shrieked, one final, searing wail of anguish, and went lifeless.

Michael lifted his head. Blood dripped off his muzzle and his lips were pulled back in a tight, menacing wolf grin. He ran his long tongue over his teeth, sucking her blood off of them until they gleamed white in the moonlight. He remained tense on his haunches, and a low growl rumbled in the back of his throat as he surveyed the carnage, his massive head turning slowly.

When his eyes landed on mine, the growling stopped, and he stared at me, panting, still licking the blood off his lips as if he wanted to savor every last drop. His back arched, his chin pointed up to the moon, and he howled. The sound began as a single note, melancholy and plaintive into the inky night sky. But then his chest arched back and his howl climbed and fell, rose into the night, carrying waves of grief and triumph. The night breeze ruffled his fur, but nothing else in the park moved. Michael paused, lowered his head, took a deep breath, and flung his chest out again, howling even louder this time, a massive symphony of sound and anguish, carrying his story into the darkness.

He lowered his head once again and met my eyes, and his eyes had a cold, hard pride I had never seen before.

Slowly, the other sounds of the forest began to come back to us. An owl hooted and a nearby fox yipped her reply. Other howling, perhaps from wild wolves, distantly echoed Michael's call.

I turned to help my family, but they were all standing unharmed, while the attackers writhed at their feet.

The Wraiths were exploding into great drifts of particles, already dissipating in the evening breeze.

The Demons were dissolving into gooey piles of tar, and slowly sinking into the ground.

My aunts and cousins dusted themselves off, checked each other's wounds, turned their heads to make sure everyone was accounted for.

I fell to my knees in front of Michael. He had a terrible whip slash on his face, and a gaping, bloody wound near his front leg. I held my hand over it, remembering the sword he had taken before he turned into a wolf.

"It will heal, right?" I asked.

He ducked his massive head into my open palm. When he lifted it, my hand was slick with his blood.

I felt lightheaded with relief and adrenaline. From a great distance, I heard my Aunt Bridget, now the eldest of the Sommers sisters, now also the reigning High Priestess of the Sommers Coven, say, in a calm, gentle voice, "Someone catch her."

And then Iz's arms came around me, holding me as I fell into blessed, deep darkness.

Chapter Thirty-Seven: Wolf Interlude Three

*T*he wolf licked the red scratch on the side of Gail's face, hearing himself let out a reflexive whine. She was alive, he could tell, from the rhythmic sound of her slow and steady breathing, and her still-strong heartbeat.

The female holding Gail stroked her hair, murmuring gentle sounds, nodding her head. She made eye contact, and he could sense that she meant him no harm.

He whined again and nuzzled Gail's chin and neck.

Then he smelled a medley of emotions emanating from the newly arrived humans, the ones that were kin to Gail as they stepped closer.

Fear. Disgust. Hatred.

For him.

He growled a warning as he turned to face them.

The woman holding Gail let out another stream of incoherent human words, this time commanding. The other women backed away, their movements wary and tense, never taking their eyes off of him.

This one would keep Gail safe. That much was clear.

This many humans made him uncomfortable. He felt it best to leave. Turning toward the forest area, he prepared to trot away, but the pain in his leg caused him to stumble unsteadily.

He heard the kind female call out and turned to look back at her.

She stood and reached toward him. He peeled back his lips to show her his teeth.

But she did not recoil in fear. She lowered her eyelids, took a step back, and bent her body in an odd little curtsy.

He stepped forward, tentative, and she placed one hand over his brow, and the other over his left leg.

A soft warmth emanated from where she touched him, a sensation that spread from the wounds and into his body.

The throbbing pain slowly faded.

He looked into her dark eyes. She nodded again, and the words she spoke had a rhythm of sorrow.

Stretching forward, he touched his nose to hers.

Then he turned, ignoring the other human females, and loped off into the cover of the wooded area.

Thursday August 10, 2017

Chapter Thirty-Eight: When I think back to all the crap I did in this world, everything looks worse in black and white

New York

MICHAEL
9:03 a.m.

"I get it," I said to Ben, who was sitting in the chair on the other side of my coffee table. "It doesn't mean I have to like it, but I get it, and I'm not going to do anything to jeopardize the status quo. Too much has already been lost."

Ben's face remained stonelike, but I could smell the anguish he held inside as he clutched the now empty paper coffee cup in his left hand as if it were a precious talisman. The last thing I remembered from the evening before was saving Ben's life, and then Darina stepping in to save mine, before she was killed.

This was a new experience for me. I normally suffered a type of amnesia, unable to remember anywhere from a few minutes to fifteen minutes from the time I started to transition into a wolf. But last night I'd managed to hold on to my human consciousness and the memories that came with it longer than I ever have before.

The coffee cup Ben held was the twin of the coffee cup he'd brought for me, along with some clothes, when he'd met me along the heavily wooded bluff south of The High Bridge. My wolf self hadn't left the safety of that area, not with Harlem River Drive running along one edge at the bottom of the steep hill and the neighborhood of Washington Heights on the other. It hadn't taken him long to find me. Or, rather, for me to find him, picking up his scent shortly after I woke in the woods.

I smiled across the converted Algonquin Hotel apartment living room at him, realizing I was clutching my own empty coffee cup similarly to the way he was holding his.

Our cups were empty, but neither of us seemed as if we wanted to admit it.

All I knew was it felt good, for a change, to have someone who knew about my condition to be there to look out for me; especially now that Gail couldn't be that person in my life. Because otherwise, getting my naked ass home would have been a challenge I would not have relished. I'd done that more times, already, than I'd liked.

"And there's still so much left to do," he said, biting gently at his bottom lip as if to try to keep it from trembling.

"But, you found the second artifact," I said.

He had explained what happened the previous night, as Isabeau and Gail had relayed the details to him. How Gail and I had killed Laxmi, who had been behind it all.

That she'd been operating under the tutelage of the goddess demon Fraus. That this demoness was likely already in the process of converting some other witch or sorcerer to do her bidding.

"Yes."

"And it's being sent to New Orleans so that Isabeau's grandmother can figure out a way to destroy it."

"Isabeau and my aunts, and...others are there already." I knew he meant Gail, but he seemed hesitant to even say her name in my presence.

"There are more Baloraye, right?"

He nodded.

Though we had secured this second artifact, and its power was being contained, there were still others in the world to find. And we needed to determine a way to destroy the ones we had found. By locating and removing this local Baloraye, we had effectively tucked most of the darkness and evil that had spilled into New York City from that proverbial Pandora's Box back inside.

But it would release the minute Gail and I met up again; even for the briefest moment. As there were active Baloraye in the world, Gail and I could not be together.

"If you love her as much as I think you do," Ben said. "You'll still be there when all of the Baloraye are found and can be destroyed."

"Even if it takes years," I said, feeling the wetness coming to my eyes. "Decades."

A flash of memory struck me.

Night. Evil, anger, hatred perfuming the air.

Surrounded by enemies.

A view of the world low to the ground. The wolf's perspective.

Locking eyes with Gail and feeling a pure and unadulterated connection, deeper than any connection we'd experienced.

That bond was eternal. Neither physical distance nor time could ever take that away.

"But that being said, there's no better time than the present for us to get started in finding the next one, right?"

Ben shook his head. "Not just yet. There are several personal matters I need to attend to with my mother's coven."

"We make a good team, you know."

He nodded. "I know. And I will be back."

"When?"

"I can't say for sure. It'll only be after I deal with my personal responsibilities. And after you," he paused as if considering how he was going to say it, "deal with what's eating at you."

"I'm fine," I said, showing a mask of machismo so fake even I knew how full of shit I really was.

"Are you?"

I looked down into my empty coffee cup, unable to meet his eyes.

He didn't have the same olfactory abilities I had. How the hell could he know?

I'd been thinking about my last moments of conscious memory as I was relishing the blood-thirsty act of pummeling that gunman in the hotel room.

A second wolf memory suddenly snapped into my mind like a cold slap in the face:

The taste of blood as I sunk my fangs deep into Laxmi's throat, the satisfying taste of her blood bubbling up into my mouth.

I'd never killed a human before. But in the span of a single week, I'd taken two lives. And been responsible for the death of my lover's mother.

Who was I?

What was I?

In the space of a little over a week, Gail had not only learned of her witch heritage and the family secrets she'd never been privy to, but she had trained herself to wield and engage with this power.

Even though I had been living with my werewolf alter ego and these supernatural powers for fourteen years, I knew virtually nothing about myself—nor how to control the transformation between man and wolf like I'd seen other werewolves do.

Ben was right. There was a lot I needed to deal with.

Pressing my lips tightly together, I fixed a stern and determined look on my face as I nodded back at him.

I knew exactly who I needed to call to help me set things straight, and figure all this out.

The man who was there when it all first went down. The man who remained in my life all these years like some elusive Hairy Wolf Mother.

Sunday August 20, 2017

Epilogue: Cue up The Lonely Woman Theme

New York

GAIL

Dear Michael,

At least, I hope the person reading this is Michael. I suppose anyone could find this letter, at any point in the future. If you are not Michael, quit reading now, nosy stranger! None of this will make any sense to you, and I will probably write something about how much I like seeing Michael naked, which is none of your damn business.

I can't tell you where I'm going. To be honest, I don't know a whole lot myself. I can't even leave you cute little hints, as much as I want to. So don't go looking for clues in this letter—there are no doodles of mouse ears to send you to Florida. This paper is not sprayed with French perfume in the hopes that you will find me at the top of the Eiffel Tower. Even if I knew my destination, I would not share it with you.

Michael, listen to me: I know you are imagining me wandering off with a backpack and my thumb out, and you're humming the end theme from "The Incredible Hulk." Knock it off. This is not the time, my love.

There is so much more to say. So much more to do. I wish we could do it together. What we didn't know, and I don't think anyone in history could have known, was that together we could defy the laws of physics.

(Do the laws of physics apply to Paranormals? I don't know. I will add that to the list of things I intend to learn.)

We buried my mother last week. It was a family service, filled with traditions more ancient than our curse. Someday I will tell you about it because, as it turns out, funerals for people like my mother are ... intense. I wish you could have been there.

I didn't know anything about her, I rarely liked her, and still, she gave up her life to save you.

To save us.

I can hear you humming those first four notes of "Lonely Man," over and over, like a broken music box. You are thinking how sad the discordant notes are, how they drift into space like loneliness. Stop it.

I don't regret one minute of my time with you. I know you are blaming yourself for everything we've lost. You're going over it in your head, endlessly, and I know you are convincing yourself that I don't want to see you again. Believe me when I tell you this: I wish we had the people we love back again, and I wish we weren't in pain, but I don't regret loving you. If I had a time machine,

I'd go back to that bookstore café on the day we met and flirt with you shamelessly all over again. I would fall for you over and over again, forever.

Know this: I'm going to figure it out.

The curse may be ancient, but what we have is bigger.

I love you,

Gail

PS—Lonely Man really is a terribly sad song. I'm listening to it on repeat as I write and honestly, those last two notes—*bom, bommm*—are so serious, so final.

I hate that tune. I refuse to let it be our theme song, Michael.

But you already knew I'd argue with you about that.

I re-read the letter for the thousandth time and folded it into a small rectangle. The words were inadequate, but it was the best I could do, given everything.

There was no way to know if Michael would ever find it. I was forbidden to contact him in any manner, at any time, supervised or not. We finally knew enough to take our enforced separation seriously.

But I figured that one hidden message, hopefully found long after I left the country, wouldn't set off any nuclear-threat-level battle, as it almost did before.

If he found it, and if enough time had passed, he would be able to handle whatever skirmish this small communication set off.

I pried the paper into a small fissure at the base of the of Bow Bridge in Central Park, where the footpath met the rising pillar of the railing, and then kicked dirt over it, packing it into the crack with the toe of my boot. I could only hope this hiding spot would stay dry enough until he found it.

I walked to the top of the bridge, waiting for a young woman to finish her proposal to her girlfriend, clapped along with everyone else watching nearby, and then leaned against the railing, staring out at the rippling water.

Michael was the writer, not me. Hopefully, he would understand that words were inadequate in a situation like ours.

He'd understand. He'd also drive himself mad with self-doubt. I could only hope that he would trust me, and my reassurances.

People passed behind me on the bridge, some stopping to enjoy the view, others on their way to other vistas. I lingered, thinking about all the ways I'd changed since I met Michael Andrews. Everything I had once understood about myself, my body, my abilities, my friendships, my family—all of it was changed now. All of it different.

Another couple paused at the top of the bridge.

"Excuse me, could you take our picture?" the man asked me, his face flushed. He leaned in when I took his camera. "It's on video," he whispered, and then he winked.

I winked back, feeling equally foolish and pleased for both of them. He dropped to one knee and his girlfriend's hands came to her cheeks.

After I returned the phone and congratulated them, I turned back the way I had come. I didn't glance at the spot where I had hidden my message to Michael.

He would find it.

The days were still hot, but I wrapped my arms around myself as if I felt a chill. My palm rested on my stomach, still flat, still unchanged.

But not for long.

Coming Next

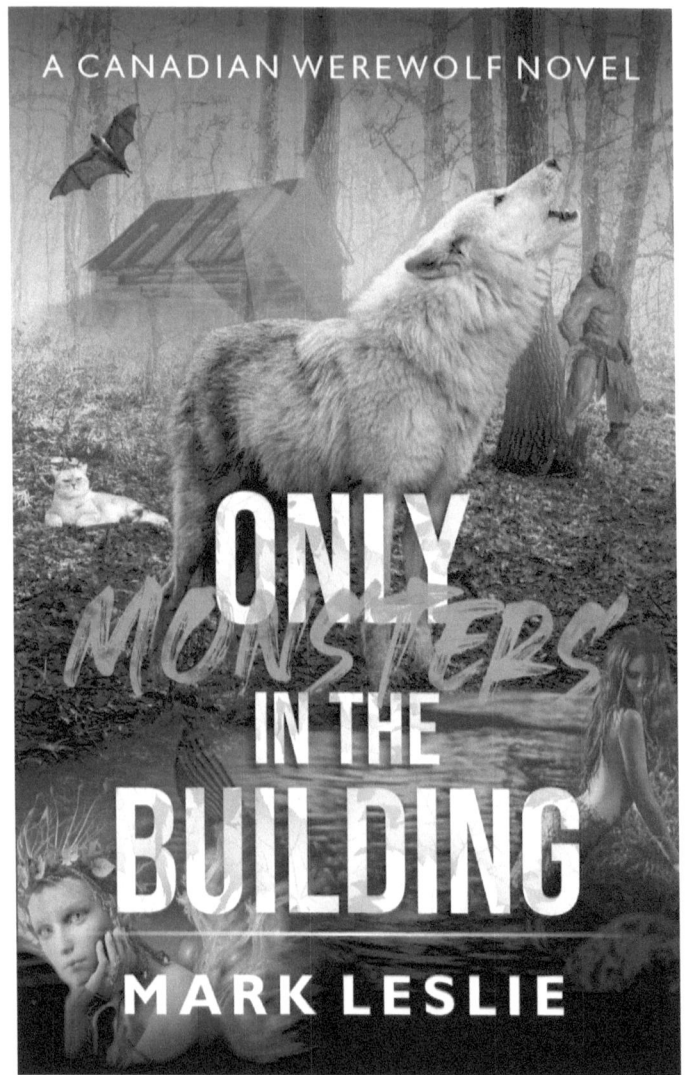

A CANADIAN WEREWOLF NOVEL

ONLY MONSTERS IN THE BUILDING

MARK LESLIE

WHAT COULD POSSIBLY GO WRONG
WHEN A WEREWOLF NEEDS THERAPY?

Michael Andrews has suffered the slings and arrows of an outrageous fortune living with lycanthropy. But an ancient curse preventing him from being with his true love has finally pushed him right over the edge.

In desperation, he checks into a secret and remote retreat in upstate New York to undergo group therapy with a motley crew of other Paranormals.

But when their therapist is found dead, Michael and the other patients (a mischievous fairy, a brooding vam-pire, a sassy mermaid, a playful werecat, and a grumpy ogre) find themselves embroiled in a classic locked room whodunnit.

Will his years of writing mystery novels be enough to help him through a case where he is one of the prime sus-pects?

Only Monsters in the Building is a humorous and mysterious adventure that will keep you laughing on the edge of your seat.

Also Coming Soon

WITCH

THE GAIL SOMMERS TRILOGY

JULIE STRAUSS

WITCH
Book One in
THE GAIL SOMMERS TRILOGY
BY JULIE STRAUSS

Learn their secrets.

Gail Sommers doesn't know who placed the curse on her family. All she knows is that the lives of everyone she loves are in grave danger if she stays in New York City.

For once in her life, Gail's stubbornness is her strength. She'll leave town in the dead of night, without a word to her family, her friends, or her lover Michael. She'll find the source of the curse, and she'll destroy it. She doesn't care who gets in her way.

The Tír Uaighe gang is close on her heels, and she doesn't entirely know how to be a witch yet. But that doesn't matter. Because now, it's not just about Gail.

It's about her baby.

And nothing pisses a witch off more than someone threatening her family.

Authors' Notes

I never expected the series would be where it currently is.

Oh, who am I kidding? I never expected this to even be a series when I first penned a short story about a guy (a then-unnamed Michael Andrews) trying to drag his naked butt home after spending a night out howling at the moon.

Almost everything about this entire series has surprised me.

But the most amazing surprise is what happened when I attended to a handful of readers who asked me to share the back-story of how Michael and Gail first met.

You see, *Lover's Moon*, book five in the series, was initially intended to be either a long short story, or, like *Stowe Away*, a novella. It was meant to be a treat for those readers who wanted more of the Michael/Gail romance; at least back when their relationship had been entirely romantic in nature.

I figured the best way to share their story was to write it as an actual romance, following all the standard tropes of that genre.

But I kept running into false starts.

Because I wasn't able to write Gail's point of view scenes as effectively as I liked. You see, like Michael, I'd fallen deeply in love with Gail, put her on a pedestal, and kept over-looking many of her flaws.

And that's where my good friend Julie Strauss came in. She not only masterfully owned the voice of Gail, but she helped draw out multiple layered dimensions to the overall universe by asking insightfully probing questions.

So, when we were writing *Lover's Moon* we already knew there was even more to Gail Sommers than the character knew about herself and about her family. We crafted the concept that she was descended from a long line of witches, but she had no clue about any of it.

We merely hinted at these details in *Lover's Moon*. And we drew upon elements about Gail from the previous novels that further enhanced that idea. It seemed almost as if, subconsciously, I'd been planting those ideas all along.

It's no secret that Julie and I had an absolute blast writing *Lover's Moon* together despite our completely different ways of approaching the entire process of writing.

So, when I first put up the pre-order for *Hex and the City*, I had intended it to be a return to the single POV Michael Andrews adventures, like the four novels before.

Of course, considering the plot I was looking at exploring, the tale needed to be told from two perspectives; particularly since Gail and Michael had to be separated and fighting their own parallel battles.

Remembering how much trouble I had writing from Gail's point of view, and, more importantly, how brilliantly Julie brought a whole new life to that character, I returned to my friend's proverbial doorstep, put on my best puppy-dog eyes, and asked if she would please consider putting aside her other writing plans and to help me by co-authoring this novel.

I am over the moon—the full moon—with delight that Julie agreed to do this.

The process was not easy. We did not see eye to eye on elements of the story, or even the approach to the writing process.

We had many spirited late-night discussions, each making a case for our vision. We laughed, argued, teased each other, compromised when necessary, dug our heels in when it was really important, and came out with a stronger friendship, better writing, and a book we are both truly proud of.

We wrote this manuscript in a similar tag-team chapter-by-chapter fashion that we wrote *Lover's Moon*. Only this time, we did not have a concrete outline. The rough outline notes (thanks to my way of typically doing things) included things like: "They fight the Big Bad in a climactic battle."

As we wrote each of our chapters, I remember, like in the previous process, both eagerly awaiting the treat that lay before me that flowed through Julie's keyboard, and consistently being delightfully surprised at the twists and plot elements Julie added.

Including the way she shocked me by having the book end with the reveal that Gail was pregnant. It was not something we discussed, but it blew my mind.

And during this entire process, magic continued to unfold. We not only ended up with what I believe is a fantastic book that helps explain some of the confusing elements of Michael and Gail's ill-fated relationship, but it also allowed me to dig deeper into the mysterious Buddy J. Samuels.

And, like in that previous novel, Julie and I discussed deeper components and "truths" about this universe that would only be hinted at in this book. Concepts and stories, and strands and adventures that we would explore in future books.

Including an entire trilogy of stories about Gail Sommers.

One of the most gratifying things about this book, apart from the incredibly rewarding collaboration with a writer I so admire and respect, is watching how Julie's idea for a stand-alone series of books about Gail Sommers launched into the stratosphere.

It exploded into shape the way Michael's love for Gail manifested the moment they first locked eyes in 2011 at that Barnes and Noble café.

In the same way I eagerly anticipated the delivery of each of the Gail-POV chapters, I cannot wait to read what adventures Julie has in store for Gail in the *Witch*, *Warrior*, and *Priestess* novels of the Gail Sommers Trilogy.

Of course, Michael has his own solo adventures and misadventures to have, including having to reel from dealing with the loss of his love plus living with the reality that he has murdered two people.

So what better way to have him face that head on than testing his ability to solve a mystery when the person tasked with helping him through his therapy is discovered murdered at a special retreat for Paranormals.

And that's one of numerous adventures for Michael that consistently nudge me from the corner of my mind where the Muse lingers with a gleeful look in her eye.

Speaking of prodding, I am so tremendously grateful for the fellow creatives who were there to poke, prod, and point me in the direction this series has taken.

Sean Costello prompted me to write the first novel.

DeAnna Knippling and Jamie Ferguson prodded me to write another story which became that second book, making it a series.

And Julie Strauss inspired me to look deeper, to consider exploring the larger worlds both within Michael and his companions, but of the world he was muddling his way through.

Oh, the possibilities. Oh, the amazing further adventures to explore.

And, finally, I'm extremely grateful for you, dear reader. Because, even though I adore writing these novels and continuing to explore this "Canadian Werewolf" universe, and would likely do it anyway, knowing that you're still there, wanting to read more, truly makes it a wholly satisfying endeavor.

Thank you for reading.

Yours in writing,
Mark Leslie
March 2023

About the Authors

Like Michael Andrews, **Mark Leslie** considers himself a beta human. However, unlike his fictional character, Leslie doesn't have an alpha-wolf persona, despite hair growing on his aging body in all the wrong places.

Mark lives in Southern Ontario and can most likely be found behind the keyboard, with his nose stuck in a book, tracking and enjoying craft beer, or sharing musical earworms and dad jokes.

You can learn more about him at **www.markleslie.ca**.

Julie Strauss is a writer, editor, and podcaster who lives, reads, writes, cooks, and gardens in Southern California with her family.

She is known in some circles as "that weird bookish lady who talks to her plants" and in other circles as "that foul-mouthed wine drinker who laughs at inappropriate moments." She loves you as a person but does not care about your cats unless you have taught them how to talk.

You can learn more about her online at **www.juliewroteabook.com**.

The Canadian Werewolf Series

This Time Around (Short Story)
A Canadian Werewolf in New York
Stowe Away (Novella)
Fear and Longing in Los Angeles
Fright Nights, Big City
Lover's Moon (*with Julie Strauss*)
Hex and the City (*with Julie Strauss*)
Only Monsters in the Building (Feb 2024)

The Gail Sommers Trilogy
By Julie Strauss
Witch (Jan 2024)
Warrior (April 2024)
Priestess (July 2024)

Selected Other Books by the Authors

Mark Leslie

Non-Fiction Paranormal
Haunted Hamilton
Spooky Sudbury (with Jenny Jelen)
Tomes of Terror
Creepy Capital
Haunted Hospitals (with Rhonda Parrish)
Macabre Montreal (with Shanya Krishnasamy)

Non-Fiction Trivia/Comedy
The Canadian Mounted: A Trivia Guide to Planes,
Trains and Automobiles

Julie Strauss

The Oro Beach Series
Almost Blue
Ruby Tuesday
Goodbye Yellow Brick Road

The Chefs in Love Collection
Hungry Heart
Moonstone Heart
Prosecco Heart